THE COMPLETE TALES OF
SHERIFF HENRY, VOLUME 3

W. C. Tuttle

HENRY RIDES THE DANGER TRAIL

THE COMPLETE TALES OF SHERIFF HENRY, VOLUME 3

W.C. TUTTLE

ILLUSTRATED BY

V.E. PYLES

STEEGER BOOKS • 2019

TABLE OF CONTENTS

The Revelation of Henry 1

Henry Rides the Danger Trail. 57

THE REVELATION OF HENRY

*Never had peaceable Sheriff Henry expected
to find himself facing a term in jail—
trapped for a robbery he hadn't committed*

CHAPTER I

TWO DEUCES MISSING

HENRY HARRISON CONROY sighed expansively, leaned back in an old rocker, and made a futile effort to put his boot-clad feet on the porch railing. Failing in this, he looked thoughtfully at Oscar Johnson, sprawling on the steps, his huge shoulders braced against a post.

Henry was middle-aged, very rotund, and only five feet six inches in height. In fact, Henry was so rotund that he had difficulty in crossing his legs, much less putting them up on the railing. Until less than a year ago, Henry Harrison Conroy's moon-like face and huge red, putty-like nose was known wherever high-class vaudeville was played.

Born in a dressing room, a trouper all his life, and at the end of his string as an attraction, when vaudeville waned he inherited the J Bar C cattle ranch in Wild Horse Valley, Arizona. With only a stage concept of the West, he accepted the inheritance; and stepped into a world of which he knew not a thing.

Wild Horse Valley laughed with and at Henry, and elected him sheriff. Not to be outdone by the voters, Henry appointed Judge Van Treece as deputy, and Oscar Johnson as jailer. Judge was past sixty, very tall and gaunt, with pouchy eyes and a long nose. Too frequent libations had made a derelict out of a once brilliant lawyer, but he still retained his dignity.

Oscar Johnson, whom Judge labeled the Vitrified Viking, was a giant Swede, with a queer sense of humor. He had faded blond hair, a button-like nose and small, innocent-looking blue eyes.

The porch of the J Bar C ranch house was crudely decorated with red and white streamers, juniper branches and a few badly lopsided Chinese lanterns.

A glimpse through the front doorway disclosed the fact that the main room was also decorated.

"I take it," remarked Henry, "that the decorations are finished."

"Yah, su-ure," nodded Oscar. "Das a ha'al of a yob, Hanry. Oll my fingers are hammered flat. Yudge vars no halp. Ay yust as soon have a yack-ass around."

Henry squinted sideways at the Chinese lanterns, closed his eyes and shuddered slightly before opening them again.

"I have always contended that decorating is an art in itself," he said quietly. "As in other things, I believe a man should confine himself to his own trade. Have you a knack for any certain thing, Oscar? I mean, outside of wrecking buckboards, getting into fights—and—and drinking fermented prune juice."

"Yah, su-ure," replied Oscar.

"What is it, if I may ask?"

"Decorating a hoose for de vedding," replied Oscar blandly.

Judge was sure the line would hold

"Yes, I suppose that is true," sighed Henry. "For instance, it is a new idea in hanging those lanterns upside down. Naturally, the candles will burn better—faster. But I don't suppose it will make a particle of difference, because some of those wild cow-waddies will shoot them out long before they set anything on fire."

"Ay vars yust thinking," observed Oscar. "You are going to marry Mrs. Horper, and Danny Regan is going to marry Leila Horper tomorrow night. Ay vars yust vishing."

"I can believe the 'wishing' statement," said Henry. "What were you wishing about, Oscar?"

"Ay vars vishing it vars a t'ree-handed game. If das Yosephine Swensen vould only—" Oscar shook his head hopelessly.

"Why not?" queried Henry. "The decorations are all in place and the minister is engaged. I would really like something to relieve the solemnity of the occasion. I really believe you and

Josephine would steal the show, Oscar. Why not ask her to marry you tomorrow night?"

Oscar sighed and shook his head.

"She say Ay am yust a bog-headed Svede, oll muscle and no brains. She vouldn't come."

"You love her, don't you?"

"Yah, su-ure, Ay lofe her."

"Then be a cave-man. Grab her by the hair and toss her over your shoulder and—"

"Ay don't vant to wrassle mit her. Anyvay, she hits too damn hord."

"Something to that, I suppose."

Josephine Swensen, Oscar's Light o' Love, was a huge, raw-boned maid, who worked at the Tonto Hotel. Their courtship had been one of hard knocks, in which Oscar received most of them.

HENRY GLANCED toward the main gate of the ranch, where Judge Van Treece was riding through. Judge hated horseback riding and ignored stirrups most of the time. He rode straight up to the porch, where he dismounted carefully and painfully. He was taking care of the office, while Henry made preparations for the coming double wedding.

"If your facial expression is any criterion, my dear Judge," observed Henry, "we are due for a calamity. Or is it an urgent need for bicarbonate of soda?"

With an exaggerated flourish of his right hand, Judge reached into a vest pocket and drew out two rather soiled playing cards which he carefully placed on the railing before Henry. They were the deuce of clubs and the deuce of spades. Henry looked closely at them, leaned back in his chair and made another futile effort to elevate his booted feet. Henry sighed and folded his hands.

"Again?" he said quietly.

"Last evening at Scorpion Bend, sir," replied Judge gravely. "It happened thusly, I believe. The Scorpion Saloon, Gambling

Palace and Honkatonk had a profitable run. I believe I said it happened last evening. My error; it was three o'clock this morning.

"The pomaded gentleman known as Silk McAllister, who guides the destinies of said place of iniquity, not trusting anyone, took the proceeds, intending to keep them in his room. On his way up the stairs, in the semi-dark, something descended upon his head. When he awoke, of course the money was gone."

"He probably was robbed," said Henry.

"Since money has no legs," nodded Judge gravely, "we would conclude that it had some assistance. Mr. McAllister was discovered by a swamper, who gave the alarm. Inside Mr. McAllister's collar, in close proximity to his left ear, were those two cards."

"The Two Deuces," sighed Henry. "I believe that is their third job in two months. Who brought the story and the cards?"

"Doc White, the stage driver. He informed me that Scorpion Bend demands action from you. They are a bit wrought up, sir."

"Naturally. We all deplore crime, my dear Judge. I suppose that the Scorpion Saloon, etc., etc., are the most wrought. I can see it as a double robbery. They robbed the players, and the Two Deuces robbed them. However, we must do something. Oscar, what would you suggest? Is there any way in which our office might discover the identity of the Two Deuces?"

"Yah, su-ure," replied Oscar blandly. "Yust find out who had deck of cards mit only two deuces."

"There you are!" exclaimed Henry. "Simple deduction, Judge. In fact, like Sherlock Holmes, I might say, 'Elementary, Doctor, elementary.'"

"Henry," said Judge gravely, "there are times when I doubt your complete sanity. Before you fell in love with Laura Harper you did have lucid moments. Yes, I believe you did. But now you are a mere star-gazer, a moon-looker, a bird-listener; unfit for the mental strain of combating crime.

"You—you could almost condone this robbery, because you do not believe the games are square. It is not for us to judge. A crime has been committed, two dangerous opponents of law and order are abroad in the land, laughing at the law, flaunting their damnable deuces in our faces."

"I like that word 'flaunting,' Judge. It has a devil-may-care swing to it. Of course, one must be careful how it is used. For instance, you could hardly say that a man flaunted a shotgun in your face. I believe it would be physically impossible to flaunt a shotgun. But two deuces—certainly. One might even flaunt a whole deck, being careful not to scatter them."

"I give up," sighed Judge. "Where is Danny?"

"Danny Regan," replied Henry, "is down at his little ranch. With the instinct of a male bird, he has gone down there to build a little nest for the honeymoon. In other words, Danny decided that he would make repairs, clean up the place, and spend his honeymoon down there. I believe he is right, Judge. It is his ranch, his bride—and his own damn business."

Judge looked sharply at Henry. "Lucid again, eh?" he observed. "Perhaps I had better tell you about that robbery at three o'clock this morning at Scorpion Bend. It happened thusly—"

"One of us must be crazy," interrupted Henry. "Which would you say, Oscar?"

"Ay am not a yudge of such t'ings," replied Oscar, "but Ay have my own opinion of both of you."

"If I might venture an opinion," said Judge, "I believe we could all do justice to a little of Frijole Bill's prune fermentations—if he has any on hand."

"Yah—su-ure," agreed Oscar heartily. "Ay have got gallon hid avay. Free-holey made it a veek ago."

"Old stuff, eh?" queried Henry eagerly.

"Yah—su-ure, Ay don't like it too new, Hanry."

CHAPTER II

FRAMED

DANNY REGAN WAS wide awake. In fact, he had only been knocked out for a short time and had awakened to find himself in a bed, undressed, bound hand and foot, and blindfolded. It seemed a ridiculous condition to the young cowboy, because, as far as he could determine, there was no earthly reason for such a thing.

Danny had spent the day at his own little ranch, south of Tonto City, cleaning and repairing the place. Despite the fact that he was foreman at the J Bar C, Danny did not neglect his own little ranch; and now he was preparing it as a honeymoon haven for his bride-to-be.

He had worked until after dark, and had just stepped from the kitchen doorway to toss away a panful of water, when someone hit him on the head. He reasoned that his unconsciousness was of short duration, because of the fact that someone was working on his bonds when he awoke.

There was a slight ache in his head, but nothing to indicate that he had been badly injured. If it were a joke, Danny decided that somebody's sense of humor was badly warped. It seemed hours that he had worked at the bonds, but to no avail. They had been put there to stay. The blindfold, too, had been well applied and was not to be slipped off.

Finally he heard someone enter the room. Apparently they were making no attempt at stealth. A husky voice said:

"You stay there at the door."

"All right," replied another voice, pitched in a rather high key. Danny wondered if it was a woman's voice.

He felt the blanket thrown back. A moment later there was a sharp tug at his feet, as the rope was cut. He was quickly turned on his face, and his wrists cut apart. Then he heard the man step swiftly across the room and the door slammed sharply.

He turned over as quickly as possible, reached up and took away the blindfold. The room was in darkness, but a hasty glance at the starlit windows showed that he was in his own bedroom. He got up stiffly, found a match, and lighted the lamp. The hot chimney indicated that the man had worked by lamplight, but had extinguished the lamp before leaving the room.

Hanging on the back of a chair were Danny's clothes, his high-heel boots beside the bed. Hanging on a nail were his chaps, belt and holstered gun. He searched his overall pockets, and discovered that his money, seven dollars in silver, was intact. His white Stetson, with the silver-studded band, hung on a post of the bed, where he had left it. He found his old silver watch in his vest pocket, and the time was nearly eleven o'clock.

"I must have been in bed since about seven," he mused. "But why in the devil did somebody knock me out, put me to bed, all tied up—and then cut me loose? They didn't take my money nor my gun. Dog-gone it, it don't make sense."

Fully dressed, he examined his sore head. The skin was not broken, nor was there any appreciable swelling. He found his horse in the corral, his saddle hanging on the fence where he had left it.

"Brownie," he told his horse, "I have heard of a lot of cock-eyed things but this beats 'em all. It may be funny when I know why it was done, but it shore don't get a laugh out of me right now. I reckon me and you better go home before somethin' else happens."

Instead of going back through Tonto City, Danny cut across the hills to the J Bar C, arriving there about midnight. Neither Oscar nor Frijole Bill Cullison, the cook, were in the bunk-house; so he went into the ranch house looking for Henry or Judge. He wanted to tell them what had happened to him. But the house was empty.

"I've got me a hunch," smiled Danny. "They started on Frijo-

le's prune whisky and have gone to town to finish the celebration. I'll just hit the hay, and talk about my troubles in the
morning."

But Danny was not to sleep long. He awoke with the lamp-
light shining in his eyes, and sat up in his blankets. There were
Henry, Judge, Oscar and Frijole, all standing there, looking at
him. Danny blinked, relaxed and slid back on his pillow.

"Go to bed, you prune-juice hoot-owls," he said sleepily.

"Ay yust vill be damned!" choked Oscar, and sat down on a
bunk.

None of the others made any remark. Finally Danny lifted
himself on one elbow and squinted sleepily at them.

"What the devil ails you fellers?" he asked. "What have yuh
been drinkin', anyway?"

"Danny," said Henry huskily, "where were you tonight?"

"Huh? Where was I? I was down at the ranch and—"

"Was Nick Borden with you, Danny?"

"No, Nick wasn't down there. I saw him about noon, but—"

"What time did you come back here, Danny?"

"Midnight. But what the devil is this all about?"

"Can you prove you were at your ranch all the time until you
came back here?"

"Sa-a-ay! This is gettin' kinda funny. Prove it? Why should I
prove it? What's wrong, anyway?"

"Danny"—Henry's voice shook a little—"the Tonto Bank
was robbed tonight, and George Gray, the cashier, was killed.
They—they didn't get much money, if any. The shots were heard,
and an investigation was made. They found Nick Borden near
the back door of the bank, unconscious from a bullet-scrape
across his head and with a small bunch of bank money in his
pocket.

"Gray wasn't dead, but he died shortly after he was found.
He was able to talk—a little. He said there were two men. One
of them guarded the back door, while the other tried to force

him to open the safe. He—he said—" Henry licked his lips and drew a deep breath. "He said he recognized you by your clothes, Danny."

DANNY BLINKED foolishly. Recognized by his clothes! Suddenly he swung around and got out of bed, his lips tightly shut. Now he knew the reasons for what had happened at his ranch house.

"That's what happened," he gritted. "They stole my clothes, robbed the bank, and then—"

"What are you talking about, Danny?" interrupted Henry.

"Somebody socked me on the head this evenin'. Oh, it's plain enough now. They blindfolded and tied me up in bed, took my clothes—and robbed the bank. Then brought the clothes back and turned me loose."

Judge was looking at Danny, a pained expression on his lean face.

Henry sighed, dug his pudgy hands deeply in his pockets and leaned one shoulder against the bunk-post.

"What the hell's the matter with you fellers?" demanded Danny. "You don't act as though yuh believed me."

"Where did you get hit, Danny?" asked Judge.

"Right here—on my head."

Danny pointed out the spot but there was no bruise and little, if any, swelling. Danny realized that. He closed his jaws tightly, shifting his eyes from Henry to Judge, reading the disbelief in their eyes.

"You fellows don't believe me—I can see that," he said wearily. "But every word of it is true. I've never lied to you."

"Danny, I believe you," stated Henry. "You are not a fool."

"What do you mean by that statement, sir?" asked Judge.

"Take a look at Danny's clothes—and ask a fool question like that. Green shirt, covered with pearl buttons, a glaringly white sombrero with silver trimmings. Chaps with conchas the size of saucers. Would any sane man wear clothes like those to a hold-up or robbery?"

"But, fool or no fool, what alibi has he?" queried Judge. "You couldn't convince any jury with abstract evidence like that."

"What's the use of arguin' about it?" demanded Danny. "I didn't rob that bank. Even if I wanted to rob a bank, I shore wouldn't take a chance—not the day before my weddin'."

Henry groaned softly, knowing that there was no earthly way to avoid arresting Danny. Several men had heard George Gray, the cashier, positively identify Danny Regan. And there was no way for Danny to prove that he had been held captive and robbed of his clothes.

"A wedding," stated Judge in a sepulchral tone, "is no alibi for a robbery and murder."

"You—you—" Henry glared at Judge malevolently. "You damned law addict. You would hang your own grandfather on manufactured evidence. Not a word, sir!"

"I was merely pointing out—" faltered Judge.

"Don't point!" snapped Henry. "It is bad form."

He turned back to Danny, who was dressing. "Are you sure there were two men, Danny?" he asked.

"Yes, Henry. I heard two distinct voices. One was—well, it might have been a woman's voice. You know what I mean—kinda nervous and high-pitched."

"A woman, eh?" mused Henry.

"That might narrow the field," suggested Judge.

"NARROW IT!" snorted Henry. "How would that narrow the field, Mr. Narrow-Minded Blackstone? Previous to this we were looking for two men who might be working together. Now we have to include married couples and sweethearts. Narrow—the devil! It could be anybody in Wild Horse Valley."

"True," murmured Judge. "George Gray said he did not see the other of the two men who had been given an order to guard the back door. It could have been a woman."

"But what about Nick Borden?" asked Danny.

"Unconscious," replied Henry. "The bullet tore his scalp rather badly but not dangerously. In a pocket of his coat they found a sheaf of one-dollar bills which had been taken from the bank."

"Nick Borden wouldn't rob a bank," declared Danny. "I'd bet my life on that. Why, Nick even quit gambling and drinkin', after he married Lola. And she's back East."

"That is true," sighed Henry. "I sincerely hope that Nick has a good alibi, when he regains consciousness. But in the meantime—"

"I've got to go to jail," finished Danny.

"You make it easier, Danny," said Henry quietly. "I have no alternative. But it will only be for a short time."

"I can talk it over with Leila in the mornin'," said Danny drearily. "Let's go."

Henry and Judge went to Tonto City with Danny, leaving Oscar Johnson and Frijole Bill at the ranch. Frijole was sixty-five years of age, five feet three inches tall, and would not weigh over one hundred pounds fully dressed. He had a skinny little face, decorated by bushy eyebrows and a huge mustache.

Frijole was a first-class ranch cook, who spent all his extra time in brewing and distilling. His *pièce de résistance* was a prune whisky which Judge declared was nothing less than a depth bomb filled with cyanide.

After the three men departed for Tonto City, Frijole and Oscar sat together on a bunk, a duo of dejection.

"Das ha'ar is hord luck, Free-holey," declared Oscar.

"Hard luck!" snorted Frijole. "This here is the squintessence of jumbileer, I'll tell yuh that. Danny ain't got a Chinaman's chance. They'll hang him so high that a buzzard would have to hire a balloon to git up there. Hard luck! Huh!"

"Ay am de yailer," reminded Oscar. "Ay have de keys to de yail."

"Uh-hah! You'd turn him loose, eh? And then they'd hang you, yuh cock-eyed Swede. If yuh don't believe me, ask Judge."

"Ay vould prove an alibi."

"Yuh would, eh?"

"Yah, su-ure. Ay vould say Ay forgot to lock the yail."

"Yeah, that would be great. They'd prob'ly carve that on yore tombstone. Forgettin' to do the right thing ain't no alibi for a Swede. How 'bout a little portion of prune whisky, Oscar?"

"Ay feel de need of a little prune yuice, Free-holey. How vars de last batch you made?"

"I ain't tested it yet, but I'm bettin' she's good. Bill Shakespeare got at the mash right away. His old crop swelled up like a balloon, and I seen him headin' for the stable, with his one tail-feather cocked up toward his comb, and—"

"Ay know oll about it," interrupted Oscar. "Das damn rooster yumped oll over me, and Ay kicked him over de fence."

"He's prob'ly gone huntin' a wild-cat," sighed Frijole. "He most allus does. I'll git the jug. Mebbe we better take off our boots, before we take any; yuh never can tell what it'll do."

NICK BORDEN was tall and swarthy, with handsome features. Just now his head was swathed in bandages as he sat in the sheriff's office. Borden, until he acquired the Smoke Tree mine, had been a professional gambler. He invariably dressed in black, from his patent-leather boots to his big sombrero.

Seated near him was Danny Regan, looking decidedly miserable. Henry sat at his desk, watching John Campbell, the prosecutor, a huge gray-haired man, who paced the room slowly.

Finally he turned to Nick Borden.

"You say you became lonesome last night, and rode to town to get some tobacco, Borden?"

"That's right, Campbell," nodded Nick Borden. "My wife has—"

"I understand that," interrupted the lawyer. "You saw no one on the street who might have seen you?"

"No, I didn't. I tied my horse across the street from the bank and came across the street, going to the store. I happened to glance into the bank window as I walked past. There was a dim light near the back of the place, and I saw a flash of something. It could have been lamplight on a gun-barrel or on silver.

"I can't explain why I did it, but I went down that alley between the bank and the hotel. The back door of the bank was open, and just as I started to look in I heard a—well, sort of commotion—and something struck me a devil of a blow. That's all I can tell you."

Campbell stopped his pacing and looked keenly at Borden.

"You can't account for that sheaf of dollar bills, eh?"

"Certainly not. I didn't have over a dollar in my pocket."

"Need money pretty bad, don't you, Borden?"

"Trying to put the deadwood on me, eh?" retorted Borden.

"It seems to be on both of you, Borden. Danny Regan's story would be laughed out of court. What do you think, Henry?"

"I think they are telling the truth, John. Either of them can lie too well to tell their stories, if they were not true."

"Thank you, Henry," said Borden soberly.

"Same here," said Danny gloomily. "I'd change my story if I could. I know it sounds crazy—but it's true."

"Well," sighed Campbell, "the inquest will be held this afternoon. If you can think of a better story, it might help a lot. Any jury in Arizona would hang both of you. Lock 'em up, Henry."

The prosecutor left the office, closing the door behind him.

"He didn't believe us," sighed Danny.

"If I didn't know you as well as I do, I wouldn't believe you either," replied Henry. "Anyway, it is a hell of a mess. Laura and Leila down here, crying their eyes out—wedding plans all shot to perdition—inquest coming up—and I haven't had a drink all morning."

"I wonder what Lola will say," sighed Borden.

I SENT a telegram out on the stage," stated Henry. "She will probably start back for Arizona, Nick."

"Ruin her vacation, Henry."

"That is true. Perhaps I should have held that telegram until after the hanging."

"You're a cheerful devil," remarked Borden.

"I know it. Well, you boys might as well go back to the cell. There is nothing we can do about it—yet."

Danny looked up quickly. "Yet?" he queried. "Henry, have you an idea?"

"I haven't any more ideas than a black-tailed jack rabbit, except an idea that I'm thirsty. Forward, march."

Henry had several drinks, and went up to John Campbell's office. "Well, did they break down and confess?" queried the lawyer.

"They broke down and cursed," replied Henry soberly. "John, we are going to postpone the inquest until tomorrow."

"Why the delay, Henry?"

"I want to send word to Scorpion Bend to have the cashier of the bank down here for the inquest; and I also want Doc White, the stage driver, here. The Two Deuces robbed the bank and the stage, if you remember. Doc White might be an alibi for Danny and Nick. Perhaps they would not fit the description of the two men who held him up.

"I believe the cashier of the Scorpion Bank saw one of the robbers. There is a chance that his description might not cover either Danny or Nick. Campbell, I'm grasping at every straw to save these two boys from coming to trial."

"Knowing that a conviction would be certain, eh?"

"Just between us," replied Henry gravely, "this country needs a good rain."

"I believe you are wasting your time, Henry."

"I've been doing that for fifty years—and I've got a lot of it left."

Judge, Oscar and Frijole were in the office. Henry took one close look at them and reared back in righteous indignation.

"A fine trio, I must say! A disgrace to Tonto Town. My deputy and my jailer—drunk."

"Didja f'rgit y'r cook?" asked Frijole owlishly.

"You are always drunk, Frijole."

"I reshent the implication, shir," retorted Judge gravely. "I am not drunk. I may be a li'l in-intoshicated—not drunk."

"Ay am yust as dronk as ha'al," declared Oscar. "Ay may be a disgrace to Tonto Town, but Ay am yust right for Oscar Yohnson. Who vants for fight?"

"At least, you are an honest man, Oscar," said Henry, "but that does not mitigate the offense. Here I am, with two of our best friends in jail, facing a murder and robbery charge, an inquest coming up—wedding plans blown to bits—and you get drunk."

Henry's voice choked with emotion and his red nose fairly gleamed.

"Af'er all that, whatcha goin' to do 'bout it?" asked Frijole.

"Where is that damn jug?"

"Henry, be calm," begged Judge. "Have a little judgment. Don't destroy that whole gallon of perfec'ly good prune whisky, I beg of you."

"Destroy it?" roared Henry. "You blear-eyed disciple of Blackstone, I'm going to drink it!"

CHAPTER III

INQUEST

HARRY BURKE, THE cashier of the Scorpion Bank, sat in one of Henry's chairs, his hat on his lap, while Henry made three distinct attempts to put his booted feet on his desk-top.

"Is there anything I can do, Mr. Conroy?" asked Burke.

"Well," replied Henry dryly, "about the only thing you can do is to wish me success, sir. Nature intended for me to bend in the middle, I suppose. Just another case of Nature proposes and man disposes. But it doesn't matter."

Henry drew a deep breath and looked critically at Burke.

"Can you," he asked, "give me any description as to physical proportions of the two men who robbed your bank and left those two deuces?"

Burke shook his head. "I'm afraid not, Mr. Conroy. The one man seemed of average height and weight."

"You saw them both?"

"No, I only saw one. The other man guarded the back door."

"You sure there were two men?"

"Oh, yes. They exchanged several words with each other."

Henry rubbed his nose thoughtfully.

"You could not identify voices, of course," he mused aloud.

"I believe they were trying to disguise their voices. The one who did the actual work had a deep, husky voice, while his companion—well, he sounded rather feminine."

Henry looked sharply at Burke.

"Might have been a woman, eh?"

"Yes, I believe it could, Mr. Conroy."

"Thank you very much, Mr. Burke. It was kind of you to come down here. You have heard that we have two men under arrest, I suppose."

"Yes, I have. I believe I understand the situation, and I am very sorry."

"That is very kind of you."

Harry Burke left the office, and in a few minutes Judge came in with Doc White, the stage driver. White was a man of medium height, sallow, with thin, tow-colored hair and pale blue eyes. He had worked for about a year at the Scorpion livery stable, before becoming a stage driver.

"Hyah, Henry," he greeted the sheriff. "What's on yore mind?"

"I rarely make confessions," replied Henry dryly.

White laughed. "You wanted to ask me somethin', Henry?"

"Yes, I believe I do, Mr. White. You knew about the arrests?"

"Yes, I heard about 'em. Tough luck for them two boys, eh?"

"Yes, I believe it is. When you were held up by the Two Deuces, you had a good chance to see both men, I believe."

"I sure did."

"A short man and a tall one, I believe, Mr. White."

"I never said any such thing," denied White warmly.

"My mistake," murmured Henry. "There usually is a tall one and a short one, I believe."

"Not in this case, Henry. Both of them fellers was average size."

"I can see that you are going to be a big help to me," murmured Henry dolefully, "You know Danny and Nick, I believe. How do they correspond with the two men you saw?"

"Well, I'd hate to say, Henry. Let it go at that. I haven't a thing on earth against either of them."

"Thank you very much, Mr. White. Kind of you, I'm sure."

"Was that all you wanted, Henry?"

"Amount—yes; quality—no."

White left the office. Judge and Henry sat down together, looking helplessly at each other.

"I have been wondering," said Judge. "Do you suppose that Danny and Nick could prove alibis for the times that the other robberies were committed?"

"I have asked them," sighed Henry. "Neither of them can remember where they were on those dates."

"I don't see why not."

"I do. Where were you on June twelfth? Can you prove where you were on that date, at ten o'clock in the morning?"

"Of course not. I don't remember—"

"But Danny and Dick *should* remember, eh?"

"I think you had better go up to the millinery shop and see Laura and Leila. They are just sitting there, staring at each other. You might at least give them something to stare at."

Mrs. Laura Harper and her daughter Leila owned the little millinery shop in Tonto City. The tragic failure of their double-wedding plans had left them stunned and heartbroken, in spite of Henry's assurance that everything would be all right soon.

"I don't want to be stared at like—like a damn freak," declared Henry.

"After looking at you, I don't believe it would help their feelings a bit," said Judge soberly. "You look like indigestion makes me feel. Henry, I believe I shall be obliged to refrain from imbibing any more of Frijole's prune concoctions. Last night I tucked my pants and shoes into bed—and slept on the floor."

"You were disgracefully drunk, sir," declared Henry. "It is all right to indulge to a certain extent, but to get in that condition is positively vulgar."

"I accept the rebuke, Henry. It is well-meant, but useless. You had no trouble, I presume."

"None at all, Judge," replied Henry gravely, "except that I never found that damn bed at all."

"I feared that. Is it any wonder that they call our office The Shame of Arizona?"

"I suppose they are right, Judge," replied Henry huskily. "Two drunken old fools, and a crack-pot Swede, trying to uphold the law and order of Wild Horse Valley. A comedian, without a laugh, a lawyer without a book, and a Swede without a—a—well, what is he without, Judge?"

"Anything," sighed Judge, "except a thirst."

"A complete cast, if there ever was such a thing. Judge, I have a feeling—"

"So have I, Henry. Just a couple to brush away the cobwebs, before the inquest this afternoon."

IT SEEMED that all of Wild Horse Valley came to that inquest. They crowded the court room to suffocation, and many were obliged to stand as far away as the sidewalk. Several men testified to hearing the dying bank cashier identify the clothing of Danny Regan, and all testified to finding Nick Borden behind the bank, unconscious from a bullet wound on the head, and that he had a package of bank money in his pocket. George Gray had told them that he had fired at the retreating robber.

Nick Borden told his unsupported story, as did Danny Regan, but both men knew that the jury did not believe them. Mrs. Harper and Leila were interested spectators; horrified when the jury advised that Danny and Nick be held for trial on a charge of murder and robbery.

Leila Harper was just past twenty, tall and slender, with dark brown hair and big, dark eyes. Mrs. Harper, in her youth, had been a beautiful woman; and she was still handsome, in spite of the fact that life had been a hard struggle.

Henry and Judge sat with them in their apartment back of the millinery shop after the inquest. Conversation was nil for a long time.

"We'll have to hire a good lawyer," said Leila wearily, speaking her thoughts aloud. "The best lawyer in the world."

"And only a week until the next term of court," said Judge. "The docket is so small that this case will be called first."

"Henry," said Mrs. Harper after another long silence, "why don't you say something?"

"I was just thinking deeply, my dear," he replied quietly. "If this case comes to trial, I do not believe that the best criminal lawyer on earth can save them. You noticed the reaction to their stories this afternoon. Absolute disbelief. Our only hope is to find the Two Deuces before the next term of court."

"A mighty difficult task, I would say," remarked Judge.

"Or," added Henry, "we might prove that Danny and Nick are not the Two Deuces."

"I should say that one idea is about as difficult as another, Henry. Have you any theories?"

Henry rubbed his big red nose violently for several moments.

"No," he replied slowly, "I haven't, Judge."

"But we must clear Danny and Nick," said Leila. "I know you can do it. Why—why, you've got to do it."

"Well," replied Henry soberly, "if that is the way you feel about it, Leila, I suppose I may as well get to work on the subject. Let us go to the office—and ponder, Judge."

"Wouldn't it be wonderful if you could prove them both guiltless, Henry?" said Mrs. Harper hopefully.

"My dear Mrs. Harper, it would be a miracle," interposed Judge.

"I think he is even capable of performing a miracle."

"I nearly did—once," said Henry.

On the way to the office Judge said: "Just what was the miracle you nearly performed, Henry?"

"Marrying Laura," replied Henry, soberly.

He locked the door of the office, drew a chair up close to Judge and outlined a plan of action. Judge looked aghast at him.

"Have you no sense of proportion, Henry?"

"Possibly not."

"I know damn well you haven't. In the first place, it would be a violation of the law; and in the second place—look at us."

"I realize all that, Judge. But have you ever heard of a man who was able to give an accurate description under those circumstances?"

"This one would. Henry, you are as crazy as a shepherd. I would never be a party to such a hare-brained scheme. It is ridiculous, I tell you. Think of the disgrace if we were apprehended."

"Think what it means if they hang Danny and Nick, Judge."

"Yes, that is true. Sooner than to allow that, I would be a party to a jail-break. Oh, I mean it, Henry."

"And have both men outlawed for life, eh? No, Judge, that is the last resort. My scheme stands, even if I have to do it alone."

"All right," nodded Judge wearily. "My whole being revolts against such an outrageous thing. It nauseates me; makes me sick."

"Try a spoonful of soda in a glass of water," suggested Henry. "It will do wonders."

"The Shame of Arizona," murmured Judge. "They don't know half of it. We will make it the disgrace of Wild Horse Valley."

CHAPTER IV

RESCUE

ABOUT FIVE MILES north of Tonto City, on the way to Scorpion Bend, the road follows along Pinon Cañon for several miles. It is a narrow grade, barely wide enough for one vehicle, with turn-out places at vantage points on the curves.

At the Tonto City end of the grade is a sharp S curve, and at the bend on the lower half of the S is a small, brushy cañon.

It was the morning after the inquest, and nearly time for the stage from Scorpion Bend. Two masked men crouched in the brush of the little cañon. Their horses were concealed in the brush, out on the mesa.

As far as garments were concerned, these two masked men were nondescript; but anyone in Wild Horse Valley, unless frightened out of their wits, would have recognized Judge and Henry behind those crude masks.

"Th-there is still tut-time to abandon the scheme," faltered Judge. "As far as a disguise is concerned, I would recognize you anywhere. Your waistline, Henry, is obvious."

"Will it be noticed, unless I turn my profile?" asked Henry.

"It would be noticed even if you turned your back, sir."

"I should have worn a Mother-Hubbard, I suppose," sighed Henry. "But we will go through with it even if the heavens fall, Judge."

"I almost wish they would."

"Stop trembling. Honestly, your outline is blurred, Judge. And do not cock that gun. You stay right here, partly concealed in the brush. I shall stop the stage, and you keep the driver covered while I gather in the empty treasure-box, leave our calling cards, and order the driver to proceed."

"Suppose it isn't empty—that treasure-box?"

"There will not be a thin dime in it. Since that robbery the stage does not carry money."

Henry looked critically at Judge, took the six-shooter from his unresisting hand and removed the cartridges.

"At least," remarked Henry, "I shall not be shot from behind."

"I—I hope there will be no shooting."

"Don't worry about the shooting—just pray there will not be any *hitting*. Listen! I believe I hear the stage! Keep your nerve, Judge, and don't forget that soprano voice."

Henry edged out to the rocky wall, where he peered cautiously. A moment later the team and stage came into the upper curve of the S, with the four horses running at top speed. The heavy stage skidded perilously near the edge, throwing rocks and gravel into the cañon, righted itself and came thundering ahead.

Henry's brain worked with lightning-like speed. If that stage made the next curve in safety, there was grave danger of a complete smash-up against the wall beside the little cañon. With a yelp of warning to Judge to save himself, Henry scuttled down the grade, running for his life.

A quick glance over his shoulder showed the equipage hurtling around the curve. Another desperate leap and a glance showed the stage careening against the rocky wall just past Judge's hiding place.

Henry realized that he could never reach the mesa ahead of that thundering juggernaut; so he did the only possible thing to save his life. Just as the lead horses were nearly upon him, he leaped off the grade, all spraddled out, his chubby arms working like flails as he sailed down into the brushy depths of Pinon Cañon.

Judge didn't know what it was all about. He saw Henry start to run down the grade, and a moment later the stage threw gravel all over him. Judge fell backwards in the brush, and when he got to his feet the stage was gone, Henry was gone, too. Nothing remained except a wisp of dust in the air.

"My Gawd!" wailed Judge. "Henry is dead."

He tore off his mask, flung it aside, and walked jerkily along the edge of the grade. He felt weak all over. What could he do? What could he say? How could he ever explain things? He was still clutching the empty revolver in his bony right hand.

"Henry Harrison Conroy is dead," he declared aloud, as though trying to rehearse his story of the tragedy. "The runaway stage killed him on the Pinon Grade. We were starting for Scorpion Bend, and had just reached the grade, when—"

"You may as well forget the rest of the story, Judge," interrupted a weak voice from down along the cañon wall.

"My Gawd—Henry!" cried Judge. "I—I thought you was dead!"

"I am still a possible casualty, Judge. The back of my belt is hooked around a manzanita snag, and the seat of my pants is resting on a six-inch ledge of rock. It might interest you to know that the belt is now beneath my armpits, and that I am clinging with both hands to my overalls, in order to keep from slipping completely through this damnable belt. Also I am looking down on the backs of circling buzzards, and unless you get our two lariat ropes, tie them together and lower same within reach of me I'm afraid that Arizona is going to lose one-third of its shame."

Judge secured the ropes, tied them together, weighted one end and managed to dangle it within reach of Henry, who tied it to his cartridge belt. While the rope was strong enough to bear his weight, Henry realized for the first time that he could never climb up that half-inch rope.

"There isn't anything to tie the rope to, Henry," said Judge.

"That makes it very nice for me," replied Henry.

"I *could* try and hoist you up," suggested Judge.

"Wonderful, Judge! And then we would both go into the cañon."

"I did not mean to do the hoisting myself, Henry. Wait a moment; I believe I have an idea."

JUDGE LED Henry's horse in close to the edge of the cañon, tied the rope to the saddle-horn, and flipped it over the edge of an old log which had been built into the edge of the grade.

"I hope the idea is good!" called Henry. "I don't believe this snag is going to last much longer. Whoa-up!"

The snag broke loose, and the rope jerked taut, yanking the horse sideways; but Judge grasped the reins, yelled assurance to Henry, and led the horse swiftly away.

Henry came out of the cañon all right, bounced over the log, arms and legs waving, and was dragged several feet along the grade before Judge could stop the horse. Judge took the rope off the saddle and came back to Henry, who was flat on his back, puffing and panting. His shirt was almost entirely gone, his overalls were ripped and torn, and he seemed one mass of scratches and bruises.

"I—I didn't think I was going to save you, Henry," panted Judge.

"Personally," replied Henry, struggling to a sitting position and shoving the belt away from the immediate vicinity of his Adam's-apple, "I don't believe you have, Judge."

"You are all right, Henry. That was a close squeak."

"You heard it, too, did you? That was when I struck that log with my stomach. I bounced six feet in the air. Well—"

Henry got painfully to his feet and felt himself over carefully.

"No bones broke," he announced.

"Superficial injuries," said Judge. "Nothing to worry about. But what about that stage? A runaway, wasn't it?"

"Well," groaned Henry, "I should hate to ride on it if Doc White drives like that. I suppose we may as well go home, before somebody finds us and asks for an explanation. I'll stay on this side of town, while you bring me some clothes and a mile or two of court-plaster. You might bring some of Frijole's Lightning Arrester, too."

"I hope you have decided that our scheme did not work, Henry."

"Nothing of the kind, Judge; we try again tomorrow."

"Again tomorrow? After what happened today?"

"Certainly. Tomorrow we will take a pulley and a heavy rope."

Henry groaned aloud when he climbed into his saddle. Every muscle in his body had been strained and bruised.

"I would have sworn that you had been killed, Henry," said Judge as they rode toward the mesa.

"I know," agreed Henry dryly. "I heard you rehearsing it."

But instead of going to Tonto City, Judge wisely led the way in a wide circle to the J Bar C. Neither Frijole nor Oscar were at the ranch. Cleaned and patched-up, with fresh clothes on, Henry relaxed in a big chair.

"And so," remarked Judge, "endeth the comedy."

"You have a strange idea of humor," groaned Henry. "My stomach is one huge purple spot, and my two knees look exactly like a pair of large sunburned potatoes. Comedy—indeed!"

"For general information," said Judge, "you were thrown off a horse instead of off a grade."

"For once in my life—the public be damned!" snorted Henry.

Judge walked over to the doorway of the ranch house, as a rider galloped in through the main gate. It was Tommy Roper, a stuttering, whisky-loving cow waddie, who did odd jobs around the livery stable in Tonto City.

"Is the sheriff here, Judge?" he called.

"Yes, I believe he is, Tommy," replied Judge. "Come in."

The lanky cowboy bow-legged his way into the house.

"Huh-hell busted loose this afternoon!" he panted.

"Yes?" queried Henry. "Why, I did not know it was tied up."

"The Tut-two Deuces held up the stage!"

"No?" exclaimed Henry and Judge in unison.

"Shore as huh-hell did. Up on Pinon Grades. Gug-got eight th-thousand dollars."

"Eight thousand," murmured Henry foolishly.

"Uh-huh. They st-stopped the stage and mum-made Doc White th-throw down the money buh-box. That Juj-Josephine Swensen was in the stage, along with a dud-drummer, and they got out to sus-see what was goin' on. Juj-Josephine throwed a rur-rock at the robbers and hit one of'em on the huh-head, and he fuf-fired his gun, and the bullet knocked Doc White's huh-hat off, and he dropped the lul-lines, and the dud-damned team ran away!"

Red-faced and out of breath, Tommy relaxed for a moment. Henry and Judge looked at each other. Two large tears slowly trickled down Henry's cheeks, unheeded.

"Was there any description of the two men?" asked Henry hoarsely.

"A short one and a tut-tall one," replied Tommy quickly. "The tall one gug-gave the two deuces to Doc Wh-White, bub-before Josephine Sw-Swensen got out and th-throwed the bub-boulder."

"Then what happened?" queried Judge gravely.

"Well, the dud-damned team ran away around the gug-grades, and out on the mum-mesa, where Doc White gug-got throwed off in a cuc-cactus patch. Then the team tut-tangled up in a mesquite pup-patch a mile farther on.

"The dud-drummer was the first one to tut-town. He said that Juj-Josephine chased him most all the way, yellin' 'Sus-save me! Sus-save me!' He said he was tut-too damn busy tryin' to sus-save himself to bub-bother with her."

BY THIS time Henry was crying softly, the tears coursing down his fat cheeks.

"Yuh don't nun-need to feel sorry for Juj-Josephine," said

Tommy. "Sh-she's all right. She says that's the lul-last damn drummer she'll ever appeal tut-to for help."

"Who could blame her?" queried Henry tearfully.

"I thought they did not ship money on the stage now," remarked Judge. "Eight thousand dollars is a lot of money."

"Th-that's what I've allus sus-said," agreed Tommy heartily.

"And still," remarked Henry cheerfully, "in a way, this incident is a godsend, Judge. It proves that the Two Deuces are not in jail."

"Yes, I believe you are right, sir," agreed Judge. "I suppose we better go to town."

Henry got painfully to his feet. Tommy looked him over curiously.

"Huh-horse throwed yuh?" he asked.

"Yes," groaned Henry, reaching for his hat.

"That's tut-tough."

The three men rode to town, where Doc White explained about the robbery. Apparently Doc had been so busy, clinging to the seat of the stage, that he had not seen Henry do his leap-for-life over the edge of the cañon.

"It's kinda funny," remarked Doc. "You remember askin' me about them two bein' a tall man and a short one, Henry."

"Yes, I remember mentioning it," agreed Henry dryly.

"Well, that's what these two were."

"I see. Is there any possible chance that one of them could have been a woman?"

"By golly, yes! One was short and skinny. Might have been a woman, at that."

Henry found Josephine at the hotel, arguing with the cook.

"Ay am not saying a vord," she told Henry.

"Afraid of retaliation?" he queried.

Josephine looked blankly at him for a moment.

"Ay don't know what that vord means—but Ay am," she replied, definitely ending the interview.

The eight thousand dollars had been shipped to the bank for

the Yellow Warrior mine, which was the largest producer in the district. Danny and Nick were jubilant. It proved that the Two Deuces were still at their old trade. Henry talked with John Campbell, the prosecutor, who admitted there was a possibility that Danny and Nick were not the Two Deuces.

"Of course," he pointed out, "there is nothing to prevent any two men from using two deuces. It merely muddles things worse, and does not in any way exonerate Danny Regan and Nick Borden."

CHAPTER V

COMPLICATIONS

OUT AT THE J Bar C, Frijole Bill sat on the edge of a bed in the bunk-house, hunched over, a painful expression on his face, while Oscar Johnson slowly poured vinegar from a bottle onto a wadded cloth on Frijole's head.

When it began to run down Frijole's face and neck, he corked the bottle, placed it on the table, and picked up a gallon jug.

"Yuh better lay off that there stuff," warned Frijole. "Couple drinks of that and you'll start braggin'."

"Ay got to have couple drinks," declared Oscar. "Ay am in a ha'al of a yam."

"So 'm I," groaned Frijole. "I ain't never goin' to listen to no cock-eyed Swede again. You'll git me hung before yo're through."

"It vars a good scheme," declared Oscar. "Ve could proof to de vorld that Danny and Nick vars not de Two Deuces."

"Shore. And go to jail for life," complained Frijole. "My Gawd, that Swedish female can throw straight. I'm scared that the whole works is in the bottom of Pinon Cañon. Gimme more vinegar."

"Voe is me," wailed Oscar. "Yosephine vould know me."

"Aw, hell! You had a mask over yore face."

"Ay know," wailed Oscar. "But Ay vars vearing a ring she gave me."

Oscar held out a huge ham-like hand for Frijole's inspection. On the second finger was a huge, nearly-gold ring, with an enormous red glass setting.

Frijole reached up, grasped his vinegar-pack in his right hand, and flung it violently to the floor.

"You can do as yuh damn please," he gritted, "but I'm rattlin' my hocks for Mexico. Why didn't yuh hang a sign on yore manly bosom, tellin' the world who yuh are? Yuh might have put a piece in the paper; so we could have had a audience. If all yore brains was nitro-glycerine, and exploded, it wouldn't blow yore nose."

"Ay am not vorrying about my nose," replied Oscar dismally. "If Yosephine—"

"Sh-h-h!" warned Frijole. "Somebody comin'! Keep yore mouth shut, will yuh?"

It was Henry and Judge. They stabled their horses and came stiffly up to the house, saw Oscar in the bunk-house doorway and came down there. Henry sniffed audibly.

"Smells like vinegar around here, Oscar," he remarked.

"Ay have been soaking Free-holey's head," replied Oscar. "De hurse t'rew him off on a rock."

Frijole poked his head out of the doorway, disclosing a bump the size of a hen's egg on the side of his head. Henry and Judge looked critically at the swelling, while Frijole, sad-eyed, gazed painfully at them.

"The horse spooked at a rattler and bogged down with me," explained Frijole. He squinted critically at Henry.

"You look kinda bunged up, too," he remarked.

"I—I *fell* off my horse," replied Henry. He turned to Oscar.

"You didn't hear about Josephine, did you?" he asked.

"Yosephine?" queried Oscar blankly. Henry looked at Judge, and his left eyelid flickered before he turned back to Oscar.

"I don't believe we should tell him, Judge. It was terrible."

"Yeeminy gosh!" gasped Oscar. "Did that stage yump—"

"Whoa!" snapped Frijole. "Git that jug, Oscar; we all need a big drink."

Oscar stumbled into the bunk-house.

"What is wrong with the Swede?" asked Judge.

"Search me," whispered Frijole. "He's been actin' queer all day."

"Yes, I suppose he has," remarked Henry.

Oscar spilled much liquor, as his trembling hands poured the four portions into tin cups. They drank solemnly, after which Henry and Judge limped up to the house. They stood at a window and watched Oscar saddle a horse and gallop away to Tonto City.

"The tall one and the short one," murmured Henry. Suddenly he jerked around and faced Judge.

"I can see it all now, Judge. Josephine recognized Oscar. That is why she refused to make any comments."

"They should both be in jail—Oscar and Frijole," declared Judge.

"The same old judicial attitude," sighed Henry. "Judge, I fully believe that those two men had the same idea as we had—to prove that the Two Deuces were still abroad in the land."

"But—but—" spluttered Judge. "But they took eight thousand dollars, Henry!"

"Very true. But only through the grace of God did we fail to get it ourselves."

"True, Henry. I am prone to forget the old adage, 'Let him who is without sin cast the first stone.'"

"I wonder how on earth Doc White failed to recognize Oscar," grinned Henry. "I should like to have seen Josephine and that traveling salesman diving back into the stage, after Josephine threw that rock. What a situation!"

"What a mess!" corrected Judge dismally.

"I never have admired that word," said Henry, "but it seems

to fit this situation better than any other, Four fools with but a single thought. Or should I have said, four fools without a single brain, Judge?"

"Words are inadequate," groaned Judge huskily. "I—I need that jug."

"Don't we all?" sighed Henry. "But not too much, Judge. Remember, we both have a guilty conscience, and we cannot afford to talk too much. Unless I am mistaken in my diagnosis of Oscar Johnson, he is more interested in finding out what Josephine might do than in feeding and taking care of the prisoners."

ABOUT AN hour later, when Henry and Judge came to Tonto City, Oscar was coming from the Tonto Hotel, his too-small sombrero sitting squarely on the top of his huge head, a vacant stare in his small, blue eyes.

"How is everything, Oscar?" queried Henry.

"She's ollright," replied Oscar absently. "She vasn't hort."

But Oscar did not stay long. As soon as Henry and Judge sat down in the office, Oscar headed for the ranch, where he found Frijole sitting on the bunk-house steps, feeding corn to Bill Shakespeare, the biggest and most decrepit-looking rooster in all of Arizona. Bill was a confirmed alcoholic, due to eating Frijole's prune-whisky mash.

Oscar sat down with Frijole and sighed dismally.

"Didja see Josephine?" asked Frijole anxiously.

"Yah, su-ure, Ay seen her," admitted the disconsolate Swede.

"Yuh mean—she recognized yuh behind that mask?"

"Yah, su-ure."

"What lovely weather we're havin'! And her bein' more than half-way religious, too."

"She go to church all de time," nodded Oscar.

"Yea-a-ah, that's fine. Told yuh to go and give yourself up, and take yore medicine, eh?"

"Yosephine is a good girl," defended Oscar.

"She didn't recognize me, did she?"

"Ay told her."

"You told her! My Gawd, I'll—Oscar, did you—"

"Ay promise not to keep secrets from her."

"Oh, that's wonderful! What a beautiful faith. Because you promised yore girl—you'd send me to jail for life. You seventeen kinds of knot-headed ignorance, don't yuh realize that she's jist the kind that would send us *both* up for life? Because she ain't got brains enough to wad a shotgun, she'd set there on the witness stand and swear me and you behind the bars."

"Ay am in ha'al of a yam," complained Oscar.

"Yeah, and you dragged me in with yuh. What's to be done?"

"Ay guess ve have to do what she says, Free-holey."

"Huh! What's she say?"

"She say she keep her mouth shut if ve give her half de money."

Frijole's jaw sagged.

"She said she'd—Oscar, are you crazy, or am I?" whispered Frijole hoarsely.

"Both," replied Oscar soberly.

"But we can't give her half," wailed Frijole. "We've got to git that money back to the owners. We can't keep it. Didn't you explain that to her, you rattle-headed hairpin?"

"Yah, su-ure. She say de bank will be lucky to get half."

"I didn't think she was that kind of a girl, Oscar."

"She is yust a damn highyacker, Free-holey."

"Yeah, I guess yo're right. Live and learn. If she tells Henry what she knows, me and you will be in jail, too."

"Yah, su-ure."

"But she won't tell if we give her four thousand dollars, eh?"

Oscar nodded slowly.

"Well, I reckon there's only one thing to do, Oscar," said Frijole.

"Give her four t'ousand dollar, Free-holey?"

"Hell—no! We'll take the eight thousand ourselves and head for Mexico. Bring out that jug; this case needs a conference.

After that we're goin' to Tonto City for supper. I'm danged if I'm goin' to wrangle any food here tonight."

They were fairly well organized when they went to town. Henry and Judge had supper with Mrs. Harper and Leila. Oscar and Frijole were in no mood for sociability. They had a few drinks and wandered around town. Neither of them wanted to go to Mexico. They didn't want that eight thousand dollars either.

"You t'ink Ay should talk with Yosephine some more, Free-holey?" asked Oscar.

"You've talked with Josephine too damn much already," snarled the little cook.

"Ay might ask her to take two t'ousand dollar, Free-holey."

"Not a damn dime! Keep away from her, the daw-gone hijacker!"

Oscar slept at the jail, and Frijole went back to the ranch with Henry and Judge. It was late when they arrived, but Frijole went into the house with them and they sat down in the main room.

Henry and Judge looked narrowly at Frijole, who drew his gun and placed it in his lap.

"I've got a little talk for you fellers," stated Frijole calmly. "And after I git it all said, I hope yuh don't act foolish."

"That would establish a precedent," replied Henry soberly. "We are accustomed to act foolish, Frijole; but go ahead."

"All right. Now don't stop me to ask damn fool questions. Today me and Oscar Johnson held up that stage and took eight thousand dollars. We wasn't after the money. All we wanted to do was to show that the Two Deuces wasn't Danny and Nick.

"Josephine Swensen recognized Oscar, and she hit me with a rock. I didn't git dumped off no horse, like I said. Anyway, we wasn't goin' to keep that money, but we brought it here and cached it. Like I said, Josephine recognized Oscar, and she told him she would keep her mouth shut if we'd give her four thousand dollars.

"I'm headin' for Mexico; Oscar can do as he pleases. But I'm handin' the money over to you fellers. You can say yuh found it, or anythin' yuh want to say, jist so the bank gits it back. That's my story, gents."

Henry and Judge sat there, shooting occasional glances at each other.

"It sounds like a fairy tale, Frijole," said Henry, "but I am forced to believe you."

"To me it is incredible," declared Judge. "Frijole, I never thought you would sink to the level of a highwayman. And to think that the estimable Josephine would lower herself to—well, plain hijacking. My faith in human nature has been ruined."

"One never knows, does one?" queried Henry brightly. "You say you have the money hidden, Frijole?"

"I shore have. C'mon, we'll git it."

Frijole led the way to the bunk-house, where he lighted a lamp.

"Mebbe this ain't the best place on earth t'hide a fortune, but I figgered it would do for one night," he told them.

He flung back the blankets on his bunk and lifted up the straw-tick. On top of the slats was a section of old canvas. Frijole stared at the canvas, looked sharply at the bottom of the tick and jerked back.

"My Gawd! It's gone!" he blurted. "Why—why, where—who—"

"Nonsense!" snorted Judge. "If you put it there—"

"I put it there!" yelped Frijole. "I tell yuh, I put it there!"

"Perhaps Oscar moved it," suggested Henry mildly.

"He never had no chance, I've been with him every damn minute, until we left him in town. Oscar never touched it, I tell yuh."

"Did you count it?" asked Henry.

"Of course we didn't count it. It was all in bundles. We never opened one of 'em. We didn't know how much it was until you told us. But where in the devil is that money?"

Henry smiled thoughtfully.

"I wouldn't go to Mexico if I were you," he told Frijole. "As far as Josephine is concerned, she will not do anything as long as there is a chance to get that money. At least, let us wait a few days."

"All right," replied Frijole, "I'll do it. But I'm goin' to keep a horse all saddled—and it ain't far to the Border."

HENRY WENT to Scorpion Bend next day. Not feeling equal to riding horseback, he climbed up on the stage with Doc White.

"Investigatin' the robbery?" queried Doc, as they drove away from Tonto City.

"Just between us, Doc," replied Henry, "I must keep up an appearance of making an investigation. I want you to point out the exact spot where the hold-up occurred. Not that it will be of any use, but I believe it is customary."

"Sure," nodded the driver. "I believe I can even find the rock that Josephine Swensen threw—if it'll do you any good."

Doc White stopped the stage at the spot, and described the hold-up in detail, while Henry listened gravely and attentively. After which Doc kicked off the brake, and they went on.

"You was an actor before you came here, wasn't you?" queried Doc.

"Quite correct," agreed Henry soberly. "In me, my dear sir, you see the foremost actor of the age—retired. If I may say so, no other actor of the speaking stage was ever as well and favorably known as Henry Harrison Conroy."

"Is that a fact?" gasped Doc.

"My boy," lied Henry grandly, "I have been commanded by a king."

"Can you imagine that?"

"It is well known," declared Henry. "For years I was a headliner with the Belasco and Conroy Circuit. My name blazed in lights. In fact, I was half-owner with Belasco, drawing a measly stipend of fifty thousand dollars a year. Can you imagine that?"

"No, I can't," admitted Doc.

"It is theatrical history. Why, I was the next-to-closing act in every theater I ever played; and I've played every theater from Bangor, Maine, to—to Madagascar."

"Where is that?" asked Doc curiously.

"Madagascar? Why—why, it is away out there—not so much of a place, of course. My remark was really a figure of speech."

As a matter of fact, Henry was a trifle vague as to the location of Madagascar himself.

"Fifty thousand dollars is a pretty good salary," said Doc.

"That was not a figure of speech," declared Henry. "Of course, my main income was from the business. We made millions."

"How didja happen to come out here?" asked Doc.

"Ill health," replied Henry quickly. "The air of Arizona has done wonders for me. Great country—Arizona."

"Do you still own half the business, Henry?"

"I own *all* of it. But I closed it all down, because I couldn't find an honest man to handle it while I came here."

"Threw a lot of people out of work, didn't it, Henry?"

"About ten thousand, I suppose."

That ended the conversation, as far as Henry's past was concerned. At Scorpion Bend Henry visited the bank from which the money had been shipped, after which he visited around the town. Late in the afternoon he met Tommy Roper, the stuttering cowboy from the Tonto City livery stable. Tommy explained that he was up there to take a new buggy back to Tonto. He was just a trifle intoxicated.

"I was tut-talkin' with Doc Wh-White over in the Nun-New York Saloon," informed Tommy. "I th-thought you'd like to know wh-what he sus-said about you."

"Personal opinions are always interesting," replied Henry.

"Huh?" queried Tommy.

"I meant that I would like to hear what he said, Tommy."

"Uh—huh. Well, he sus-said you was the bub-biggest liar he ever sus-seen."

"My goodness, Tommy! That is interesting. Proceed."

"Huh?"

"Go ahead. What else did he say about me?"

"Well, huh—he said you nun-never got fuf-fifty thousand dollars a year, and he sus-said that the outfit you worked for never ex-exis—exis—never was."

Henry rubbed his nose thoughtfully.

"I—I sus-said to him," continued Tommy confidentially, "that you was mum-mum-my friend, and he sus-said, well, 'you bub-believe him, I wo-won't.'"

"Very nice of you, Tommy," nodded Henry. "I appreciate it."

"And then," continued Tommy, "he sus-said that you wasn't no gut-great actor. He—he sus-said you was juj-just a red-nun-nosed mug, who fuf-filled in be-be-between the dud-dog acts."

"That is calumny," murmured Henry.

"Th-that's what I th-th-thought, tut-too," agreed Tommy. "If I was you, I wouldn't never sus-speak to the sa-sa-sa-sap-sucker again."

"That would be punishment enough, I suppose. Tommy, I would like to buy you a drink."

"Th-thanks a lot," replied Tommy, "bub-but I've gug-got to take that bub-buggy back to Tonto sus-safely. Mum-much obliged."

"How about me riding back with you, Tommy? I do not care to stay here all night."

"Th-th-that suits me fuf-fine," agreed Tommy. "I shore huh-hate to have to tut-tut-talk to myself fuf-for tut-twenty-fuf-five miles."

"I am not surprised," said Henry.

CHAPTER VI

FORTUNE TELLING

JUDGE VAN TREECE awoke from his siesta on the porch of the J Bar C ranch house. Apparently there was a terrific commotion in the bunk-house for several moments which died down to an occasional yelp or explosive profanity.

Judge merely scratched his chin, brushed away a fly, and wondered why Henry went to Scorpion Bend that day.

Presently he saw Oscar striding down to the stable, where he saddled a horse and rode away toward Tonto City. A few minutes later he heard a slight noise, twisted his head, and saw Frijole Bill standing near the corner of the porch.

Frijole's shirt was minus both sleeves, and he had one discolored eye. He looked at Judge, spat dryly, and limped around to the steps, where he sat down wearily.

"I told that damn Swede that somebody stole the money," said Frijole. "He—he took it kinda hard."

"I believe that," agreed Judge. "You seem to have taken it rather hard yourself, Frijole."

"I reckon I should have wrote him a letter," sighed the cook.

"Swedes are temperamental," said Judge.

"Jist like dynamite in hot weather, Judge. He thought I stole it from him. Gawd, he's shore hard to convince."

"Where has he gone now?" asked Judge.

"Oh, he's gone to tell Josephine that the money has been stolen."

Judge scratched his chin, drew a deep breath, and mumbled something.

"What'd yuh say?" asked Frijole.

"Oh, I was merely offering up a little prayer for the soul of Oscar Johnson."

"Do you believe in prayers, Judge?"

"Absolutely."

"I reckon I ain't never pointed none of mine in the right direction. I 'member one time up in Colorado, when a mighty big bear run me up a danged little tree. There I was, swayin' on the topmost bough, while the bear stood up and pawed bark. Well, I shore prayed a-plenty that time. I ain't never been no great hand to ask favors, but I shore needed assistance that time.

" 'Course I couldn't git down on my knees, and not be bear-bait, and I could not clasp my hands, like the preacher does. All I could do was hang on, gaze up, and do m' askin' thataway. For fifteen, twenty minutes I didn't do nothin' but hang on and ask.

"I was gittin' cramps in my legs and a sickenin' feelin' in my stummick. I says, 'I reckon there ain't nobody listenin' to me, bear; so it shore looks like me and you was goin' to git awful close to each other.' Then I happened to look real sharp, and I seen that the bear had a collar around his neck.

"Judge, that danged bear was a pet! He didn't want food—he wanted to play with me."

"That was the answer to your prayer, Frijole," declared Judge.

"Yea-a-ah? That's how it works, eh? Well, I'll tell yuh, it shore learned me to kinda rely on m'self. After that experience, every time I felt like I ort to pray, I took another look to see if it didn't have a collar around its neck. Most allus it did."

"I have never realized that you were a philosopher, Frijole."

"Well, I ain't never claimed just what I am, Judge. Paw was a Presbyterian and Maw was a Methodist. That makes me sort of a mulligan, don't it?"

"Or hash," smiled Judge. "Well, I suppose I better go back to the office. With a Swedish highwayman as a jailer I suppose it is up to me to take care of the prisoners."

"When's Henry comin' back, Judge?"

"Tomorrow, I suppose."

"Uh-huh. You comin' back for supper?"

"No, I do not believe I shall, Frijole."

"Uh-huh. Well, I won't start no supper for Oscar until he gets back. If Josephine takes that loss as hard as Oscar did, he'll be in a hospital before suppertime."

Oscar came back intact, but disconsolate.

"Vorse dan ever," he told Frijole. "Ay explain about somebody stealing de money, and she laugh at me. Ay ta'al her ve have told everything to Hanry, and she say Hanry and Yudge are yust as big crooks as me and you, Free-holey."

"That shore makes us all even," remarked the little cook. "Mebbe she thinks that Henry and Judge stole the eight thousand."

"Yah, su-ure. Ay suggested it to her."

"*You* did?"

"Yah, su-ure."

"Well, I'll be a pink-eyed elephant! Ain't you jist a whole wagon-load of bright ideas? It's a wonder to me that you ain't President of the United States."

"Ay varsn't born in dis country," stated Oscar blandly. "Ay am not American—Ay am Svede—man."

"If you'd stayed home, they might have made you King of Sweden."

"Yah, su-ure."

"All right," sighed Frijole. "I know when I'm whipped. But what other bright ideas did Josephine have?"

"Va'al, she says she vants four t'ousand dollar, or she ta'al Yohn Campbell, de pro-se-cuting attorney."

"Well, I'll be a bald-headed armadillo! Why, Oscar, that would git Henry and Judge into trouble!"

"Yah, su-ure; she knows it."

"Well," sighed Frijole, "I reckon we better catch a couple extra horses. It'd shore look funny to see all four of us headin' for Mexico. But what in hell would she do with four thousand dollars?"

"Va'al, she say dat four t'ousand vould be plenty for us to stort hoose-keeping on, Free-holey."

"My Gawd!" gasped Frijole in amazement.

"Yah, su-ure," nodded Oscar. "Ve get married."

"And raise a flock of hijackers, eh?" snorted Frijole. "Wash yore face and hands, you—you—you—"

Frijole swallowed painfully.

"The mulligan's ready," he finished hoarsely.

It was late in the evening when Henry and Tommy reached Tonto City. Henry slipped quietly away from the livery stable and was gone for about an hour before he came back, saddled his horse and went out to the ranch alone. Frijole was in the house, reading a dog-eared novel.

"I was hopin' you'd show up," said Frijole. "Oscar told Josephine about somebody stealin' that money, and she thinks you and Judge took it. She says she'll git her half or she'll tell John Campbell."

"Well, my gracious!" exclaimed Henry. "Misery, thy name is woman!"

"This 'n's name is Josephine," corrected Frijole.

"But where on earth did she get the idea that Judge and I took that money?"

"Oscar suggested it, Henry."

"Oscar! He—" Henry struggled for words. "Of all things!"

"Yuh didn't, did yuh?" queried Frijole.

"You, too," said Henry wearily. "Do I need to deny it?"

"Yuh don't have to—no. But don't forgit that me and that damn Swede are responsible for that eight thousand. If you got it, it's all right, too. I've got four horses down in the stable, in case Josephine does tell Campbell."

"Four horses? What for, Frijole?"

"For you and me and Judge and Oscar—to ride to Mexico."

"Well, that is mighty thoughtful of you, Frijole, I sincerely hope we do not have to use them."

"Same here," nodded Frijole. "But I wouldn't trust Josephine. She wants that four thousand, so her and Oscar can git married."

Henry stared at Frijole for several moments, as though slow to grasp the meaning of Frijole's statement. Then he said quietly:

"Frijole, have you ever seen a strong man have a complete mental breakdown, becoming more and more hysterical until he exploded with the very, very dullest of well known thuds?"

"No, I don't reckon I have, Henry," replied Frijole soberly.

"Then I think you better go to bed."

"Yeah—all right. I jist waited up to tell yuh the news."

"Thank you, Frijole—good night."

THE NEXT day being Saturday, Henry went to Tonto City early. He found Judge and Oscar in the office. Judge's lean face was blazing with wrath when Henry came in, while Oscar, bland of countenance, sagged back on the single cot in the office.

"There you are!" snorted Judge. "The fat is in the fire, Henry! That howling example of feminine femininity, Miss Josephine Swensen, fiancée of this Swedish cross between a missing-link and a broken-oar, says that if she doesn't get her share of that robbery, perpetrated by Oscar and Frijole, today—today, mind you—she will take the information to John Campbell, along with the information that you and I stole the money from Oscar and Frijole. Think that over, Henry."

"Well," replied Henry quietly, "it is a nice day for it, Judge."

"Nice day! Do you realize what the law will do for us—guilty or not guilty—on such evidence?"

"Yes, I believe there is some sort of a penalty. Frijole seems rather wrought up over the situation. In fact, he has four horses ready for us to ride to Mexico."

"Mexico? What on earth would we four do in Mexico?"

"Well, my dear Judge, we couldn't do much worse than we have done here—if the evidence is true."

"I will grant you that. But, damn it, I do not care for Mexico."

"Needs must, when the devil drives, Judge."

"Yosephine," corrected Oscar quietly.

Henry rubbed his nose and considered Oscar.

"Josephine will miss you when you are in Mexico, Oscar."

"Ay am not going," replied Oscar.

"I see. You prefer jail, do you?"

"No. Ay am going to turn state's evidence."

For several moments no one spoke. Only the labored breathing of Judge Van Treece broke the stillness of the little office.

Finally Henry said quietly:

"I wonder if there is any of Frijole's liquor left in that jug in the closet."

"I do not care for a drink," said Judge huskily.

"Neither do I," replied Henry. "But there are times when something desperate must be done; and that is the most desperate thing I can suggest right now."

Oscar drank with them and walked over to the doorway, where he looked up the street.

"Yudas Priest!" he gasped. "Ha'ar comes Yohn Campbell!"

"You go over there and sit down!" snapped Henry. "And if you so much as open your mouth I'll hit you so hard that it will shake Stockholm."

Oscar obeyed meekly. It was the first time that Henry had ever spoken to him in that manner, and Oscar was a trifle shocked.

Henry looked narrowly at the big lawyer, who smiled pleasantly.

"I knew you went to Scorpion Bend yesterday, and I wondered if there was anything new on that latest stage robbery, Henry," said Campbell.

Henry drew a breath of relief. "No, there isn't, John. In fact, I haven't a clue of any kind to work on. There is no doubt in my mind that the two men are laughing at our puny efforts! No matter what the evidence against Danny and Nick, the Two Deuces are not in jail."

"Perhaps not," nodded Campbell. "But until we capture the real Two Deuces and force them to confess that they shot George Gray, I am very much afraid that Danny and Nick will face a murder trial."

"It appears that way," sighed Judge.

"They haven't retained counsel yet, have they?"

"Not yet," replied Henry.

"Court convenes next Wednesday," reminded Campbell, "and this is the first case on the docket, Henry."

"Ay vould like to ask a question," said Oscar.

"You keep out of this, Oscar," snapped Judge. "When two gentlemen are talking—"

"Va'al, Ay yust vanted to know if—"

"You don't need to know anything," exclaimed Judge. "Keep still."

"Perhaps I could—" began Campbell.

"Don't pay any attention to him, John," advised Henry nervously.

"Ay yust—"

"No!" roared Judge. "Not a word, Oscar. John Campbell is not at all interested in you."

Campbell laughed and flicked some ashes off his cigar.

"Well, I suppose I might as well go back to the office," he remarked. "I hate to see this case come to trial without those two boys being well represented."

"Oh, they will be represented—or not need representation," assured Henry.

Campbell walked away. Henry and Judge turned fiercely on Oscar.

"You vitrified Viking!" roared Judge. "What in the devil did you want to ask Campbell?"

"Va'al," replied Oscar soberly, "Ay yust vanted to ask him how much a vedding license costs."

"Judge," said Henry after a long silence, "where did you put that jug? That Swede may rob me of years, but he cannot rob me of thirst."

They had a drink and Judge put the jug away.

"Ay am vorried," declared Oscar. "Ay vish you two vould go and talk with Yosephine. She tell me that today is de dead-line."

Judge looked soberly at Oscar, his eyes narrowed thoughtfully.

"I wish I was strong enough to wring your neck, Oscar," he said.

"Yah, su-ure," agreed Oscar. "Ay have t'ick neck."

"And head," added Judge.

"Su-ure. Ay vear seven and a half hat."

Henry sighed audibly and walked over to his desk, where he picked up his belt and gun. Carefully he buckled it around his ample waist and jerked the holster around on his leg.

Oscar watched him narrowly and anxiously.

"Ay have not made up my mind yust what to do, you know," he said slowly. "Ay don't vant to cause any trouble."

"That suits me all right," replied Henry. "But keep away from Josephine. That woman is pure dynamite."

"Yah, su-ure."

HENRY PUT on his hat and went up the street. It seemed as though everybody in Wild Horse Valley was in Tonto City. Many of them smiled behind Henry's back, but he did not care. He talked with Mrs. Harper and Leila, but offered no hope of getting Danny and Nick out of jail. Leila was baking a cake to take to the prisoners.

An hour or so later Henry wandered into the Tonto Saloon. Judge and Oscar were there, with Frijole, who was so intoxicated that he did not recognize Henry.

John Campbell, Doc White and three other men were playing a desultory game of poker. It was Doc's off-day from driving the stage, and he loved poker. Three of the men left the table, and Henry sat down in one of their chairs. He picked up the deck and idly shuffled the cards. Judge came over and stood near the table.

"Let me tell your fortune, Judge," suggested Henry.

Judge smiled and shook his head.

"Poppycock," he remarked.

"My fortune telling is absolutely reliable," said Henry. "I will admit that a large percentage of fortune telling is poppycock, but mine is not. I never fail to tell the truth."

Doc White laughed shortly.

"Fortune teller, eh?" he sneered. "Was that how you made fifty thousand dollars a year, Henry?"

"Sorry, but it was not," murmured Henry. "But I can tell fortunes."

"Tell Judge's fortune," urged Campbell.

"I could," agreed Henry, "but that would hardly be a fair test of my powers. Anyone may prophesy the future. That part of it is a hit or miss proposition. A man's past is easier to prove. Judge and I have been associated for months. Naturally, I know much of his past; so any fortune telling with Judge would be from what I know. The cards might corroborate this, but no one would believe me."

"That's just a lot of damn bunk," declared Doc White.

"It is not bunk," denied Henry warmly. "The cards do not lie."

"I thought you was an intelligent man, Henry."

"I think I am," replied Henry soberly. "I may be wrong."

"Do yuh think you could tell my fortune?" queried Doc.

"Certainly."

"I think you're crazy. I'll bet you twenty dollars that you can't."

"You are taking an unfair advantage, Doc," said Henry.

"You wouldn't bet on it, eh? I thought you'd reneg."

"You misinterpret my meaning," said Henry quietly. "As I said a while ago, the only fortune telling which may be proved is of a person's past. If I accepted your twenty-dollar wager, what would prevent you from denying the accuracy of my revelations—and taking my money? That is why the bet is unfair to me."

"Wait a minute!" snapped Doc. "With me, a bet is a bet. If you can tell me—aw, what the hell! I've seen—"

"Just a moment," interrupted Henry. "I believe that in every man's life is some one thing which impressed him most. It may have happened in childhood; possibly later in life. It would be something that only that man would know about. Surely, it would not be anything that *I* would know.

"Perhaps something like that has happened to you, Doc. If I can tell you what it was, after reading the cards, will you admit it?"

Doc reached in his pocket, selected a twenty-dollar gold piece and tossed it on the poker table.

"Twenty dollars' worth," he grunted. "But I'll be buyin' drinks for the house—on your money, Henry."

Henry turned and called to the bartender:

"Frank! Bring me a new deck, will you? Blue-backs, if you have then; that is my lucky color."

"You'll need luck," grinned Doc. "I happen to know something about this fortune tellin' game myself."

Someone tossed the new deck on the table, and Henry shuffled them carefully. He made mystic passes with the deck, and numbed unintelligible words, while the crowd stood around and smiled.

Finally he was ready to make the layout.

Taking two cards off the top of the deck, he placed them together, face down.

"Those are your fortune cards, Doc," explained Henry. "I place the next card on the opposite side, face down. That is your occupation card."

"A little different layout, but the same old bunk," grinned Doc.

"Sorry," murmured Henry. "But do not forget your agreement."

"I back my bet," declared Doc.

Henry slowly dealt out two rows of seven cards each, face up. He placed the rest of the deck on the table, staring intently at the fourteen cards.

Slowly he lifted his eyes and looked at Doc.

"That is certainly strange," said Henry. "I haven't seen that layout for a long time. Doc, how long have you been driving stage?"

"What the hell has that got to do with it?" asked Doc. "Anyway, you're tellin' this fortune."

"It doesn't show you as a stage driver; so you haven't been one long enough to influence the cards."

"Of all the damn bunk!" snapped Doc.

"There is no bunk about it," denied Henry. "Those cards show—"

HENRY KNITTED his brows thoughtfully. Then he reached over a pudgy right hand and placed it on the lone card, face down, "This card will settle that question," he stated and turned it over.

"The joker!" blurted someone.

"The joke's on Henry," declared Doc.

"Wait a moment," begged Henry. "There is no joke connected with this card."

Henry leaned forward, one hand on the table, looking at Doc.

"Doc, how long ago were you a ventriloquist in vaudeville?"

Doc White jerked back in his chair, staring at Henry. Then he seemed to grip his nerves and his eyes narrowed venomously.

"What the hell are you talkin' about?" he asked tensely.

"The cards don't lie," replied Henry coldly. "Take a look at your fortune cards!"

With a flip of his fingers, Henry turned over the two

concealed cards—the deuce of spades and the deuce of clubs. The calling cards of the Two Deuces!

"Two Deuces," said Henry slowly. "One always out of sight, with the voice of a woman—except when *you* get held up, Doc. If you—"

With the snarl of a trapped animal, Doc kicked his chair backwards, coming halfway to his feet, clawing a gun loose from his pocket. From beneath the table a forty-five roared, the bullet lifting splinters and cards from the table-top.

Doc White's clawing hand jerked away, and he pitched forward across the table, sprawling almost into Henry, who promptly fell over backwards in his chair, crashing down, with his two feet waving in the air.

Doc White was struggling on the table, when Oscar, with a whoop, swooped down on him, clasped him in his brawny arms and lifted him bodily off the table.

"Did dis ha'ar yigger shoot Hanry?" he roared anxiously.

Judge and Campbell were helping Henry to his feet, and he stood against the table, his nose redder than it had ever been seen in Tonto City.

"Close work!" he panted. "Wasn't sure that bullet would stop him, shooting through the table-top."

"My God, Henry, you drew quickly!" panted Judge, his face drawn.

"I had the gun in my lap all the time, Judge."

Oscar placed Doc White on the pool table, and someone went for the doctor.

"No—use," whispered Doc painfully. "I'm—glad."

"Glad to cheat the law, Doc?" asked Campbell.

"Why not?" whispered Doc. "Where's Henry?"

"Right here," replied Henry. "Want to talk, Doc?"

"You win, Henry. I—I didn't think you'd tumble to the scheme."

"Your mistake was in describing the men who robbed you, Doc. Why didn't you give one a high-pitched voice?"

"My—mistake," whispered Doc. "I—I wanted to—make—it—harder."

"You confess that you alone was the Two Deuces?" asked Campbell.

"I—swear—Campbell, I—killed—George—Gray—and—"

"I guess I asked that question just in time," said Campbell quietly. "It clears up the whole mystery—thanks to Henry."

Henry threw back his shoulders, shoved his hands deeply into his pockets, and there was a trifle of swagger in his walk as he went toward the doorway, where a crowd had gathered. Oscar came up to him, rather timidly, it seemed.

"Can Ay do somet'ing for you, Hanry?" he asked.

Henry squinted at him thoughtfully and replied:

"You can go out to the ranch, put up fresh decorations, and try to hang the Chinese lanterns right side up this time."

"Can that son-of-a-gun read the cards!" gasped Frijole in a hoarse whisper.

"There is one thing we forgot," said Campbell. "We forgot to ask Doc White what he did with all the money. That was a bad—"

"I think I've got about thirteen thousand of it in my office safe," stated Henry. "That will cover most of the losses."

"In *your* safe?" gasped the prosecutor.

"Yes, John. I read the cards last night, and they said that the money was inside an empty five-gallon demijohn in Doc White's kitchen. I shall turn it over to the bank for distribution."

"You read the cards," parroted Campbell. "Wonderful!"

"Miraculous," corrected Henry. "I suppose we may turn Danny and Nick loose?"

"Go ahead," said Campbell. "I'll fix the papers later. But what about that last stage robbery, Henry? Doc didn't do that."

"Merely some cheap imitators," replied Henry blandly. "We have the money back; and they have had a severe lesson.

"I believe we may declare the case closed, John."

"That suits me perfectly, Henry."

Halfway across the street Judge halted Henry.

"How in the devil did you do it—with those cards?"

"I palmed the deuces and the joker from the other deck."

"I see. But why suspect Doc White?"

"Judge, there were only three people on that stage who could have recognized Oscar and Frijole. Certainly, neither Josephine nor that drummer came out to the ranch, searched the bunk-house and recovered that money."

"By George, that is right! Simple deduction, of course. But what about the ventriloquist part? I don't see how you guessed that."

"Merely the fact of a high-pitched voice from an invisible person, Judge. After I felt sure that Doc White stole that money from the bunk-house, I became interested in him. So I rode to Scorpion Bend with him, and lied vigorously about my vaudeville career. I created the Belasco-Conroy circuit, gave myself a half interest, and drew fifty thousand dollars a year.

"Doc knew I lied. In Scorpion Bend he drank enough to tell what a liar I was. He swore that the Belasco-Conroy circuit never did exist, and that I was only a small-time act, following a dog number. That hurt me a little, Judge. The truth very often does hurt.

"However, it proved to me that Doc White's knowledge was not that of the layman. Last night I burgled his shack, found the missing money, and also some treasured copies of a well-known theatrical publication which contained pictures and publicity for Doc White, Ventriloquist Extraordinary."

"I am very glad," said Judge warmly. "I am a man of above-average mentality, I hope; but you almost had me believing in fortune telling, Henry."

"Evidently I put on a good act," smiled Henry. "There goes Laura and Leila toward the jail, all excited. Let us hurry."

From behind them came Tommy Roper's voice, and they stopped.

"I—I juj-just wanted to gug-get it sus-straight," stammered Tommy. "Fuf-first you tut-take off tut-two cards and put 'em fuf-face down. Those are the fuf-fortune cards. Then you—you—you tut-take one cuc-cuc-card and—"

"That is all there is to the trick, Tommy," replied Henry gravely.

"Th-th-then what do you dud-do?"

"It all depends on whether you are a gun-man or a foot-racer, Tommy."

"Sh-sh-shoot or rur-run, eh?"

"That seems to be the grand finale," nodded Henry, and went with Judge toward the jail, where Laura and Leila were waiting anxiously. The Two Deuces of Wild Horse Valley had passed into history; and Oscar Johnson was putting up the decorations.

At the Tonto Hotel, Josephine heard the news, without emotion. Win, lose, or draw, it was all the same to her. She picked up her tray and went calmly to the kitchen for another order of hash.

HENRY RIDES THE DANGER TRAIL

*Death stalked the range along Wild Horse
Valley and it was up to Sheriff Henry
to solve three mysterious murders*

CHAPTER I

ACCIDENTALLY SHOT

CHARLES H. LIVINGSTONE, attorney-at-law, sat on the edge of a chair in the sheriff's office at Tonto City. Charles Livingstone was huge, pompous, well-groomed. He rested his gloved hands on the curve of a heavy cane, and fixed inquiring eyes upon Henry Harrison Conroy, the sheriff of Tonto.

"I can hardly understand your indifference to this transaction, which will bring more money and more people to your town," said the lawyer. "The Beloit interests have done little toward the exploitation of the Golden Calf and Shoshone Chief. This syndicate will operate on a big scale, Mr. Conroy."

Henry Harrison Conroy was of tub-like proportions, with a round, moon-like face, and a huge putty-like nose. That nose was famous. For years it had been featured in vaudeville, with the tub-like Henry and his squinty eyes behind it. When vaudeville waned, fate, in the form of an Arizona inheritance, brought the erstwhile comedian to Tonto City, where a deceased uncle had left him the J Bar C ranch.

Henry did not understand Arizona; and Arizona did not understand Henry, with his spats, cane, derby hat and flaming nose. So Wild Horse Valley, in sort of a humorous spasm, elected Henry Harrison Conroy sheriff. Henry, in turn, appreciating the humor of the situation, appointed Judge Van Treece as deputy and Oscar Johnson as jailer.

Judge Van Treece was sixty, several inches over six feet in height, with a long, lean, pouchy-eyed face, and a great thirst,

*"Don't make
a noise!"*

HENRY
HARRISON
CONROY

which had ruined his career as a lawyer. Drunk or sober, he retained the dignity and solemnity of a Supreme Court judge.

Oscar Johnson, erstwhile horse-wrangler at the J Bar C, was a giant of a Swede, with a flat face, small, blue eyes and a button-like nose. Oscar's ability never to do anything right was an unceasing joy to Henry.

Just now Henry's booted feet were on his desk-top, and he was tilted back perilously in his rickety office chair.

"My indifference to your statement, sir," replied Henry, "is entirely due to a sense of balance. Once in a great many attempts I am able to put my feet on the desk-top. Since I lost my lap, a certain hinge, located in the center of my body, seems to have—well, tightened up a bit.

"Any attempt on my part to exhibit emotion might upset my balance. I assure you, I am not unappreciative—but I'll be damned, sir, if I am going to applaud, at my own peril."

"But, are you comfortable in that position?" queried the lawyer.

"Comfortable? Of course not! It is merely a satisfied sense of having accomplished something."

The lawyer smiled thinly. "I believe I understand."

"I am glad," sighed Henry. "So few people do understand. You are the attorney for Howard Beloit?"

"Yes. I have handled Howard Beloit's interests for several years, and am in sole charge of the negotiations on this big deal. This syndicate is paying one million dollars for the two mining properties."

"Cash?" queried Henry.

"One-half cash," replied the lawyer. "Mr. Beloit is not in very good health, and as soon as this transaction is completed, he and his daughter will leave for Europe."

"Then Mr. Beloit is coming here?" asked Henry.

"He and his daughter, Gale, will be here—possibly tomorrow.

She is a lovely girl. It will be her first visit to a—well, a town of this character. It will also be Mr. Beloit's first visit to Tonto City."

"A town of this character," sighed Henry. "I want to resent that half-hidden slur against Tonto City, Mr. Livingstone; but I hardly know just what to use as a talking point. I will admit that Tonto is—well, rather rough. The combination of cowpuncher, prospector, miner, gambler—and a sprinkling of city folks—all thrown together on one crooked street. Well, I suppose the less we say about it, the better it will all seem. Not bad, when you get used to it."

The lawyer nodded solemnly. "I suppose that is true. They tell me that after many years on the theatrical stage, you became an Arizonan over night."

"I have, sir," replied Henry gravely, "been an Arizonan all my life—unknowingly. In me, you see the Spirit of Arizona."

"Except for the dialect."

"Yea-a-ah?" drawled Henry soberly. "Well, I'm a-tellin' you, Mister, there ain't a cow-poke this side of *Mejico* that can't understand what I'm a-talkin' about."

At that moment Judge Van Treece came into the office, his lean face very grave. He merely nodded to the lawyer, and turned to Henry.

"We have, as they say," he remarked, "a man for supper, Henry."

Henry's eyes widened a little. "Wait a moment, Judge," he said slowly, "while I get my feet off this desk-top. Your words portend evil—and I am in no position to be upset, mentally or physically. Ah-h-h-h-h! That was well-done, if I may be excused for boasting. Proceed, Judge."

"It appears," stated Judge ponderously, "that Tommy Roper, that stuttering horse-wrangler from the livery stable, together with a certain Lester Allen, a drifting cowboy, who has only been here a few days, went to Scorpion Bend yesterday.

"Tommy admits that they both got very, very inebriated. In plain words, they got so damn drunk that on their way home, they got lost. With only one road to follow, they got lost. They went somewhere. Tommy doesn't seem to know where it was. He rather gurgles about a blond angel, who shot Lester.

"I will admit that it does not make sense. Tommy says that he and Lester left this place, and later found the road to Tonto City. And at about the time Tommy discovered this fact, Lester was nearly dead from loss of blood. Tommy roped him to his saddle, and when they reached Tonto City, Lester Allen was dead."

"My goodness!" exclaimed Henry quietly. "A blond angel. That is rather remarkable, Judge. I did not know they ran in different shades. And this particular angel had a gun? Well, I suppose that with the type of people we are sending up there these days, even an angel needs protection."

"You jest," complained Judge. "Don't you understand that we have a murder on our hands, Henry? The man is dead!"

AS JUDGE glared at Henry, Oscar Johnson and Tommy Roper came into the office. Tommy was of medium height, sallow, buck-toothed. Just now he looked particularly disheveled and rather frightened.

"He yust says he vants to say a few words," explained Oscar.

"Yuh—yeah," admitted Tommy.

"I was afraid of that," murmured Henry. "Tommy, try and be calm; so you may tell us exactly what happened."

"Well, I'll tut-tell yuh," gulped Tommy. "Mum-me and Lul-Lul-Lul—"

"That's all right," assured Henry. "You and Lester Allen went to Scorpion Bend yesterday. You both got blind drunk, lost the way home, and Lester got shot by an angel."

"Bub-bub-blond angel," corrected Tommy.

"With wings, Tommy?"

"I dud-didn't see any wuw-wings."

"Perhaps she wasn't an angel."

"Well, maybe she wa-wa-wasn't. That was my im-imp-imp—that's how sh-she struck me."

"Oh, she struck you, did she?"

"He means that was his impression,"interposed Judge gravely.

"I see," murmured Henry. "Was she flying around, merely floating, or sitting on a limb, Tommy?"

Tommy scratched his head violently for a few moments.

"I th-th-think she was in a huh-huh-house."

"You *think* she was? How did you gain that impression?"

"She sh-shot through a wuh-wuh-window."

"I see. Well, it is barely possible that the window had some direct connection with a house. In fact, I do not believe that angels carry windows. Tommy," Henry looked keenly at the young cowboy, "I am under the impression that you and this departed cow-waddie were too drunk to know what happened."

"Uh-huh," agreed Tommy. "But Lul-Lester was dud-drunker'n I was."

"On what do you base that statement?"

"Huh?"

"What makes you think he was drunker than you were, Tommy?"

"Well, he dud-didn't dud-duck."

"That is reasonable. Too drunk to duck a bullet, eh?"

"Uh-huh."

"Have you any idea where you were when the blond angel shot through a window at you?"

Tommy shook his head violently.

"Where were you when you discovered that Lester Allen had been shot?"

"On the Pup-Pup-Pup—"

"On the Piñon Grades, eh? How did you know he had been shot?"

"He wouldn't tut-take a dud-drink. I—I said, 'Gee, Lul-Lester, you mum-mum-must be in tut-terrible sh-sh-shape,' and then I seen the bub-blood on his shirt. I got my rur-rope and tied him on his sus-sus-saddle."

"I see. How much whisky did you have when you left Scorpion Bend?"

"We huh-had fuf-fuf-fuf—"

"Four quarts, eh?"

"Uh-huh."

"Tommy," Henry stepped over and placed a pudgy forefinger on the cowboy's chest, "are you sure that the blond angel isn't an hallucination, and that Lester Allen was accidentally shot by you, or by himself?"

"Huh?" queried Tommy blankly.

"My mistake," murmured Henry. "You and Lester Allen both carried guns, did you not?"

"Uh-huh."

"Allen didn't have one," said Judge. "Tommy hasn't any now."

"The Mum-Marshal in Sco-Sco-Sco—"

"The Marshal of Scorpion Bend took your guns away," finished Henry.

"Uh-huh. We for-forgot to gug-get 'em."

"The accidental alibi is shattered," sighed Henry. "Tommy, my advice to you would be to go to bed and have a good sleep."

"Uh-huh. Th-thank yuh, Huh-Henry."

"You are very welcome, I am sure. Good-day, sir."

"An interesting case," murmured Livingstone.

"Unusual, to say the least," replied Henry.

"Yes, indeed. Well, I must be going, Mr. Conroy. Good-day, everyone."

"W'at de ha'al did that yigger vant?" queried Oscar.

"That yigger," smiled Henry, "is Howard Beloit's' lawyer, who is here, waiting for Howard Beloit and the syndicate, which is to buy out the Golden Calf and the Shoshone Chief mines. His name is Charles H. Livingstone."

"A TREMENDOUSLY big deal," said Judge. "I believe the price is one million dollars. I understand that Beloit is in bad health, and wishes to dispose of all his mining properties."

"Have you ever met him?" asked Henry.

"I have never met him, but I have seen him a number of times. His interest in mining is only from an investment angle. I believe that a syndicate would be preferable to Beloit, because Beloit has made no effort to exploit the property."

"Who in de ha'al ever seen an angel with a seex-shooter?" asked Oscar. "Ay don't believe it vars an angel."

"Have you a better theory, Oscar?" queried Henry.

"Ay don't know what in ha'al a t'eory is, but Ay t'ink Tommy is fu'ling. Angels don't carry seex-shooters; dey carry horps."

"Have you ever seen an angel, Oscar?"

"Ay have seen de pictures of 'em. Oll Ay have ever seen varsn't over a year old. Yust little, fat babies, vit only a yee-string."

"Quite correct, Oscar," said Henry. His chin quivered and there was a suspicious moisture in his eyes.

"Ay t'ink Tommy is yust as cuckoo as a ship-horder."

"Judge," said Henry, a quaver in his voice, "unless something is done immediately, I shall start screaming and pounding on the wall. There is only one antidote, you know."

"At once, sir," replied Judge gravely.

They put on their hats, walked outside, and went straight to the Tonto Saloon.

"Vit only a yee-string," choked Henry.

"That impossible Swede!" grunted Judge. "Why on earth you ever keep him, Henry, is more than I can understand."

"Oscar is one of my excuses for drinking too much, Judge."

"The man is positively psychopathic."

"Don't tell him—he will be bragging about it."

"Very true. But what about this tale of an angel shooting a cowboy."

"Well," replied Henry, squinting at the mirror of the back-bar. "I don't quite understand it, of course. I agree with Oscar when he states that angels carry harps, not six-shooters. But times are changing, Judge. That particular angel might not care for music."

"There are times, sir," said Judge gravely, "when, in my opinion, there is little to choose between you and Oscar Johnson."

They filled their glasses, bowed gravely to each other, and drank their liquor, with an exaggerated flourish. Drinking, to them, was a ritual. It amused Tonto City.

"I believe," stated Henry, "that my duty is to go down to the doctor's office and examine the corpse."

"Why?" queried Judge. "The man is dead. The bullet went completely through him, on the left side. He needs a shave and a haircut. There are no known relatives. His pockets contained thirty-five cents and a jackknife, together with a half-package of tobacco and a few crumpled cigarette-papers."

"Under those circumstances, Judge, we will have another drink or so. I admit that I am a little baffled, Judge. I can't quite reconcile myself to the fact that a blond angel is flying around Wild Horse Valley carrying a six-shooter—even if they do say that *anything* might happen in Arizona. I believe, sir, that we have a real mystery."

"Mystery!" scoffed Judge. "You can find the same mystery in any insane asylum in the state. Remember, Henry, those two boys had four quarts of whisky when they left Scorpion Bend."

"But no guns," said Henry. "Do not forget that item, Judge."

Oscar came striding in and stopped beside them.

"Ay am going to take Yosephine to de dance at Scorpion Bend tonight," he announced, "and Ay vant to take de bock-board."

"No," replied Judge quickly.

"All right," said Henry. "Be careful, Oscar."

Oscar gave Judge a malevolent glance and walked out. Judge lifted his glass.

"To the biggest fool in Arizona," he said.

"To you, sir," said Henry heartily.

CHAPTER II

HOLD-UP

ABOUT ELEVEN O'CLOCK next morning, Josephine Swensen and Oscar Johnson came riding around the Piñon Grades in the J Bar C buckboard, returning from a night of dancing at Scorpion Bend. Josephine was about thirty-five years of age, huge and raw-boned, with a lean face and a long nose.

On top of her mop of taffy-colored hair perched a small hat, with a single feather sticking straight up in front. They were sitting as far apart as possible in the seat, both looking straight ahead. Oscar was minus his collar, one sleeve of his coat was nearly ripped loose at the shoulder, and there was a slight swelling over his right eye.

"Ay yust vant to say," remarked Josephine, "that if Ay ever go to anodder dance, Ay hope Ay can go with a yentleman."

Oscar's little, blue eyes shifted sideways for a moment.

"Yah, su-ure," he muttered. "Ven he comes out of de horspital, you can have him."

"You are yust a bog-headed Svede," declared Josephine. "You yump on Olaf for not'ing."

"For not'ing, eh? You t'ink Ay am going to let him yiggle out in de middle of de dance-holl with my girl? Everybody laughing like ha'al. Who de ha'al do you t'ink you are—a koochie-hoochie dancer?"

"Huh!" sniffed Joscphine. "Olaf is a yentleman. He say dis is de last vord."

"You damn right, it vars de last vord!" snorted Oscar. "You ought to be ashamed of yourself, Yosephine. Ay don't vant to take a lady to a dance, and have her viggling. Your vaist split up de back, and somebody yalled, 'Look out, everybody, Yosephine is getting loose!'"

Josephine reached over, grasped the lines and jerked the team to a stop on the narrow grade, and got to her feet. Oscar got up, too.

"Ay am going to get out and valk," declared Josephine. "Ay vould not ride any longer."

"You are going to stay in das ha'ar boggy, or I'll—"

Oscar should have known better than to have opposed her. At least he might have prepared a suitable defense for her left swing, which caught him square on the jaw, knocking him over the wheel, and almost off the grade.

He took the lines with him, and the jerk on the bits, combined with the crash of his fall, caused the half-broke team to leap wildly. The lurch flung Josephine over the back of the seat, where she landed on her broad shoulders in the back of the buckboard, her legs waving wildly in the air.

In order to save himself, Oscar relinquished the lines, and the equipage faded away around the next curve, with Josephine still wig-wagging frantically with her pedal extremities.

Oscar clawed his way off the rim of the cañon, and sat up in the road, rubbing his sore jaw, while his two blue eyes, as round as dimes, stared down the grades.

"Va'al, Ay suppose it is good-by Yosephine," he said inanely.

But Oscar's farewell to Josephine was a bit premature. The equipage managed to round two successive curves before Josephine, unable to shift her position, except by turning a backward somersault, did just that. Her turn was complete, and she landed in a sitting position in the middle of the road. A moment later there was a terrific crash, as the runaway team met a solid obstruction, which proved to be the rear end of the stage, which should have been nearly to Tonto City by this time.

Oscar came, running heavily. Josephine was still sitting in the middle of the road, but Oscar went right past her, staring at the few remnants of the buckboard left on the grade. The running team had tried to pass the stage on the outside, and were somewhere, down deep in Piñon Cañon. The stage team was cramped in against the solid rock wall.

Oscar stopped near the stage. Here was an elderly-looking, well-dressed man, and a very beautiful young lady, both of them rather dazed and frightened. The man said huskily, "I am Howard Beloit."

"What de ha'al has that got to do with anyt'ing?" retorted Oscar.

He walked out to the edge of the grade and stared off into the depths.

"Ay am going to get ha'al for dis," he said mournfully.

"They—they shot the driver," faltered Howard Beloit. Oscar looked blankly at him for several moments.

"Huh!" he snorted. "Runavay hurses don't shoot people."

"It wasn't the horses," explained Beloit. "The stage was held up and robbed. They killed the driver, and we have been here for hours."

"Yiminy yee!" snorted Oscar.

"It was terrible," added the young lady, trembling visibly.

"Yah, su-ure," agreed Oscar. He looked back at Josephine, who was on her feet, feeling herself over for possible injuries. Then she limped on up to them, her hat, minus the feather, cocked over one eye.

"De hurses vent over de grade, Yosephine," said Oscar. "These people tell me that Yhonny Deal is dead, and de stage is robbed."

"I should vorry," replied Josephine, bracing herself against a rear wheel. "Oll Ay vant is to get home, where Ay can pick de slide-rock out of my seestim."

Oscar went and looked at Johnny Deal, the driver. Johnny had been shot squarely between the eyes.

"He tried to resist them," explained Beloit, "so they killed him. They took the money-box. Then they took the jewelry off my daughter and myself—and climbed back over the rocks."

"How many?" asked Oscar.

"Three of them. They were masked. What is to be done?"

"Ay guess ve better got to Tonto City. Vait!"

With little effort Oscar picked up the body of the driver, swarmed up over a front wheel, and laid it on the top of the stage.

"You certainly are strong," said the young lady.

"My grandfadder vars a Wiking," replied Oscar loftily. "Yosephine, you go in de stage vit de young lady. Das faller vill ride up ha'ar vit me."

Meekly the mighty Josephine entered the stage, and Howard Beloit climbed to the seat beside Oscar, who kicked off the brake, swung the four horses into line, and they went rumbling along.

"Thank God you came," murmured Beloit. "It was a terrible situation. Did your team run away?"

"Yah, su-ure. You never have been ha'ar before?"

"No, I have not. And I hope I shall never come again. It has been a terrible experience for my daughter."

"Oh!" grunted Oscar. "Ay t'ought she vars your wife."

"Ridiculous!" exclaimed Beloit.

"Yah, su-ure," agreed Oscar. "Most of them are."

Howard Beloit smiled slowly, as he drew down the brim of his gray hat.

"Your wife seemed a bit upset," he remarked.

"Yosephine? She ain't my wife."

"Sweetheart—perhaps."

"Ay am too much of a yentleman to say anyt'ing," replied Oscar.

HENRY, JUDGE and Charles H. Livingstone, Beloit's lawyer, were at the stage-station when the stage arrived. There was always a crowd at the station to welcome the daily stage, and they listened in amazement to the news of the hold-up and murder.

Livingstone hurried Beloit and his daughter to the hotel,

while Henry and Judge helped several men take the body down to the doctor's home. They hurried back to the office, where Oscar told them what he knew about it.

"But where is my buckboard and team, Oscar?" asked Henry.

"Va'al," replied Oscar wearily, "Ay am afraid dey are in the bottom of Piñon Cañon, Hanry."

"I don't believe I quite understand."

"It vars like dis, Hanry. Yosephine got sore, because Ay knocked ha'al out of Olaf Yorgensen at de dance. On de vay home she shot off her face, and after vile she socked me on de yaw. She knocked me out of de bock-board, and de team ran avay.

"Yosephine fell out, too, and de team smashed into de back end of de stage, and de whole vorks vent into de cañon. Ay am very sorry, but it yust happened."

Henry pursed his lips, squinted his eyes and looked at Judge, who seemed to be struggling for words.

"A strange courtship," he murmured. "An exchange of socks, if I may wax humorous over the loss of a perfectly good team and buckboard. Pardon me, Judge, but you should never let your blood-pressure rise above your common sense. Relax at once, sir."

"Relax!" howled Judge. "Why of all the—"

"After all," interrupted Henry, "the horses and vehicle belonged to me."

"Yah, sure," added Oscar. "You don't own 'em, Yudge. Hanry don't care a damn."

"I don't, eh?" Henry's jaw snapped shut, and his nose flamed.

"Careful, Henry," advised Judge maliciously. "Remember the old blood-pressure."

At that moment Charles Livingstone, Howard Beloit, and John Campbell, the local prosecuting attorney, arrived at the office.

"Well, Henry," said Campbell grimly, "it seems that trouble has come again to Wild Horse Valley."

"It is damnable," declared Livingstone, thumping the floor with his cane. "Mister Beloit and his daughter were robbed!"

"I understand that," nodded Henry quietly. "I am sorry, sir."

"Sorry? Is that all you intend doing if I may ask?"

"What would you do, sir?" queried Henry.

"Why—why, I would—well, what would any sheriff do?"

"Never having been *any other sheriff,* I do not know."

"You will never catch them—sitting here, Mr. Conroy."

"I realize that. Neither will they sit at the scene of the murder and robbery, waiting for me to come and get them. If I have been correctly informed, it happened nearly three hours ago. No doubt the criminals are familiar with the country, and had their getaway all planned in advance. Only in fiction does a sheriff race to the scene of the crime, follow the trail of the outlaws, and corner them in a blind cañon."

"Well!" snorted Livingstone. "Well, I—I suppose you are right."

"Hanry is olvays right," declared Oscar blandly.

"Vitrified Viking!" snapped Judge.

"Just what did you and your daughter lose, Mr. Beloit?" asked Henry.

"I have the list right here," interposed Livingstone quickly. "Five hundred dollars in cash, a four-carat diamond ring, a two-carat stickpin, a three-carat diamond ring, and a platinum wrist-watch set with diamonds. The jewelry was valued at about twenty-five thousand dollars."

"A jewel robbery on Piñon Grades," murmured Henry. "Queer."

"I do not see anything queer about it," said Livingstone.

"Perhaps not," agreed Henry. "But we are simple folk in Wild Horse Valley. Diamonds and platinum mean little. It doesn't seem to me—But, however, that is beside the case. Mister Beloit and his charming daughter were robbed. Mister Beloit, can you describe the three men?"

"I am afraid not," replied Beloit.

"No, I didn't believe you could," sighed Henry. "You saw them shoot the driver?"

"NO, I did not. My daughter and I were still in the stage. I heard one of the robbers order the driver to keep his hands quiet, and a moment later the shot was fired. They then ordered us outside. One man noticed the jewels, and ordered us to remove them."

"Very efficient, I presume, Mister Beloit?"

"Very," replied the millionaire dryly. "They told us to get into the stage and close the door, before they left. But I took a chance, opened the door a few inches, and saw them climbing up over the rocks on the upper side of the road."

"Your charming daughter was frightened, I presume."

"Nearly to the point of collapse."

"Yosephine collapsed, too," said Oscar. "Yust end-over-end."

"In reply to that," said Henry, "I can say that there have been three events that I would give much to have seen. One was the defeat of Napoleon, another was Washington crossing the Delaware, and the third was Josephine turning a back flip-flop from the rear end of a runaway buckboard."

"It vars a spectacle," nodded Oscar.

"It's a wonder it didn't kill her," said Campbell.

"She landed on de wrong end for that," explained Oscar blandly.

"Well," said Livingtone, "we seem to be getting nowhere."

"I believe I can see the sheriff's point of view," said Beloit.

"If you are satisfied, Mister Beloit; we may as well go back to the hotel."

"We shall leave no stone unturned," assured Judge briskly.

"Thank you, gentlemen," said Howard Beloit.

The three men left the office. Oscar shrugged his shoulders.

"Who in de ha'al is going to turn over stones?" he wanted to know.

Judge glared his indignation at Oscar. Henry wiped some tears from his eyes before getting up from his chair.

"Has Frijole Bill been in lately?" he asked.

"Yah, su-ure," replied Oscar. "Free-holey was ha'ar before Ay vent to Scorpion Bend, and he left a gallon of prune yuice. Ay locked it in a cell in de yail."

"Get it," ordered Henry. "I must relax, or go all to pieces."

"Like Yosephine," said Oscar. "But Ay t'ink she stayed oll in von piece. She says she vanted to get home and pick oll de slide-rock out of her seestem."

"Get that prune whisky—quick!" gasped Henry, holding his middle with both hands. "I've stood all I can."

Henry sniffed suspiciously of the prune whisky before drinking from the tin-cup. Frijole Bill was prone to make mistakes; and in one instance he delivered a gallon of pure horse-liniment. However, he and Oscar drank it all, and Oscar declared it to be "yust as good as anything."

"Mister Howard Beloit is not exactly impressive, Henry," said Judge, smacking his lips over his cup of home distillation.

"He seems rather a sad dog," replied Henry. "My impression is that this sadness probably dates beyond the loss of money and jewelry."

"Livingstone told me a little of Beloit's history," said Judge. "It seems that about ten years ago Beloit was in moderate circumstances. He had a son, sixteen years of age, at that time. Rather a wild youth, I presume. At any rate, he ran away from his father, and has never been heard of since.

"Shortly after that, Beloit married a wealthy widow. It was her money, combined with Beloit's ability, that built up the Beloit millions. Livingstone says they had done everything possible to try and locate this son, but to no avail. Gale, the daughter, is not Beloit's child; she is his step-daughter."

"How soon do they expect to complete their deal here?" asked Henry.

"Livingstone says that the representative of the syndicate should be here now."

"Bearing a check for half-a-million, I presume."

"Those are the terms," nodded Judge.

"Do you vant any more of das ha'ar yuice?" asked Oscar.

"Lock it up," advised Henry. "After that you better go and make your peace with Josephine. I'd hate to see that romance go on the rocks."

"Ay don't know what a romance is," grinned Oscar, "but Yosephine vent on de rocks, sitting down awful hord."

"I believe I could use another drink," said Henry. "You have a drying effect on me."

CHAPTER III

GALE BELOIT

DON BLACK, TOP-GAMBLER at the Tonto, sauntered into the hotel for a late breakfast. The young gambler was immaculate, as usual, clear-eyed, in spite of late hours, and always reserved. Black was handsome, and rather young to be in charge of the Tonto gambling room, but very efficient. His well-shaped head was covered with dark, curling hair, and he wore a small mustache, waxed to needle-like points.

Henry Harrison Conroy was at one of the tables, and with a curt nod, Don Black sat down across the table from the sheriff.

"Big play last night?" asked Henry.

"Very," nodded the gambler.

Josephine Swensen came to get Black's order, standing there, like a Statue of Liberty, with a tray poised high. Henry looked anxiously at the tray, while Josephine intoned the menu.

"I trust and hope that you are none the worse for wear, after yesterday's incident, Miss Swensen," said Henry.

"Ay varsn't vorn, Ay vars dumped," replied Josephine.

"My mistake," breathed Henry huskily.

"Your excuse is accepted," said Josephine curtly, and hurried for the kitchen. Henry wiped his eyes and looked after her.

"I understand she is your jailer's sweetheart," said Black.

"I believe it is something like that. Still, I cannot quite discover any sweetness, nor do I think there is any heart concerned in the proposition. It may be love; who knows?"

"Oscar looks like a capable person," smiled the gambler.

"Capable of doing everything wrong. He has smashed my buckboard five times, crippled three horses, and yesterday he let the team run away on Piñon Grades, smash into the rear of the stage, and do a high-dive into the cañon."

"Rather a reckless person, eh?"

"Brainless," corrected Henry. "But I love every ounce of ivory in his head. He is the most reliable person I have ever met."

"Reliable? I thought you said he did everything wrong."

"That is real reliability. I can count on him never doing anything right. You or I might make a mistake and do something wrong; but Oscar never makes a mistake and does anything right."

"I see," laughed the gambler.

As Josephine came through the swinging doors, Gale Beloit came from the little hotel lobby. She wore a brown coat, riding breeches and polished, brown riding boots. Her garb was something new in Tonto City. She sat down, turned her head and looked square at the handsome gambler for a moment.

Black's cold, dark eyes examined her critically, until she turned away. He looked at Henry, a slight smile on his hard lips.

"That is Gale Beloit, daughter of Howard Beloit, the millionaire," explained Henry quietly.

"Something new in Tonto City," observed Black softly. "Pretty."

"A very beautiful young lady," agreed Henry. "Very rich, I believe."

Josephine interrupted, with Black's breakfast. While she was assembling the dishes on the table, Charles H. Livingstone, the Beloit attorney, came briskly in, his cane hooked jauntily over his wrist. He went straight to Gale Beloit, and talked with her for several moments.

As he turned away from the table, starting toward the doorway of the lobby, he saw Henry. He stopped short as though to speak to Henry, but suddenly jerked around and started ahead, crashing squarely into the hurrying Josephine.

The trayful of empty dishes crashed to the floor, as Josephine went staggering into a table, with Charles H. Livingstone clawing at her. But only for the moment was Josephine off balance. Then she grasped the lawyer by the collar, started a round-house swing with her right fist, and hit him a terrific smack between his left ear and his eye.

Charles H. Livingstone, already off balance, went flat on his back. Gale Beloit screamed softly, as she got to her feet.

"Ay may be yust a Svedish vaitress," observed Josephine, "but Ay von't let no dudes paw me around."

She stooped over, gathered up the broken dishes and walked triumphantly from the room, while Charles H. Livingstone sat there on the floor, gasping foolishly, his left eye swelling rapidly. Gale went to him, and he got slowly to his feet.

"What on earth happened?" he asked weakly.

"That—that creature struck you," explained Gale indignantly.

"My gracious! Why, I—I must have accidentally collided with her."

Henry was crying into his napkin as they walked out together, but there was no change in Black's expression. Josephine, unperturbed by the incident, came briskly out with Gale Beloit's breakfast. She glanced at the empty table, looked all around the room, and finally placed the tray on a table.

"Ay suppose she vent out to put leen-i-ment on de dude," said Josephine to no one in particular. "Va'al, ha'are it is, if she gets hungry."

Henry got to his feet, gasping a little.

"Excuse me, Mr. Black," he said hoarsely. "I feel that I must go to some secluded spot, where I may roll."

He went out through the lobby, wiping his eyes.

"Something wrong, Mr. Conroy?" queried the clerk anxiously.

"Horse-radish," whispered Henry hoarsely.

"On the breakfast table? I shall speak to Josephine at once."

"And may the Lord have mercy on your soul," muttered Henry.

HENRY HURRIED back to his office, where he fell weakly into a chair. Oscar was sitting on the cot, cleaning a Colt six-shooter. Henry eyed him with disapproval.

"Loaded?" queried Henry.

"Ay have not had drink today," replied Oscar coldly.

"Is that gun loaded?"

"Do you t'ink Ay am a fule?"

Henry got up, took the gun from Oscar's fingers and removed the cartridges.

"By Yimminy!" snorted Oscar in amazement. "Ay t'ought Ay took 'em out! Oh, Ay remember now."

"Old Reliable," muttered Henry. "Where is Judge?"

"Yudge? Oh, he vent out a while ago. He said he vars looking for some glue."

"Glue? What on earth is he going to do with glue?"

"Ay don't know, Hanry. Yudge says it is about time ve got some glue to vork on."

"Glue to work on," muttered Henry. "That seems rather queer."

"Yah, su-ure," agreed Oscar blandly, as he peered down the muzzle of the six-shooter. "Yudge says ve never catch murderers without some glue."

"Clue!" exploded Henry.

"Yah, su-ure; that is what Ay said."

Henry gasped audibly, turned away and stood in the doorway, looking across the street. He saw Charles H. Livingstone come from the livery stable, driving a team hitched to a top-buggy. He drove up to the hotel, where he stopped for several minutes, talking with Howard Beloit, and then drove on in the direction of Scorpion Bend.

About five minutes later he saw Gale Beloit, accompanied by Tommy Roper, the stuttering cowboy, ride from the stable, horseback. Tommy led the way out of town, heading for the hills to the north.

Danny Regan, Henry's foreman, rode in and stopped at the office. Danny was a young, red-headed cowboy, with freckles, a slightly upturned nose and a wide grin. Danny's tastes ran to gaudy raiment and silver-trimmed leather.

"Hyah, Sheriff," he grinned, as he looped his tie-rope around the pole of the narrow hitch-rack.

"Good morning, Daniel," smiled Henry.

"You ain't caught them murderers yet, have yuh?"

"Not yet," admitted Henry. "We left the jail open all night, but it was still empty this morning. How is everything at the rancho?"

"Fine. A keg of Frijole's experiment blew up last night, and almost wrecked the kitchen. Frijole thought somebody was tryin' to dynamite the house, and went out through a closed window."

"I believe I drank some of the same stuff yesterday," smiled Henry. "Frijole is wasting his talents; he should be head chemist for some munitions manufacturer."

"That's right," grinned Danny. "What's new on the murder and robbery?"

"Not a thing, Danny. Mr. Livingstone, the lawyer, doing his

own driving, headed toward Scorpion Bend a while ago. And the beautiful Miss Beloit has gone for a canter, accompanied by Tommy Roper."

"Accompanied by Tommy Roper?"

"As self-conscious as the sheep-herder, who accidentally sat down on a rattlesnake," added Henry gravely. "I have no doubt that Tommy's ears have already burned holes in his hat."

Danny chuckled, and hitched up his chaps.

"I reckon I'll go up and see Leila," he said.

"I would," advised Henry. "With every eligible young cow-waddie in the country making eyes at the rich Miss Beloit, Leila might suspect you."

"She don't need to worry," replied Danny. "Leila and I understand each other."

"So far," amended Henry seriously. "Oscar thinks he understands Josephine, too. Their case is the only one on record, where it was love at first *sock*."

"That's true," grinned Danny. "Well, I'll be back later."

LAURA HARPER and her daughter Leila operated the little millinery shop of Tonto City, and had their living quarters at the back of the shop. Leila and Danny had been engaged for over a year, while Laura and Henry had been engaged for several months. Every time they set a date for a double wedding, something happened to postpone it. Just now, no date was set.

Tommy Roper left Miss Beloit at the hotel, and came back to the stable, leading her horse. Judge and Henry were at the office, when Tommy came over there, swaggering a little over his own importance.

"Dud-didja see me?" he asked.

"Everybody in Tonto City saw you, Tommy," assured Henry.

"Gug-good! She's sure a sus-sus-sweet girl."

"You must have made an impression on her," said Judge gravely.

"Huh?"

"You must have made a hit with her, Tommy. There must be a dozen young fellows around here who would have given anything to ride with her."

"I gug-guess I did," admitted Tommy. "Why—why, she even gug-gave me fuf-five dollars."

"No!" exclaimed Henry.

"Sh-she sure did; I sus-said I didn't want any mum-money, and she sus-said it was wu-worth it."

"She must be very emotional," said Henry soberly.

"Uh-huh," nodded Tommy. "She's gug-got lotsa money, tut-too. Said she wu-wu-wouldn't mum-miss the money at all. I—I'll betcha if I tut-took her to a dud-dance, she'd pup-pay tut-ten dollars, just as-as easy."

"No doubt about it," nodded Judge.

"What did she talk about?" queried Henry.

"Sh-she didn't tut-talk much. She said she lul-liked to th-think, when she was ridin', and I sus-said I did, too."

"One must have one's period of concentration," said Henry.

"Huh?"

"Surely you understand what I said, Tommy."

"Uh-huh. Bub-but I wasn't sh-sure what you meant. Sh-she asked me who Don Bub-Black was. I sus-said he was a tut-tut-tin-horn gambler in the Tut-Tonto Saloon. I sus-said he's good-lul-lookin', but he's gug-got a huh-heart of stone."

"What did she say to that?"

"Well, she-she asked me if that was a fuf-figure of speech, or if it actually was pup-pu-petterfied."

Henry's boots hit the floor, and he reached quickly for his hat.

"I must get out in the air, Judge," he declared hoarsely, and went out, slapping one knee with his hat.

"Has he gug-got a wu-wu-weak heart?" asked Tommy.

"Wu-wu-weak heart?" parroted Judge. "Oh, pshaw, you've got me doing it, too!"

Judge grabbed his hat and followed Henry up the street, leaving Tommy to stare after them in amazement.

CHAPTER IV

SUDDEN MURDER

PLAY WAS RATHER heavy at the Tonto Gambling House that night, but most of the games broke up about midnight. Don Black slept on a cot in a room, which he used as an office, and, for lack of night banking facilities, he kept the day's receipts in a small safe in the room.

With every patron gone, and only a night bartender and the usual quota of swampers, cleaning up the place, Black sat at a table and checked up the money. Placing it all in a canvas sack, he called a good-night to the bartender, took the sack and went into his room, closing the door behind him.

As he stepped over near the safe, his back to the window, he realized that there was a draught from the window, which was always fastened shut. He placed the sack on a table near the safe, and glanced quickly into a mirror, which hung on the wall near him.

It gave him a view of the window, which was open, and the muzzle of a rifle protruded into the room, its round bore centered on Don Black. The steel-nerved young gambler picked up the canvas sack, opened the top and drew out a package of currency, which he examined. Then, as though speaking his thoughts aloud, he said, "Twelve thousand cold dollars! What a play!"

Then he knelt down to open the safe. From behind him came the soft slither of cloth on wood and a husky voice said quietly:

"Stand up slow, keep your hands away from yuh, and don't make a noise."

Don got slowly to his feet, obeying the order, and turned

around. Just inside the window stood a masked man, the rifle-butt tensed at his hip. For several moments they eyed each other silently. The canvas sack was on the floor in front of the safe.

"Move aside a little," ordered the man quietly, and Don obeyed.

The man looked critically at Don, who did not wear a gun in sight.

"I reckon yuh better put your hands up, pardner," decided the masked man. "Yuh might be packin' a gun."

Slowly Don's hands came up, and when his right hand was just above waist-level, it spurted flame, and the room shook from the concussion of a heavy shot. The masked man jerked back, and the rifle slid from his hands. Then he pitched forward on his face, as Don Black stepped swiftly aside.

Someone out in the saloon yelled sharply. Don Black flung the door open, as the bartender and swampers came running.

"Get the sheriff and a doctor," ordered Black. "Quick!"

"A stickup?" queried the bartender.

"Yes," replied Black quietly.

Henry, Judge and the doctor arrived at the same time. The man was dead. He was a stranger to Wild Horse Valley. Although they made a search of the town, there was no sign of any strange horse, which the man might have ridden to Tonto City.

After the body was removed, Henry went into the private room with Don Black.

"I am willing to swear that I have never seen the man before in my life," declared the gambler.

"That's all right," nodded Henry. "It is merely a case of a hold-up man being shot down, while in the act of committing robbery."

"I didn't mean that—exactly," stated the gambler. "I may be all wrong in my hunch; but I don't believe that man came merely to rob me."

"I do not quite understand, Black."

"Well, I explained about that rifle barrel through the window. The man never said a word until after I took some money from the sack and mentioned a large amount, aloud. I played a hunch, Sheriff. I believe that man was there to murder me.

"Smile, if you like. Perhaps he realized that if he shot me from outside the room, the sound of the shot would alarm everybody, and he would not have time to get the money; so he decided to get the money first."

"Merely a gambler's hunch," murmured Henry.

"Exactly—merely a gambler's hunch."

"But why on earth would a total stranger seek to murder you?"

Don Black shrugged his shoulders.

"Who knows? I've been trying to puzzle that out for the past thirty minutes. Of course, a gambler *does* make enemies. But I do not know of a single person who might hate me badly enough to hire a gunman to kill me."

"Well," sighed Henry, "I suppose we may as well go to bed. We may find somebody in the country who has seen this man. If I were you, young man, I would walk warily. If your hunch is right, the one who hired this gunman might hire another one very easily."

"I realize that," nodded Black.

"Good-night."

"Good-night, sir."

"At least," sighed Judge, later on, as they undressed, "this is not a mystery."

"I believe I shall adapt myself to a sleeve gun," smiled Henry. "The one Black used was a single-shot, forty-four; and small enough to conceal in the palm of a hand. He had the gun in his right hand, and as the robber told him to put up his hands, it was very simple for Black to lift his hand and fire the shot."

"Simple for Black, perhaps," replied Judge. "What we need, Henry, is a six-shooter which shoots shotgun cartridges."

"And something to rest it on," added Henry gravely.

HENRY WENT to the livery stable next morning to have a talk with Tommy Roper. Henry was still curious about that "blond angel." Tommy told him that Livingstone had not returned from Scorpion Bend. Tommy grinned foolishly when Henry asked him about the blond angel, but was unable to add any details to what he had told.

"I sus-seen her," declared Tommy. "It was kinda like a dud-dream, I gug-guess."

"Maybe it was," sighed Henry. "But haven't you any idea where you and Lester Allen went that night? You must have some idea."

"I mum-must, bub-but I ain't," declared Tommy. "You know huh-how it is, Henry."

"Being dumb, I suppose. Oh, yes, I know how *that* is. You saw the man who was killed at the Tonto last night?"

"Uh-huh."

"Did you ever see him before?"

"Nun-nossir, I nun-never did. He's a st-st-stranger of mine."

"Thank you for all the information," said Henry gravely.

"I'm gug-glad to help you any tut-time," replied Tommy.

Henry went back to his office, where he found Judge reading an ancient tome on mining laws.

"Pack up the liniment bottle, Judge," ordered Henry, "we are riding to Scorpion Bend."

Judge groaned and laid the book aside. Putting his glasses in his pocket, he looked wearily at Henry.

"Is this county too poor to pay rental for a horse and buggy?" he asked.

"We go astride our noble steeds, sir," replied Henry firmly.

"But—"

"But me no buts," interrupted Henry. "It may be that we will leave the traveled ways, seeking, sir."

"Seeking? Seeking what, if I may ask, sir?"

"Blond angels, perhaps."

"I see," groaned Judge wearily. "I must rack my bones, skin my ancient shins, and bruise my anatomy, following the will-o'-the-wisp of a drunken cowboy. The longer I live in Arizona—"

"The more garrulous you become," finished Henry.

"It is well enough for you to talk, upholstered, as you are."

Still complaining, Judge saddled his horse and rode away with Henry. Judge usually ignored stirrups, and refused to wear chaps and spurs. He invariably removed his cartridge belt, looped it around the saddle-horn, and let his holstered gun dangle. Henry rode in full panoply, his short legs encased in bat-wing chaps, huge spurs on his high-heel boots; and on his head he wore a huge, black Stetson sombrero, surmounted with a wide, silver-studded band.

They rode to the scene of the hold-up and murder, where Henry dismounted and searched the ground, moving stiffly in his heavy chaps, while Judge looked on with amused tolerance. Henry went to the edge of the grade, from where he surveyed the wall on the upper side of the grade.

"They went up over that jumble of rocks," said Judge. "If you care to examine the road, back there about a hundred feet, you might locate the spot where Josephine sat down."

"Thank you, sir," nodded Henry gravely. "Very kind, I'm sure. I would deduce that the three outlaws had their horses concealed back there in the brush, not too far from here. They would not use the road in making their getaway. Perhaps they circled toward Scorpion Bend. If not, where would they go? What, if anything lies to the north of here, Judge? By that seemingly inane question, I mean, is there any ranches, or habitation, within a reasonable distance?"

"To my knowledge—no," replied Judge. "Possibly three miles north of here lies the old ghost town of Erin, which has no inhabitants. Perhaps there is nothing left of the town."

"I have heard of it," said Henry. "Perhaps that is where Tommy

Roper saw his blond angel. By jove! Judge, it may have been a blond ghost, instead of an angel. They look alike, you know."

"I know nothing of the kind, sir," denied Judge. "In fact, I know nothing of the occult. I, sir, am a realist."

"You are a damn, grouchy, old lawyer," declared Henry. "The only time you are fit for human companionship is when you have absorbed about a quart of one-hundred-proof."

"Why speak of love?" queried Judge dryly.

"True enough," sighed Henry. "I forgot to bring some. Well, I suppose we may as well go on to Scorpion Bend."

"There are no blond angels in Scorpion Bend," said Judge.

Henry chuckled, as he yanked his cinch tighter, whereupon his crop-eared sorrel kicked viciously, striking the sole of Judge's dangling left foot, and nearly unseated him.

"Stop that, you rubber-legged disgrace to the equine species!" yelped Judge, flexing his shocked leg. "Henry, I can never understand why you ride that warp-brained creature."

"This horse," declared Henry, "understands my every wish."

"He does, eh? Am I to assume that you wished him to kick me?"

"I would not say that, Judge. You must give the horse credit for having a few likes, or dislikes, of his own. Whoa, Socrates."

Henry arrived pantingly in the saddle.

"Truly a noble steed," he murmured.

"A bow-legged moron from the horse kingdom, you mean," corrected Judge, giving Socrates a malevolent glance. "And why on earth do you insist on going to Scorpion Bend? What is there to do in that village of vice—except to torture our old bones on uncomfortable beds?"

"I resent that 'our old bones,'" replied Henry. "Classify your own bony structure, if you must, but leave my bones alone, sir. I am as tough as a mesquite root, and as resilient as a—a—well, I do not seem able to pick a simile just now. If you can touch off a spark in that loose-lipped, pot-bellied—"

"This, sir, is a horse!" snapped Judge.

"Well," sighed Henry, "that is all a matter of opinion. Suppose we venture on, Judge."

"Unfortunately you are the boss," replied Judge. "Whither thou goest, I shall go—whether I approve or not."

"Well said, thou good and faithful servant," smiled Henry. "We go to Scorpion Bend—and who can say what we may find?"

"Bed-bugs, for one thing," muttered Judge.

IT WAS late in the afternoon when they arrived in Scorpion Bend. Stabling their horses, they went to a restaurant for supper, after which they eventually sauntered into the Scorpion Saloon, Gambling House and Honkatonk Supreme.

They found the dignified Charles H. Livingstone at the bar, cane dangling from his arm, and apparently a sizeable amount of liquor within his system. He greeted them cordially.

"I feel that we are especially honored, sir," replied Henry gravely.

They poured, bowed and drank.

"Ah-h-h-h!" breathed Henry. "Nectar of the gods."

"How are your negotiations coming along, Mr. Livingstone?" asked Judge. The lawyer's face clouded a bit.

"I came here," he replied, "expecting to meet the man who is representing the syndicate. A telegram notified me that this man, because of illness, will be several days late. I was about to return to Tonto City, when I received a telegram from Mr. Beloit's secretary, who is in charge of the San Francisco office, saying that he will arrive this evening, bringing some very important papers for Mr. Beloit's signature. Naturally, I stayed to meet him."

"Naturally," agreed Henry. "As I have always contended, one leg is not enough to stand on, gentleman; so fill up the glasses."

They poured, and drank again.

"Gen'lemen," stated Livingstone, "the more I see of Arizona, the more I am inclined to make a def'nite statement. I say—and

I believe that you gen'lemen will bear me out—that the more I shee of Arizona, the more I am inclined to make a def'nite statement."

"You are absolutely right, sir," declared Henry seriously. "It is wonderful of you to say this—and I am sure that Arizona will be proud to know what you have just said."

"I shall write to the Governor," declared Judge. "It is magnificent of you, Mr. Livingstone."

"It is nothing 'tall," assured the well plastered Mr. Livingstone. "It was in my heart of hearts. Shall we drink to Arizona?"

"After that, I believe we should," replied Henry.

They poured, bowed and drank once more. The passenger train from the West came to Scorpion Bend, but none of the trio paid any attention. Mr. Livingstone tried to sing a song. It was something about "Hail, hail, the gang's all here, and we'll have a hot time in Old Lang Syne." The tune was a combination of all three songs.

While Mr. Livingstone, with both hands clenched, his mouth stretched to full capacity, was trying to hold a high note, somewhere on the street a shot rang out. But a shot on the street of Scorpion Bend was no novelty.

"Some exuberant cow person starting for the ranch," said Henry. "Now, Mr. Livingstone, if I had a voice like yours, I would do something with it."

"Except sing," added Judge dryly.

"Opera has of'n called me," confided Livingstone.

"And found you, sitting there with a bob-tail straight," said Judge callously. "I know just—"

A bareheaded man dashed into the saloon, saw Henry, and came quickly to the bar.

"A man has just been shot and killed in front of the Scorpion Hotel," he blurted. "Someone said you was here."

They left Charles H. Livingstone at the bar, and hurried across the street, where a crowd had gathered. A doctor had already arrived on the scene, and was making an examination of the victim. He got to his feet, as Henry and Judge arrived, and said to Henry, "This man was killed instantly, Sheriff. Someone shot him with a load of buckshot."

"A very, very efficient weapon," murmured Henry. "Does anyone around here know who this man is—or was?"

"He came in on the train a few minutes ago," volunteered one of the crowd. "I seen him get off the train."

"Here's what he was a-carryin'," said a cowboy, handing Henry a leather brief-case. "He dropped it into the street."

Henry looked at the gold lettering imprinted on the case, which showed the name Arthur M. Miller.

"Did anybody see the flash of the shot?" he asked. No one replied, except that one man said:

"I was in the hotel, and it sure sounded like it was real close to the doorway."

TO THE right of the hotel doorway was a recessed doorway to a vacant store building. Evidently the assassin had stood in that doorway, fired the shot at a distance of about thirty feet, and then stepped quickly into the darkness of an alley.

Henry turned to the doctor. "Will you have the body taken to your office, please, Doctor? I will talk with you later about it."

Henry and Judge went into the alley, where Henry lighted matches, as he examined the well-packed ground. Nearly behind the hotel he found a ten-gauge shotgun shell, which had been fired recently. It was apparent that the assassin had fled quickly, and had waited until he was some distance away before reloading.

The crowd was still in front of the hotel, but Henry and Judge went straight to the Scorpion Saloon, where they found Livingstone at the bar.

"What was the name of Mister Beloit's private secretary?" asked Henry.

"His name," replied Livingstone owlishly, "is Arthur M. Miller."

"It was," corrected Henry. "I use the past tense, because Mr. Arthur M. Miller is dead."

"Eh?" Livingstone jerked slightly.

"Shot down a few minutes ago," nodded Henry soberly.

"My God!" gasped Livingstone.

"Are—are you sure?" he faltered.

"Very sure, sir. His name is on the brief-case, which he carried. Did he know someone here? Someone who might want to kill him?"

"I do not believe he ever was here before. Perhaps he met someone he had previously known."

"Have you told many people that Miller was coming here tonight?"

Livingstone shook his head slowly. "I do not remember mentioning it to anyone. Perhaps I may have mentioned that Mister Beloit's secretary was coming—but not his name. No, I'm sure I haven't."

"I see," murmured Henry. "Well, perhaps the contents of the brief-case will give us some information, although I doubt it."

"Where is the case?" queried Livingstone.

"I have put it in a safe place," replied Henry. In reality it was lying on a shelf behind the hotel counter.

They left the saloon and went to the hotel, where Henry had the brief-case locked in the hotel safe. After making some inquiries, Henry and Judge went to the home of the owner of the general store, which was the only store in town handling ammunition.

The storekeeper examined the cartridge shell carefully and shook his head.

"We don't handle that cartridge," he told Henry. "I don't believe anybody in Wild Horse Valley stocks that brand. Ten-gauge, eh? Never have any calls for tens. Don't reckon I've sold a box in two years."

Henry thanked him, and they went back to the hotel. They found Livingstone in front of the hotel, apparently sober now.

"I am driving back to Tonto City," he told them. "I want to break the news to Mister Beloit. You see, he was very fond of Miller. I am rather broken up over it myself. Have you any clues?"

"Well," replied Henry gravely, "you might tell Mister Beloit that we are on the ground—and have the situation well in hand."

"Thank you, I shall do that."

As they stood there, watching Livingstone hurry down the badly-lighted street, Judge remarked quietly:

"If I were asked for an opinion, I would say that you and Livingstone are just about mentally equal."

"And still," replied Henry, "I believe we are both shrewd."

"All of which might throw the balance in favor of Mister Livingstone."

"Perhaps you are right, Judge. I suppose there is nothing to do, except go to bed."

"And fight bed-bugs," sighed Judge. "They will come for miles to feast upon me."

"Possibly," nodded Henry. "But my opinion would be that they come to sharpen their teeth—not to eat."

CHAPTER V

A NEW ESCORT

HENRY AND JUDGE came back to Tonto City the next afternoon and found that the man who had been shot by Don Black had been identified by a miner at the Yellow Warrior.

"I knowed him well," the miner told Henry. "His name is Ben Greer. He was a pretty bad boy over in New Mexico. They was crowdin' him pretty close; so he pulled his freight. I got a card

A bullet smacked into Frijole's horse

from him a year ago, and he was in San Francisco, workin' for some outfit, I dunno what doin'."

"You say he was a bad boy?" queried Henry.

"He sure was. He killed a gambler over in New Mexico, and they was lookin' for him for shootin' up a deputy sheriff when he faded out of there."

"How did he happen to send you a card?"

"Well, he asked me if I knowed whether there was a reward still out for him."

"On a postcard?"

"Yeah."

"He must have been a brainy sort of a chap," said Henry.

"Yeah, he was pretty smart," admitted the miner.

Henry talked it over with Don Black, the young gambler.

"Possibly I'm wrong," said Black. "The poor devil was probably making a play for the money. But," he smiled wryly, "it still gives me the shivers when I think of that rifle barrel—about a foot of it—through that window, covering me. And it looked as steady as a rock, too.

"That's what made the play look so queer. Why didn't he

shove in against the window and order me to toss him the money, instead of waiting? He had me dead to rights in that little room. I don't understand it, Sheriff."

"Have you ever been in San Francisco, Black?"

"Certainly."

"Is there anybody there who wants you killed?"

"Of course not. I haven't been there for several years, anyway."

"I guess it was an attempted hold-up, Black. Anyway, we are holding an inquest this afternoon. Merely as a matter of form. However, by the way, have you seen anything of the beautiful Miss Beloit?"

Don Black flushed slightly, but grinned.

"That is askin' quite a lot, don't you think?" he countered.

"Oh, I didn't know," replied Henry. "She asked about you."

"Well," smiled Black, "millionaires' daughters are allowed a certain amount of curiosity, I suppose. Naturally, they are out of my line. I saw her riding with Tommy Roper again today."

"Poor Tommy," sighed Henry. "He doesn't understand that she is paying him to ride with her, merely as a guide. By the way, you used to ride nearly every day."

"Oh, I haven't quit—merely lazy. Go ahead and say it."

"Say what?"

"That I might be earning that money instead of Tommy Roper."

"I would not play poker with you, Don," smiled Henry. "You can see through the backs of the cards."

BELOIT AND Livingstone came to the office, where they talked with Henry about the murder of Arthur Miller.

"Someone must have made a mistake," declared Beloit. "Miller was an inoffensive person, and I am sure no one held a grudge against him. Perhaps he resembled someone else. As soon as the inquest is over I shall have Livingstone arrange to ship the remains back to San Francisco. It is a terrible personal loss to me, Mr. Conroy."

"I can imagine that, Mr. Beloit. You have sent telegrams to his relatives?"

"Mr. Livingstone is handling all that. By the way, did you bring Miller's brief-case with you?"

"No, I did not," replied Henry. "It is in a safe place. No doubt it will be opened at the inquest in order to see if there is anything in it that might throw light on this tragedy."

"That is a wise move," replied Beloit.

"Was there some important reason for Miller coming here?"

"Miller seemed to think there was," said Livingstone. "In his telegram he said that he needed Mr. Beloit's signature on some important papers, so would bring them himself."

"Have you any idea what those papers were, Mr. Beloit?" asked Henry.

"Miller did not say," replied the millionaire.

"Well," sighed Henry, "I suppose, as Mr. Beloit suggests, somebody mistook Miller for someone else and killed him. There does not seem any reason why anybody should have killed him in that manner, except through a mistake."

"That is the only possible solution," agreed Livingstone.

"I trust your daughter is enjoying Tonto City, Mr. Beloit," said Henry.

"Oh, very much. She rides every day, with that quaint, stuttering cowboy as a guide. They are out today, I believe. Of course, we will both be glad when this deal is settled and we may go on."

Henry sauntered over to the livery stable, where he found Tommy, pitchfork in hand, sitting on an inverted water pail, his shoulders hunched dejectedly.

"I thought you were out riding, Tommy," said Henry.

"Huh!" grunted Tommy.

"The beautiful lady decided not to ride today?"

"Oh, she—she wuw-went ridin' all rur-right."

"Alone?"

"Nun-not exactly. She—she wu-went with Dud-Don Black."

"Oh, I see-e-e. Riding with the handsome gambler."

"Uh-huh—th' dud-dad burned tut-tin-horn."

"Perhaps," smiled Henry, "you piqued her curiosity when you spoke of his heart of stone."

"I ain't the kind that pup-peeks," denied Tommy warmly. "I sure huh-hope he charges huh-her tut-ten bucks. I tut-tole her he mum-might be ex-ex-ex—costly."

"What did she say, Tommy?"

"Oh, sh-sh-she just laughed. Wo-wo-women ain't got mum-much sense."

"She is a very beautiful young lady," observed Henry.

"She's all—all right," admitted Tommy, "if sh-she wouldn't act like a da-da-da—fool. The idea! Gug-goin' out rur-ridin' with a tut-tin-horn ga-ga-gambler."

"With a heart of stone," added Henry.

"Uh-huh," sighed Tommy. "I've got a dud-damn good notion to qui-qui-quit this juj-job and go away—sus-sus-some place."

"Why not get drunk, and find another blond angel?"

"Huh? Oh, I gug-guess I ain't lucky with bub-blondes."

FAR OUT on the rim of Mummy Cañon, Gale Beloit and Don Black had halted their horses.

"It is all so interesting," said Gale. "Tommy Roper has explained a lot of things about the cañon, and he promised to take me down to those old cave dwellings some day."

"Why not today?" queried Don. "I've been down there. We'll have to leave the horses up here and walk down. The trail is narrow, but not dangerous. What do you say?"

"I'd love it," smiled Gale.

They dismounted and tied their horses. Don had no trouble in locating the narrow trail, which led down to the upper caves.

"Keep in as close as you can to the wall," he told her. "Watch the trail, so you won't stumble; and if you want to, take hold of my belt."

"I am not afraid," she told him.

"That's fine, Miss Beloit. You demonstrated your nerve when you rode out of Tonto City with a professional gambler. I hope your father will not be too severe with you when he hears about it."

"Are professional gamblers so bad?" she laughed seriously.

"Bad enough, I suppose," he laughed shortly. "To me, it is merely a way of making a good living."

"I am sure it can't be too bad," she said. "Shall we start down?"

A MILE east of where Gale and Don went into the cañon, Oscar Johnson and Frijole Bill Cullison, the cook and handyman at the J Bar C, came riding along the cañon rim. Frijole was sixty-six, five feet, three inches tall, and would weigh about one hundred pounds on a wet day. His face was small and thin, and entirely out of proportion to his huge mustache.

"Ay don't like das ha'ar yob," declared Oscar gloomily. "Hanry says for us to find a new boggy team. Ay am not hurse-wrangler any more—Ay am de yailer."

"Yeah, you big bat-eared Swede!" snorted Frijole. "You killed that team on Piñon Grades, and now yuh yelp like hell because you've got to help bring in another pair of broncs. If I'd been Henry I'd have spiked the seat of yore pants in that quicksand spot in Wild Horse River."

"Ay yust told you that Yosephine socked me on the yaw."

"Jist between me and you, I'd git rid of that female, Oscar."

"Free-holey, have you ever been in love?"

"In love? Me? I hope to tell yuh, I have! Didn't I steal five horses so I could trade 'em for the daughter of Three Eagles, up in Wyomin'? I'll tell yuh, I did. Her name was Whisperin' Wind. What a squaw she was! But her old man was a caution to cats. My, my!"

"You stole five hurses to buy a squaw, Free-holey?"

"I hope to tell yuh, I did."

"Did you get her?"

"No, I didn't. Yuh see, Oscar, I made a damn bad mistake. The five horses I stole already belonged to her father. I might have got her, at that, but she couldn't keep up with me. Them Arapajo squaws ain't built for runnin'."

"Ay don't like Inchuns," declared Oscar. "Love is vonderful."

"Yeah, I reckon it is. But fer me, I'll take a clingin' vine. I want somethin' to protect—not somethin' that might take a swing at my jaw any minute. I'd jist as soon have a kickin' horse."

Oscar rubbed his chin thoughtfully.

"Yosephine is a vonderful girl," he declared.

"She's a hell of a good heavyweight fighter," amended Frijole.

"Ay see two hurses," said Oscar, pointing ahead at the spot where Gale and Don had left their steeds.

"Yeah, that's right," agreed Frijole. "But we ain't lookin' for saddled horses. Somebody's prob'ly down in the cañon, lookin' at the old caves."

"Yah, sure," nodded Oscar. "Das sorrel hurse is de von what de millionaire girl rides every day. By Yee, das odder hurse is de von what belongs to Don Black."

Frijole smiled broadly. "I reckon Don Black is gamblin' for a bigger pot than usual," he said.

They stopped and looked at the two horses, tied to a snag, before going on. They were possibly a hundred and fifty yards beyond the two horses when a rifle shot sent the echoes clattering from the cliffs along the cañon walls. Both men drew rein and looked at the cañon. After a moment Frijole shrugged his shoulders.

"Black's prob'ly showin' the lady how good he can shoot."

"Yah—sure," agreed Oscar.

They rode on a short distance when Frijole looked back. Gale was running across the cañon rim, stumbling as she reached the horses.

"What the hell!" snorted Frijole. "Somethin's wrong, Oscar."

The girl was into her saddle, spurring away from the cañon,

before the two men realized what she intended doing. Frijole yelled at her, but she apparently did not hear him.

"I'll be danged if I like the looks of this!" snapped Frijole. "Somethin's wrong, I'll betcha. We better go back there and take a look."

"Yah, sure," agreed Oscar.

They swung their horses and started back, when Frijole exclaimed:

"Hey! Look! Two men on the rim, Oscar! Right at the trail—"

AT THAT moment a bullet smacked into Frijole's horse and it went into a nose dive, throwing Frijole, who landed sprawling in some low brush. Oscar flung himself off his saddle and went flat on the ground as a bullet whined over his head. Oscar's frightened horse galloped ahead a few yards, swerved to the right, and went end over end when a well-placed bullet broke its neck.

"Yeeminee!" wailed Oscar. "Are you hort, Free-holey?"

"Got m' damn knees skinned," complained Frijole, as he rolled in behind a rock, drew his six-shooter, and flexed his legs, testing them for a possible broken bone.

"How'd you git off?" he asked.

"Ay yust fell off," replied Oscar blandly. "Who in de ha'al is doing all dis shooting?"

Zing! A bullet ricocheted off the rock in front of Frijole. Another shot rang out and Frijole's old hat, which dangled from a low bush, jumped convulsively.

"Ay can't see damn soul," declared Oscar, huddled behind a rock.

Frijole peeked over the top of his rock and got his eyes filled with gravel from a low shot.

"Aw, shut up!" snapped Frijole tearfully. "Do yore own lookin', will yuh? I wish I had a rifle. Danged six-gun ain't worth nothin' at that distance."

Oscar lifted his gun over the rock, guessed at directions, and fired twice in quick succession.

"You won't hit anythin' thataway," declared Frijole.

"Ay von't get hit either," replied Oscar.

"Somethin' to that, too," agreed Frijole grimly, as he eased up and took a careful peek past a corner of the rock. Then he sat up, leveled his gun and began shooting.

"Are dey coming?" queried Oscar.

"They're goin'!" yelped Frijole. He fired his last cartridge, swore softly and began stuffing more shells into his smoking gun.

"While we was ground-hoggin' it, they made a sneak," stated Frijole. "They had horses up there behind that bunch of mesquite."

"Did you hit anyt'ing?" asked Oscar anxiously.

"Hell, yeah! Yuh don't think I could shoot against the side of a hill and not hit *somethin'*, do yuh? Yo're iggerent as hell."

"Ay meant, did you hit a man?"

"I did not!" Frijole got painfully to his feet. "Do you think I could hit a man at two hundred yards, with a six-gun—and him runnin' like hell?"

"Could you tell who he vars, Free-holey?"

"Yeah, I reckon so. I think he had blue eyes, and a mole on his nose."

"Are you yoking, Free-holey?"

Frijole arose in indignation.

"If you had ten times as much sense as you've got you wouldn't be quite half-witted, Oscar," he declared. "Am I yoking? Sufferin' sidewinders! Two dead horses—and seven miles home. Well, what are you thinkin' about?"

"Ay vars yust vondering."

"Yuh was, eh? Wonderin' about what?"

"Ay vars yust vondering if dose boggy hurses are on dis side of de cañon, or on de odder side."

"Now that's a hell of a deep problem," declared Frijole sarcastically. "Mebbe I better leave you here to figger it out while I walk back to the ranch. When you've decided you can come down and break the news to me. If yuh can't arrive at a decision before yuh starve to death yuh might consider that this here cañon has got two ends, as well as sides."

"Yah, su-ure," agreed Oscar. "But den, at the same time, ve must figure dat de hurses might not stay in von place."

"I give up!" snorted Frijole. "Let's hang up the saddles and head for home."

"Ay believe it is closer to Tonto City."

"Yeah, mebbe yo're right, at that. C'mon, let's git goin'."

Both horses had been killed. Oscar and Frijole removed their riding rigs, hung them up in a tree, and started on foot for Tonto City.

"Ay hope to get a shot at dem fallers some day," said Oscar.

CHAPTER VI

AT PEACE

HENRY HAD MANAGED to get his feet on the desk-top again. It had been an infinite amount of labor, and he sagged back in his office chair, sighing deeply with satisfaction. Judge sat in an old chair, tilted back against the wall.

It was quiet in Tonto City. Flies buzzed up and down the window panes, and one horse-fly zinged and buzzed his way around the room. Judge eyed it malevolently, but Henry paid no attention.

"Complete inaction—and so much to be done," sighed Judge.

"Go do it," breathed Henry, "and stop bothering me."

"No wonder they call us the Shame of Arizona."

"Stop slandering the office," whispered Henry. "Relax. You are continually under a strain. Why should we try to do it all? The cemeteries are filled with men who tried to do everything."

"But, damn it, Henry; after all, we are the peace officers of Wild Horse Valley."

"Granted, my dear sir. So, is it any crime for me to desire just a little peace?"

Judge squinted apprehensively at the buzzing horse-fly, lifted his right hand as though to swat the insect, changed his mind and settled back.

"Jests," he muttered. "Always a jest. Murders, robberies—all unsolved—and you jest."

"Jes' so," murmured Henry comfortably, "Jes' so. Judge, do you believe in reincarnation?"

"I do not, sir."

"I do. I shall likely be a patient old horse, sway-backed and pot-bellied. And you, sir, will be one of those damnable horse-flies, continually forcing me to switch my tail in selfdefense."

Judge grunted disgustedly. Henry pricked up his ears as a horse galloped down the street and went into the livery stable, hoofs rattling loudly on the plank driveway.

"Hurrying—always hurrying," sighed Henry. "And what is the good of it all? Life is queer. As the rooster said, 'Yesterday, an egg; tomorrow, a feather duster. What's the use?'"

"After all, sir, you were elected to combat crime."

"I realize it, Judge. If it were not for you, my good friend, I would become a sloth, a panderer to my natural laziness."

"I do not see what I have done to change you," said Judge.

"You do not?"

"Certainly not."

"After all these months of hard labor?"

"Not a particle, sir."

"Then why in the devil don't you stop annoying me, sir?"

Henry pricked up his ears again and glanced toward the doorway. Someone was running heavily across the street. His boots clattered on the wooden sidewalk, and into the doorway skidded Tommy Roper, his mouth and eyes wide with excitement.

"Gug-gug-gosh a'mighty!" he gasped. "Cuk-cuk-cuk-cuk—"

"Tommy," said Henry sternly, "have you laid an egg?"

Tommy worked his jaws convulsively.

"Quick!" he exploded, "Mum-Miss Bub-Bub-Bub—"

"Beloit?" prompted Henry.

"Uh-huh."

Henry's feet hit the floor with a bang.

"What happened to her?" he asked anxiously.

"Nun-nun-nothing," panted Tommy.

Henry and Judge exploded sighs of relief.

"Then what in the devil is wrong with you, Tommy?" asked Judge.

"Dud-Don Black has been sh-sh-shot."

"Where—how?" blurted Judge.

"Wait a minute," interrupted Henry. "I would like a clear and concise report on this incident. Miss Beloit was with Don Black this afternoon. Tommy, is Miss Beloit in town?"

"Uh-huh," gulped Tommy. "She-she went to the ho-ho-hotel."

"There we shall go," declared Henry. "Come, Judge."

THEY FOUND Gale Beloit at the hotel, with her father and Charles Livingstone. Quite a crowd had gathered in the little lobby, and the girl was trying to tell her story.

She said that she and Don Black went riding, out to Mummy Cañon, where Don offered to take her down to the old cave dwellings. They went down there, where they searched for turquoise beads and spent some time in enjoying the scenery. Don was standing on a narrow parapet, overlooking the cañon, when a bullet struck him, knocking him off the parapet and into the cañon.

Frightened for her own life, Gale ran back up the narrow trail to the horses, mounted and raced all the way back to town.

She said that only a few moments previous to the shot she had looked over the edge of the parapet and noticed that it was a long distance to the bottom.

"Do you suppose that the shot could have been accidental?" asked Henry.

"Why, I wouldn't know," replied the girl.

"Did it sound loud?"

"I don't remember. I was so frightened."

"Ma'am," said one of the cowboys, "which cave was it?"

"It was the second one—I remember that."

"She's pretty deep right there," sighed the cowboy. "If he went over that ridge he ain't hardly hit bottom yet."

He turned to the crowd.

"I want every one of you men to go with me. It is rather late in the day, but we will go into the cañon and, if possible, recover the body. If he is not dead we can get him to medical assistance as quickly as possible. Get your horses."

"We better take a blotter along," said a cowboy. "If he fell all the way into that dad-blamed cañon he's a grease spot now."

"I think that one of us should stay at the office," suggested Judge, as they turned down the street.

"In case Don Black should come back—you mean?" queried Henry.

"Not exactly, Henry; but Oscar is not here and—"

"Well, those assassins wouldn't do a thing like that, Judge."

"Wouldn't do a thing like what?"

"Come in and give themselves up. No, I believe that the jail will be perfectly safe, if we leave it alone for the afternoon."

"Old legs, stumblin' around in a cañon," muttered Judge.

"All right, Grandpa," said Henry. "You stay here. When I get as old as you are I will probably need a lot of rest. Hide the keys to the cells, and don't let anybody in until I get back."

The posse of twelve men met Oscar and Frijole about two miles out of Tonto City, limping along on blistered feet.

In a few well-chosen words, sprinkled with profanity, Frijole told them what had happened to himself and Oscar.

"Why," queried Henry, "didn't you both ride Don Black's horse?"

Oscar and Frijole looked foolishly at each other.

"By Yee, Ay never t'ought!" exclaimed Oscar.

"Well, I'll tell yuh," said Frijole, "I got me in trouble a couple times, takin' horses that didn't belong to me. How'd I know Don Black was dead?"

"Admit that you were so frightened that you never thought," said Henry.

"Keno," grinned Frijole. "What'll we do, Henry?"

"Go on to Tonto. You are both too sore-footed to help us."

THE POSSE went into the cañon about a mile from the cliff dwellings and came down the bed of the cañon. Several of the men were familiar with the cañon, and led the way directly to a spot below the old dwellings.

Apparently the walls were almost sheer, but they did not find the body, although they searched until dark before going back to Tonto City.

"We will search again tomorrow," Henry declared. "It is possible that the body lodged on a small shelf, or was snagged and held up there. By working top and bottom we may accomplish something."

Back at the hotel room with Judge, Henry bathed his sore feet in hot water and talked things over with Judge.

"I am thoroughly convinced that someone deliberately murdered Don Black," stated Henry. "He was right when he said that man intended to murder him, but was overcome by cupidity when he saw all that money."

"That is plausible," nodded Judge. "I am glad they did not molest the girl."

"Yes, that was fortunate," agreed Henry.

"And you have lost two good horses."

"I am glad it was horses, instead of men, Judge. This shooting is very mysterious. I am sure that Don Black had no idea what it was all about. I wonder what is at the bottom of it."

"We will never know, Henry," sighed Judge.

"Never is a long, long time, my friend. I wonder if the men, or man, who shot Black have any connection with the men who shot Johnny Deal, the stage-driver, and Arthur Miller. By Jove, Judge, we are having an epidemic of crime!"

"So you have discovered that too, have you?"

"Yes, I believe I have."

"Good! It has taken a long time, Henry."

"They have been rather broad in their selections. A secretary to a millionaire, a gambler, and a stage-driver. Their affections seem to be scattered. That is worth thinking about."

"Miss Beloit was badly frightened," said Judge. "It was a terrible experience for one so young, She nearly collapsed. I believe her father chided her for riding with a gambler. But she is an only child and he indulges her, I am afraid."

"I believe you told me that she is not his child."

"That is true. But there seems to be the same affection, as though she were his own child. Howard Beloit strikes me as being a very lonely man. He rarely leaves the hotel, where he spends most of his time reading. Mr. Livingstone tells me that Beloit is not a little exasperated over the delay in the arrival of that syndicate representative."

"Well," replied Henry, "I am too young and virile to break down my health in worrying about Mr. Beloit's troubles. Toss me that towel, Judge. And if you can find a fork I would like to test my feet. I feel that they are well done."

THE SEARCH next morning was fruitless. As far as they could see there was no body lodged on any of the narrow ledges, nor on any of the few old snags which grew out from the rocky walls.

They were back at noon. Charles Livingstone had already gone to Scorpion Bend; so Henry and Judge hired a livery-rig to take them to Scorpion Bend, where they were going to hold an inquest over the body of Arthur Miller. Livingstone had already told Judge that Beloit would not attend the inquest.

It was late in the afternoon when they arrived, but they decided to hold the inquest, anyway. There was no direct evidence; so a hastily summoned jury decided that Miller had been murdered by a person unknown, who probably had made a mistake in his victim.

After the inquest was over, Judge said to Henry:

"By jove, we forgot that brief-case!"

"And you a lawyer," chided Henry.

"I will admit that I forgot it. Why, that might contain something of value to our investigation."

"I think it did," replied Henry soberly. "As a matter of fact it had been taken from the hotel safe. The hotel keeper was as surprised as I was when he opened the safe and did not find it."

"You mean—the safe was robbed?"

"Of the brief-case," nodded Henry. "That was why I did not mention it at the inquest."

Judge scratched his lean chin thoughtfully for several moments.

"I believe we need a drink, sir," he stated soberly.

"At times you appear lucid," declared Henry. "The worthy Mr. Livingstone is already at the Scorpion bar, so we may as well join him. I cannot say that I crave his companionship, but, damn it all, sir, he does get drunk like a gentleman."

Two hours later, out in the darkness in front of the livery stable, Henry, Judge, and Charles Livingstone were all trying to fit themselves into one buggy seat. Finally Judge said:

"Please, gen'lemen, please. I've made sheven trips around thish equipage already. Every time Henry sits down he squeezes me out entirely. I sugges' that Henry sits down firsht and remains as quiet as posshible."

"A ver' good sugges'n," agreed Livingstone. "I've been squeezed out five times. Are you 'greeable, Misser Conroy?"

"I bow to shuperior wishdom," announced Henry. "I will even hol' my breath, drawing myshelf as compac' as posshible. Ready?"

They all managed to stay on the seat this time. After a reasonable period, Henry suggested:

"Will shomebody speak to the horsh?"

"Giddap!" snorted Judge.

The horse started with a jerk, and went down the dark road at a smart clip, heading for Tonto City, the buggy squeaking and clattering along behind. They went around a sharp curve, throwing the buggy into a skid on the gravel, but it straightened quickly.

"I don't like to make remarks," stated Henry, "but I don' think that such speed is exactly proper, especially on curves."

"Tha's exactly my shentiments," agreed Livingstone heartily. "Thish road is not built for speed. Did you put the bottles in the buggy, Misser Van Treece?"

"I never overlook any details," declared Judge.

"You know," stated Henry, "I jus' remembered that *we* had a horsh and buggy, Judge."

"Tha's right!" exclaimed Judge. "Can you imagine—forgetting our horsh and buggy."

"Merely a small detail," declared Livingstone loftily. He felt around and found a quart bottle.

IT WAS rather difficult to drink from a bottle in that lurching buggy, but they managed to do it. They went around another curve, nearly losing Livingstone, who was obliged to lose the bottle in order to save himself.

"As I mentioned before," said Henry, "the driving is ter'ble."

"I have been prac'ing law for thirty years and I never shaw worsh," declared Livingstone.

"Well, gen'lemen, why don't you control it?" asked Judge. "All complaints and no action."

"Wait a minute," begged Henry. "Jus' who in hell is driving thish horsh?"

"Aren't you?" asked Judge.

"I chern'ly am not. Aren't you?"

"I am not, shir. Are you, Mr. Livingstone?"

"I am not. Anyway, I am on the wrong shide."

"My Gawd!" exclaimed Henry. "We are adrift, without rudder or shail! What'll we do-o-o?"

"Be phil'shopical," replied Judge. "Can't stop; can't get out. Horsh sheems to be doing well enough. Shuppose we open 'nother bottle. If anything happens it might be a long time between drinks."

"All right," replied Henry, grabbing for his hat as the buggy gave an extra heavy lurch. "I'll fin' bottle."

It required some time for Henry to locate a bottle in the bottom of the buggy, and a longer time to open it.

"You know," said Judge, "for shome reashon I sheem to have more room than I had previously to thish time. Can you account for that phenomenon, Henry?"

Henry drank deeply and handed the bottle to Judge. It was so dark that Judge had difficulty in acquiring the bottle.

"Judge, there is an anshwer for every phenomenon, if you happen to dishcover it. The anshwer to your little private phenomenon is thish: we have losht Mr. Livingshtone."

"My goo'ness!" exclaimed Judge. "Stop at once, sir; we must recover him."

"That, my dear shir, is a matter entirely between you and the horsh. Pers'nally, I have stopped. I am not going to jump out; and the horsh shows no disposition to stop; so, I believe Mr. Livingshtone is left entirely to his own reshourses."

"Have you," asked Judge, "any idea where we are, sir?"

"At present we are here. Judging by a forward motion, we are changing our latitude and longitude. Where we will be is of no more concern than where we are jus' now."

"Exac'ly," agreed Judge. "It is so damn dark that I cannot see my hand before my face."

"That fact is nothing to complain about, Judge. You have lived with that particular hand for over shixty years. You know exac'ly what it looks like. Let us have 'nother drink, and conshider all 'rangements for our funerals. I have a feeling that we are merely traveling willy-nilly over the landscape, and you know the extreme danger of traveling willy-nilly in Arizona."

"Very true," agreed Judge. "Find the bottle."

Miraculously enough, Charles Livingstone was unhurt when the sudden lurch of the buggy flung him into some bushes. He lost his hat and cane, and was unable to locate them in the darkness. However, he staggered and stumbled along the road, fortunately in the right direction, and reached Scorpion Bend an hour later.

The moon came up about midnight. It flooded the old ghost town of Erin, with its dilapidated buildings. At an old, sagging hitch-rack stood a dejected-looking horse, hitched to a buggy. The horse was not tied. And in the buggy, sprawled together, faces upturned to the moonlight, slumbered Henry and Judge, an empty bottle between them. Peace officers—at peace.

CHAPTER VII

A LIVE GHOST

IT WAS LATE afternoon at the J Bar C ranch. Delicious odors of steaming mulligan permeated the air as Frijole puttered around the stove, a flour sack tied around his thin waist. Frijole was a *chef supreme* when it came to concocting a mulligan. Seated at one side of the kitchen, tilted back in a chair, was Tommy Roper, his battered sombrero perched on one knee.

Frijole laid aside the huge ladle and squinted quizzically at the stuttering stable hand from Tonto City.

"Well, I'll tell yuh, Tommy," he said slowly, "I invited yuh out here to fill yore skin with mulligan and beans—not to set there, a pitcher of gloom. If you'd use the small set of brains that Gawd A'mighty screwed into yore head you'd re'lize that millionaire females don't commit matrimony with stable hands."

"Uh-huh," admitted Tommy gloomily.

"Uh-huh," mocked Frijole. "That wasn't from your heart—it was reflexion action in yore damn neck. Wait a minute!"

Frijole reached under the table and drew out a jug. Tommy watched him as he poured two tin cupfuls of the liquid. Frijole handed Tommy one of the cups.

"Pour it inside yuh, cowboy," advised Frijole. Tommy sniffed at the cup.

"You—you know dud-damn well I don't dud-drink any more," he said.

"You ain't—up to now," amended Frijole. "There's a turnin' point in every man's life—and yo're right at the bend. A couple shots of that stuff and yore love ain't what it was. Here's how."

"I—I gug-guess I am kinda dud-desperate," admitted Tommy.

He finished the drink and sat there, tears streaming from his eyes, as the powerful stuff went down his throat. He wheezed like a wind-broken horse, but managed to stay in his chair. Frijole watched him critically and filled up the cup again.

"That's shore a test for any man," he said. "This stuff is exter proof. Yuh know there's one thing I like about it, Tommy: it keeps yuh from carin' what folks say or think. Take two drinks of this and you'll go to a dance with yore shirt-tail hangin' out. How."

"How," whispered Tommy. The second one wasn't so bad. Apparently the first one had a cauterizing effect on the throat. Tommy slapped his hat off his knee and grinned vacantly.

"I fuf-feel like a mum-mockin' bird," he declared.

"Shore," agreed Frijole. "But jist stick to hoppin' from limb to limb, 'cause, no matter how yuh feel, you won't be worth a damn as a flyer. It's been tried before."

"I fuf-feel like I—I had wings," declared Tommy.

"Stay with yore perch, cowboy—you ain't. I think I hear Oscar comin'."

IN A few moments the big jailer came clattering into the kitchen, sniffing at the delicious odors of the mulligan.

"Hallo, Tommy," he boomed. "How are you, Free-holey?"

He flung his hat into a corner and leaned against the doorway.

"Hanry and Yudge got back from Scorpion Bend," he announced. "Yudging from what dey looked like, Ay would say dat de inquest must have been a ha'al of a t'ing. Both of dem lost their hats, and dey come home in de wrong boggy."

"Sober?" queried Frijole.

"Yust as sober as usual."

Oscar looked keenly at Tommy, as he noted the tin cup near him.

"Tommy," he said, "Ay t'ought you vars going to be a to-tat-ler."

"What the hu-hell's he talkin' about, Fuf-Frijole?"

"He means he didn't think you drank."

"Oh! Well, I dud-don't, and I dud-do."

"That's right," agreed Frijole. "He either takes it or leaves it alone. Yuh see, Oscar, he's all busted up over a female."

"I was," corrected Tommy expansively. "This pup-pup-prune-juice cuk-cuk-cured me."

"Yeeminee! You vars in love and dis prune yuice put you out, eh?"

"He ain't out—yet," corrected Frijole. "Yuh see, Oscar, he's been a-ridin' with Miss Beloit and she likes him so well that she's been payin' him five dollars a day. Then she slips a cog and goes a-ridin' with Don Black. After Don gits knocked off this here mortal coil, as they say, she ain't been near Tommy. I can't quite figure whether it's filthy lucre or love. Anyway, the boy's kinda down; so I brought him out here."

"Yah su-sure. Ay know yust how he feels. Va'al, let us have a drink."

"Women are pup-pup-poison to me," declared Tommy. "All my lul-life I've been honest and up-up-up-right, sus-sober as a juj-judge; and wh-wh-what have I gug-got?"

"Yust a small yag," replied Oscar solemnly. "How is de mulligan, Free-holey?"

"Be ready in about fifteen minutes."

"Good. Yust time for five or six more drinks."

They had two more. Then Frijole wanted to sing; so they adjourned to the main room, where Frijole got his guitar. There were only two strings on the instrument—but who cared? Tommy had a fair, barber shop tenor, Frijole a rasping baritone, while Oscar bellowed what might be construed as a whisky-bass.

The coffee boiled over the stove, the mulligan burned, and the beans baked to a crisp, while sweet music blended with the odors of burning food. In fact, the ranch house had the pleasant odors of an incinerator. The one oil lamp in the room guttered for lack of oil, but no one cared. A string broke, but the music went on.

Tommy was half lying on the old sofa, looking owlishly at Oscar, who was standing in the center of the room waving the jug and chanting an old Swedish song, while Frijole, emitting encouraging discords, was trying to beat time on one string.

Oscar's voice suddenly faded, his blue eyes snapped wide open. He was staring at the doorway between the kitchen and the main room.

"Yee-minee!" he gasped in a choking whisper. "Ay will never take anodder drink of prune yuice!"

Then he turned and hurled the partly-filled jug through a window, narrowly missing Frijole, who was heading for that same window, guitar in hand. The two crashes were nearly simultaneous—first the jug, secondly, Frijole.

Oscar glanced back at the doorway and began backing toward the window, his lips moving queerly.

"Now, Ay lay me down to sleep," he was mumbling. "Ay hope de Lord—Oh, yumpin' Yee!"

THE STRAIN was too much for Oscar. He whirled and plunged head first through the already smashed window, and went galloping away.

Tommy was unable to get off the sofa. His mouth opened and shut, like a fish out of water. Finally he mumbled:

"A huh-huh-huh-heart of sus-sus-sus-stone, Mum-my gosh!"

Standing in the doorway was Don Black, one shoulder braced against the side of the doorway. His face was pasty-white, clothes torn, his eyes wide. Perhaps he realized the humor of the situation, and tried to smile, but it was only a grimace.

"Sorry," he whispered.

"Yuh-yuh-yuh damn rur-rur-right I am," whispered Tommy. "You're the fuf-first gug-gug-ghost I ever sus-seen—close to."

"I'm no ghost, Tommy," declared Don Black weakly. "At least," he amended, "I don't think I am."

"Cuk-cuk-can't yuh be sure?" asked Tommy anxiously.

"I think so. Somebody shot me, didn't they?"

"Sh-sh-sure. You—you was killed dud-day before yesterday."

Don nodded wearily. "I thought so."

"Yuh do-o-o-o? Mum-my gug-gosh!"

Strength was returning to Tommy's limbs and he estimated the distance to that gaping window.

"Yes," said Don Black. "Something knocked me oft that ledge, and I snagged on an old manzanita about a dozen feet below. I managed to get off the snag and onto a narrow ledge, under the cliff. I've got some broken ribs, I think, along with a cracked head. I've been too sick to do anything, I guess. That bullet hit the side of my cartridge belt and glanced off. I had to walk, and it was—"

Then Don Black let loose and slumped to the floor.

"Can yuh imagine that?" marveled Frijole from the broken

window. He had a glasscut over the bridge of his nose and across one cheek.

"Wh-where's Oscar?" asked Tommy huskily.

"I dunno," replied Frijole. "If he kept his speed and direction he's jist about passin' the immigration officers at the Canadian Border right now."

Frijole came around to the door and entered the house. Still a trifle dubious, he approached the unconscious gambler, touched him fearfully, and then grinned widely at Tommy.

"He didn't lie, Tommy; he ain't dead. I know live ones, y'betcha."

They put Don Black on a bed and removed his clothes. The gambler was a mass of bruises and small cuts, and his left side was a huge, purple splotch. The bullet had scored deeply into his heavy cartridge belt, tearing a half-dozen of the cartridges from the loops.

Shocked to sobriety, the two men went to work, patching up the cuts and cleaning him up as well as they could.

OSCAR WENT all the way to Tonto City, where he swore to Henry and Judge that the ghost of Don Black came to the J Bar C, all eyes and clammy skin, chased him through a window and all the way to Tonto City. Henry smelled of Oscar's breath.

"I suspect an overabundance of prune juice, Oscar," he said.

"Ay am not dronk," declared the winded Oscar.

"Well, what became of Frijole and Tommy?" queried Judge.

"Das ha'ar ghost kill 'em both—Ay bet ten dollar!"

"Ghosts do not kill people," argued Judge.

"Yudge," queried Oscar, "did you ever see von?"

"Certainly not!"

"You vait until you see dis von. Yeeminee, he looks bad!"

"Are you sure it is Don Black?" asked Henry curiously.

"Yust as sure as anyt'ing. Ay cross my hort."

"When a Swede crosses his heart, drunk or sober, it means

something, Judge," declared Henry. "We better investigate this particular ghost."

"Oh, well, if you insist; but we will find that it is hallucinations."

"Ay don't know who de ha'al dat is," stated Oscar, "but dis von is Don Black."

Don Black was sitting up, trying to partake of nourishment, when Henry, Judge and Oscar arrived. In addition to his injuries he was nearly starved to death. He was able to explain what happened to him. That is, he knew something about it. He remembered regaining consciousness, hanging on an old snag, and had been barely able to drag himself to the comparative safety of a little ledge where he had been hidden from the searchers, and evidently unconscious during the search.

"I believe my hunch was right, Henry," he said.

"There is little room for argument, Don. But who?"

Black shook his head. "Who knows? Frijole told me what happened to him and Oscar, and that Miss Beloit escaped any injury. I am glad of that."

"Sh-sh-she's all right," added Tommy. "Tut-too damn much money, that's all."

"I guess you're right, Tommy," smiled Don.

"Sh-she wouldn't mum-mum-marry a gambler."

"I believe," remarked Henry, "that we should shelve all discussions regarding affairs of the heart and devote a little time to deciding what would be best for Don Black. What do you propose to do, Don?"

"Why, I suppose I shall go back to work, as soon as I am able."

"And furnish them another target?"

"I hope not, Judge."

"Don, do you still insist on denying that you have any idea who might be behind this?" queried Henry.

"I haven't the slightest idea."

"Some tough yiggers," sighed Oscar.

"There seems to be an ungodly stench about this place," sniffed Judge.

"Free-holey burned de molligan," said Oscar.

"Uh-huh," added Tommy. "I sus-smelled it juj-just about the tut-time I seen the gug-gug-ghost. It kinda sus-smelled to me like bub-brimstone."

"I think we better all sleep here tonight and think this all over in the morning," said Henry. "It may look different then."

DON BLACK decided to take Henry's advice and stay at the J Bar C, at least until he was well enough to resume work. He declared that he did not need a doctor, and it was decided that no one mention the fact that he was alive.

In Tonto City, John Campbell, the prosecutor, talked with Henry. The county commissioners were beginning to get uneasy over the number of unsolved murders, and asked Campbell to talk seriously to the sheriff about the condition of things. Campbell, of course, did not know that Don Black was alive, nor did Henry tell him.

"If they are uneasy, John—what about me?" queried Henry.

"They think you are not making any effort to solve any of the crimes," replied the lawyer. "They point out the fact that you spend very little time trying to run down these criminals."

"I should be very glad to run," declared Henry. "If any of them can show me which way to run I shall be very grateful. I suppose that Mr. Beloit has complained about not recovering his jewels and money."

"No, I do not believe he has. They talked with him yesterday, and he said it was merely an unfortunate incident."

"I wonder how much longer he is going to be here?"

"Possibly a week longer. Mr. Livingstone came in from Scorpion Bend last night and he said that a telegram informed him that the syndicate's agent would be here within a week. Beloit is getting impatient, I suppose. He rarely leaves his room."

"I shall not weep any bitter tears when they leave," said Henry. "They brought trouble; and I hope they take it away."

"How do you mean?" asked Campbell.

"It started with the stage robbery and the murder of the driver. Since then it has been fairly consistent."

"Merely a coincidence, Henry."

"As Jonah said, when the whale swallowed him," added Henry dryly.

Campbell smiled thoughtfully. "I suppose. Well, of course, I can understand the murder of the stage driver. He reached for his gun and they killed him. But I can't understand the killing of Lester Allen, the wanton murder of Arthur Miller—and the murder of Don Black, which seems to have been deliberate.

"Miller was unknown in this country. Livingstone, I believe, was the only person in Scorpion Bend who knew that Miller was coming. He was there, waiting to bring Miller to Tonto City. Don Black says he did not know this man, Ben Greer, whom he shot in the saloon office. Black told you that he believed the man was there to murder him.

"Tommy Roper swears that he hasn't any idea where he and Allen went, nor who shot Allen. And now," Campbell sighed deeply, "we are sure that somebody murdered Don Black. But where on earth is his body? He was shot off the cliff. Miss Beloit saw him go down. And yet there is no body to recover. Henry, it stumps me."

"Thank you, John," replied Henry dryly. "I feel now that I am not the only person who is up a stump. And our commissioners want me to run down something. I'm very sorry."

"I wouldn't worry too much, Henry. Sherlock Holmes was only the brainchild of a writer. If we could commit our own crimes we might find a clever way to solve them."

"Not a bad idea," agreed Henry. "Commit a crime, solve it ourselves, and then hang ourselves. But I am afraid it would be unpopular with officers of the law, John."

"I'm afraid so. Well, we shall have to do the best we can. I am not expecting anyone to do the impossible."

Charles H. Livingstone came down to the office.

"I am thoroughly ashamed of myself," he told Henry and Judge. "A man of my position doing such an asinine thing. But where did you go?"

"We awoke next morning in the deserted town of Erin," smiled Henry. "There we were, in the main street, the horse calmly leaning against an ancient hitch-rack, while a number of crows, sitting on the top of a sagging, false-fronted building, made unkind remarks regarding our presence."

"Yes," added Judge, "and I remember that you sat there and quoted 'The Raven' for their benefit."

"I brought your horse and buggy back to town," said the lawyer.

"Which makes us all even," smiled Henry. "What word, if I may ask, have you received from the syndicate?"

"Their agent will be here within a week, Mr. Conroy. Has anyone discovered the body of Don Black?"

"No. Queer that they should murder him and then steal the body."

"Why would they steal his body?"

"Why on earth would they murder him?" countered Henry.

"It is all very queer."

"Not if we knew the answer. No doubt it is as plain as the— well, as the nose on *my* face."

"That," declared Judge, "would make it a little too evident, Henry."

After Livingstone left Henry leaned on his desk thoughtfully.

"Judge, I am going back to Scorpion Bend today," he announced.

"For Heaven's sake, why?"

"The old strain of bloodhound within me is calling. It may be a cold trail—but who knows?"

"A new use for an old nose," said Judge. "Bloodhound! Henry, you have the nose, but your ears do not droop enough."

"Who knows?" queried Henry quietly. "Ere I return there may be a decided droop. Beware of prune whisky, and see that Oscar's gun is not loaded."

CHAPTER VIII

MISSING TELEGRAMS

DON BLACK SPRAWLED in an easy chair at the J Bar C. Danny Regan and Frijole Bill had gone out to get the buggy team, which Frijole and Oscar had failed to get, when their horses were shot at Mummy Cañon.

Don was impatient to get back to work, but he could realize the wisdom of staying under cover for a few days. He was stiff and sore, and still rather weak from his experience. He was as puzzled as anyone over the attempts to murder him. He had had plenty of time to think deeply over the situation, but there was not one thing in his past life which would warrant anyone starting such a feud against him.

He lighted a cigarette, picked up an old magazine, and was about to select a story, when a slight noise near the kitchen door caused him to put the magazine aside and step into the kitchen. As he walked into the kitchen doorway he met Gale Beloit, face to face. She was clad in riding clothes, and had left her horse near by.

At sight of him she stopped short. Every vestige of color left her face, her eyes wide, as she stared at what she believed to be a ghost. She flung out one hand, as though grasping for support, and went down.

Don started toward her, checked himself quickly and stepped back. He wanted to run out there and pick her up, but caution blocked him. She stirred and lifted her shoulders. Quickly he

Oscar took one look at Henry and dropped the lamp

stepped back into the kitchen, went into the main room, where he could peer between the curtains, and watched her get to her feet.

She was staring at the kitchen doorway for several moments, before she went shakily to her horse. Unable to mount there, she led the animal down to the corral fence, where she managed to get into the saddle. She drew rein, and again she looked at the empty doorway, before galloping away toward Tonto City.

Don sighed and went back to the easy chair.

"I suppose that was a dirty trick," he told the empty room. "She will swear that the J Bar C is a haunted place, and we'll have a lot of ghost hunters out here. Just imagine—a tin-horn gambler failing to be gallant to the beautiful daughter of a millionaire. But, as Henry says, anything can happen in Arizona."

Danny Regan and Oscar came back with the horses, and Don Black told them what had happened.

"I think you done exactly right," grinned Danny. "Ghosts don't run out and help faintin' girls."

"She's a mighty sweet girl," murmured Don.

"Shore," agreed Danny. "But yo're supposed to be dead."

"That's true. I hope she don't mention it to Tommy Roper. He's so crazy about her that he might tell her the truth."

"Yah, su-ure," agreed Oscar heartily. "Ay t'ink Ay vill go in town and have talk vit Tommy."

"What'll you talk with him about?" asked Danny.

"Ay yust vant to varn that stottering yigger."

"Oh! Well, it might help a little, Oscar. I believe I'll go along. She might have spread the news all over Tonto."

HENRY, RIDING alone, reached Scorpion Bend late in the evening. He ate supper and then went up to the depot. He knew Elmer West, depot agent, who greeted him warmly, and wanted the latest crime news.

"The very latest thing, Elmer," replied Henry soberly, "is that we do not know any more about it than you do."

"I guess it is quite a puzzle. What can I do for you, Mr. Conroy?"

"Elmer, this is official business. You keep a record of all telegrams received, I believe."

"Yes, sir, we do. They are all imprinted on our flimsy-book."

"Good. I would like to see copies of all telegrams received by Mr. Howard Beloit or Charles H. Livingstone."

Elmer removed the book from the little hand press and placed it on the counter. As he started riffling the flimsy pages, his telegraph instrument began clicking his station call. He shoved the book across to Henry, and went to his desk, where he opened his key, acknowledged his call, and began writing a telegram.

Henry searched the pages of the flimsy, a quizzical scowl on his fat face. Elmer finished the telegram and came back.

"Find what you wanted?" he asked.

"As a matter of fact, Elmer," replied Henry, "there isn't an imprint of any telegram here received by either of those two gentlemen."

"You must have missed them," smiled Elmer. "I happen to know that I printed them myself. Wait a minute—let me find them."

But Elmer did not find them. Deep in the binding were the cut edges of several pages.

"You will note, Elmer," said Henry, "that someone has cut those pages out entirely; someone who did not want any visible record of those telegrams."

"I'll be damned if I understand this!" exploded Elmer indignantly. "Why would anybody do that?"

"What time do you close your office?" asked Henry.

"About ten-thirty at night, following the leaving of Number Four. That is the last passenger train to make a stop, until five o'clock in the morning. But the place is locked."

Henry smiled and shoved the book aside.

"It is very evident that I am not the only person interested in those telegrams," he said quietly.

"I'll be damned if I understand it!" snorted Elmer.

"And *they*," added Henry, "might be damned if I did. It seems that I get all my bright ideas about forty-eight hours too late. However, there is no use of crying over spilled milk. Thank you very much, anyway, Elmer."

"Well, you are mighty welcome," replied the puzzled agent. "Wait a minute. Are you going back to Tonto City?"

Henry nodded. "Yes, I shall be going back, Elmer."

"Well, here is a telegram which just came in. No use waiting for the stage to take it back, I suppose. It's for Miss Beloit."

He copied the telegram, placed it in an envelope, but did not seal the flap. Henry pocketed it and went down the street to the livery stable, where he proceeded to read the telegram by the light of the stable lantern. It read:

JUST ARRIVED HOME FOUND OUT WHERE YOU ARE AND AM ON MY WAY STOP CAN NOT IMAGINE WHY YOU DID NOT TELL ME BUT SUSPECT

THAT SOMEONE INTERCEPTED LETTERS STOP
DEVOTEDLY

JIMMY

"Cupid enters," muttered Henry. "The devoted swain arrives home, finds that his light o' love has been spirited away, discovers her whereabouts, and gallops to the rescue. And like a fool in love, he sends a telegram to her. Hm-m-m-m. Well, who am I to play the rôle of an alarm clock and rudely interrupt love's young dream? I am very much afraid that the fond father and the watchdog lawyer will never see this telegram."

He moistened the flap of the envelope, sealed it carefully and put it in his pocket.

"My horse, varlet," he said sharply to the stable boy.

"Yeah, sir," replied the young man. "The name's Edgar."

"The name is Socrates," corrected Henry.

"I know your horse—he kicks. My name's Edgar."

"Well, don't blame *everything* on the horse."

CHARLES H. LIVINGSTONE came straight to Judge after hearing Gale's story. Judge listened gravely.

"Hallucinations, my dear Livingstone," he declared. "Overwrought nerves, of course."

"But the—the body has never been found, Van Treece."

"True. Perhaps the spirit has returned, trying to show us where it left its earthly envelope."

"Balderdash!" exclaimed Livingstone.

"Exactly," smiled Judge. "You know as well as I that it was only an hallucination."

"Yes, I suppose it was."

"There seems to be a doubt in your voice, Mr. Livingstone."

"*Corpus delicti,*" murmured Livingstone.

"Very true," replied Judge. "Without the corpse we are unable to prove death. We have Miss Beloit's unsupported word that she saw Don Black shot off the cliff. Is it possible that the young lady is in the habit of *seeing* things?"

"No, no, I do not believe that," replied Livingstone quickly. "Miss Beloit is a very normal, intelligent young lady."

"Hm-m-m-m," mused Judge. "What was she doing at the J Bar C ranch?"

"Why, I suppose she was merely out for a ride, and—I really did not ask her why she went there. Is Mr. Conroy out of town today?"

"Gone to Scorpion Bend," replied Judge.

"Anxious, no doubt, to clear up some of these mysteries."

"I believe he has some pet theory."

"I see. Well, I shall try to assure Miss Beloit that what she saw was merely an hallucination, caused by nervousness."

"Until I see an exodus from the J Bar C," smiled Judge, "I shall have little faith in the ghost idea. Those boys are not ghost-proof."

After Livingstone went away, Judge closed the office, saddled his horse and went out to the ranch. Oscar and Danny were gentling the new buckboard team, while Frijole cooked supper. Don Black was still resting and reading, Being rather curious about the ghost report, the boys gathered around Judge in the kitchen.

"We've got to keep Don under cover," declared Judge. "Livingstone isn't so sure that Miss Beloit did not see Don in the flesh. If John Campbell finds out about it, he will cause an awful howl. And if it is known that Don is alive, his life is again in danger."

"The whole thing is so damn unreasonable," declared Don.

"You mean the fact that someone wants to murder you?"

"Exactly, Judge. No reason why."

"They can't put me in jail—but here I am," quoted Judge.

"You know what Ay t'ink?" queried Oscar.

"It might be interesting."

"Ay t'ink dis ha'ar country is full of tough yiggers."

"That is a very good angle," admitted Judge. "I believe you are right, Oscar."

"Where is Henry?" asked Danny.

"He rode to Scorpion Bend today, Danny. He said that he had a theory which he wanted to prove or disprove."

"I wish he wouldn't go places alone, Judge. There's enough of us to do jobs like that for him. After the things that have happened lately, I figure there's a bad gang in Wild Horse Valley. And if Henry got on their trail, they'd wipe him out as quick as a flash."

"That is true enough, Danny," admitted Judge. "We must talk to him."

"It won't do any good," declared Oscar. "Das Hanry is yust as bull-headed as a—a Svedeman."

"Henry is going to love that," said Judge soberly.

CHAPTER IX

ENTER JIMMY SLOAN

HENRY CAME BACK from Scorpion Bend with that telegram in his pocket. Judge told him about the ghost incident at the J Bar C, and Henry proceeded to forget the telegram. In fact, he had decided to forget it. Judging from the telegram, this man, who signed himself Jimmy, was very much in love with Gale Beloit, and apparently there was a plot to keep the lovers apart.

"I'm going to be an absent-minded Cupid," decided Henry. "Let the young man appear in Tonto City—and see what happens."

The telegram had been sent en route to Scorpion Bend; so there would not be a long wait for eventualities. Henry told Judge about the missing pages from the telegram-copy book at Scorpion Bend.

"That *is* interesting," declared Judge. "But what does it mean?"

"Who knows? Perhaps there is some sort of a plot against Howard Beloit and his daughter. Millionaires are considered legitimate prey, I believe. And still, it is very queer. Why on earth would anyone steal copies of those telegrams? My main idea in going up there was to read the telegram which Arthur Miller sent to Howard Beloit."

"Mr. Beloit explained about that," said Judge. "He said that Miller wired that he was bringing some important papers for signature."

"I know he did. Now what in the devil do you suppose Miller had in that brief-case which was stolen from the hotel safe? And what, if any, effort has Howard Beloit made to ascertain what was in that brief-case?"

"Livingstone could probably inform us regarding that, Henry. However, I do not believe it is any of our business. Our interest is in apprehending the criminal—not in trying to see if Howard Beloit is running his business properly."

"I accept the reprimand, sir," replied Henry quietly. "But, as the rooster said when he swallowed a length of barb-wire, there are certain things that stick in my craw."

"I understand," smiled Judge, "that Laura and Leila have cooked up a great snack of macaroni and cheese. Danny is coming in, I believe. If properly approached, they might invite us to supper."

"By Jove, Judge, we have neglected them of late! Let us declare a holiday."

"But a sober one," warned Judge. He craned his neck toward the doorway. Frijole Bill had just ridden up to the doorway, bringing a bulky object in a gunny-sack.

The little cook came clattering in and placed the object on Henry's desk-top.

"Three days old, if she's a minute," he announced.

Henry removed the jug from the sack, drew the cork and smelled of it carefully.

"It won't jump out," assured Frijole. "I kinda experimented

on that batch, I was runnin' kinda short on prunes; so I cut me some maguey, soured it along with the prunes, and distilled the whole works together."

"How did Bill Shakespeare like the mash?" asked Judge.

Bill Shakespeare, the ranch rooster, an inveterate drunkard, always got inebriated on Frijole's used mash.

"Bill liked her fine," replied the little cook. "He shore got on a whizzer this time. Yuh know, there's a couple skunks down the wash that's been annoyin' the chickens. Bill don't pay no attention to 'em as long's he's sober. But today, after he was all zizzed up, he went down that dry-wash like a feller on ice skates.

"Well, I was plumb scared that Bill was huntin' hisself a wild-cat. Mostly allus, when Bill gets drunk, he goes out choosin' wild-cats. But he's gittin' too old for such pastimes; and I'm scared they might team up on him. Well, I follered him, aimin' to head him off, if he was trackin' a bob-cat, but he wasn't. I finds him down the dry-wash, settin' on the limb of a mesquite, right over the top of a hole where them skunks hived up."

"A skunk pelt would be nice," murmured Henry.

"Not after Bill got through with it," grunted Frijole.

"Personally," remarked Judge, "I believe *you* ate that mash, instead of Bill Shakespeare."

"Judge, you pain me," declared Frijole, "You don't reckon I'd lie about anythin' as small as a rooster, do yuh?"

"At any rate," said Henry quickly, "Frijole does not insist on you believing him, Judge. I do believe him. After drinking his prune whisky all these months, I believe Bill Shakespeare did exactly as Frijole told it."

"Yes," nodded Judge, "there is some supporting evidence, of course. I believe I shall retract my doubting opinion, and give full credit to Bill Shakespeare."

"That's fine," grinned Frijole. "Bill will be glad to hear it."

"You will tell him?" snorted Judge.

"Shore. I never have any secrets from Bill."

Judge grabbed his hat and started for the doorway.

"Find out about the macaroni and cheese, will you?" asked Henry.

"If I ever get back to normal," replied Judge huskily.

THE USUAL crowd was waiting for the stage from Scorpion Bend, next day. Charles H. Livingstone, faultlessly attired, swinging a new cane, came sauntering up the sidewalk. He nodded to Henry, but ignored the rest.

A few minutes later the stage came into town, swung in a U-turn, and drew up at the stage-depot. On the seat with the driver was a tall, good-looking young man, well-dressed. He smiled grimly as he swung down from the seat and faced the Beloit lawyer.

"Hello, Charles H.," he said. "How are you?"

For several moments Livingstone groped for words. Finally:

"What in the devil are *you* doing here, Sloan?"

"A free country, isn't it?" he retorted.

"I suppose it is. But why are you here?"

"To see my fiancée—if it is any of your business."

"Well, you won't see her. Mr. Beloit won't let you see her. In fact, Gale doesn't want to see you; so you may as well go back."

"I think you're a damn liar, Livingstone," declared Jimmy Sloan. "In fact, I told Howard Beloit a year ago that you were a liar. You want Gale yourself."

"Me?" Livingstone's laugh was harsh. "Why, I am old enough to be her father."

"I don't believe that a public street is the place to debate," said Jimmy Sloan. "Suppose we go to the hotel."

"All right," agreed Livingstone. "But you are not going up to see Gale until she says she wants to see you. I'll go up and tell her that you are here."

"And scheme some way to prevent me from seeing her, eh?"

"You will have to take that chance, Sloan."

"Oh, all right—go ahead."

Henry had heard all the conversation, so he sauntered into the little lobby, interested in the outcome. Jimmy Sloan registered, while Livingstone hurried up the stairs.

When Sloan finished signing his name on the dog-eared register, he said to the proprietor:

"Did you deliver a telegram yesterday or today to Miss Beloit?"

"No, I don't reckon I did, Mr. Sloan."

"Probably not," muttered Sloan grimly. He leaned against the counter, looking anxiously toward the old stairway.

"Miss Beloit is a mighty nice girl," volunteered the hotel man.

"I think so," replied Sloan. "Ah-ha!"

Charles H. Livingstone came rapidly down the stairs, and over to young Sloan.

"Miss Beloit refuses to see you," he announced. "She says there is no reason on earth why she should see you. That is final."

"And you ask me to believe that?"

"It is true, whether you believe it or not. And another thing," Livingstone turned to the proprietor. "Mr. Beloit asks that you refuse a room to this young man. Mr. Beloit will pay you for the extra room; so you will not lose on the deal."

The hotel keeper was puzzled. Nothing like that had ever happened to him before.

"Shucks, I dunno what to do," he said. "I ain't got no right to refuse a room to a decent person, have I?"

"You have that right," declared Livingstone, and the next moment he went reeling across the room, fell backward over a chair, and landed on his head and shoulders against the wall. Jimmy Sloan had hit him with a very expert straight left-right on the chin.

Then he turned to the desk, and said calmly: "Room two eleven, isn't it?"

"My Gawd!" gasped the hotel keeper. "Yeah, I reckon it is."

Jimmy Sloan picked up his bag and trotted quickly up the stairs.

HENRY, LEANING against the doorway, looked quizzically at the form of Charles H. Livingstone.

"What'll I do-o-o?" wailed the hotel keeper.

"Count ten," replied Henry soberly. "If he don't get up inside the count of ten—young Sloan wins, I suppose."

Then he turned and walked down to the office, rubbing his nose thoughtfully.

"A beautiful punch," he told Judge. "Perfectly timed, well executed. In fact, I have never seen better."

"Granting all that," admitted Judge, "Livingstone has just cause for an assault charge."

"You forget that I was a witness to the proceeding, Judge."

"You would testify for Sloan?"

"As Frijole would say, I hope to tell yuh I would."

"Yes, I suppose you would. But you do not know the circumstances. Perhaps they are justified."

"No man is justified in saying what he said, publicly."

"Perhaps not. You say the young man secured a room?"

"He took his key and went upstairs," chuckled Henry. "Our friend Livingstone was still in the Land of Nod, with his feet over a chair. Judge, it was wonderful."

"I suppose," sighed Judge. "Just my bad luck, missing things like that. Shall we sample Frijole's latest outrage?"

"That is a good idea, Judge. We shall drink to love—love, which knows not locksmiths; to Mr. Sloan and his good right hand."

"I believe, Henry, that Mr. Sloan can take care of himself."

"I hope to tell yuh he can," chuckled Henry.

Later in the afternoon, over at the Tonto Saloon, they saw Jimmy Sloan, a glass of whisky in one hand, a handful of silver dollars in the other, bucking the roulette wheel. But Charles H.

Livingstone was missing from his usual haunt—the draw poker game. Perhaps his jaw was too sore.

CHAPTER X

MYSTERIOUS DEATH

NEXT MORNING, AS Henry was finishing his breakfast at the hotel dining room, Howard Beloit and his daughter came into the room for breakfast. They nodded to Henry as he walked out. He went to the desk and inquired about Jimmy Sloan.

"Dog-gone it, that feller shore had me worried," grinned the hotel keeper. "I was scared there'd be more trouble between him and Mr. Livingston. But I reckon they patched things all up between 'em last night."

"Is that so?" queried Henry. "Where is Sloan this morning?"

"Oh, he went back to Scorpion Bend last night. Mr. Livingstone ain't back yet."

"Did he go to Scorpion Bend, too?"

"Yeah, he did. He took Mr. Sloan up there."

"Remarkable," muttered Henry. "So they buried the hatchet."

"Yeah, I reckon they did."

"What time did they leave here?"

"Why, I reckon it was about ten o'clock."

Henry walked down to the livery stable, where Tommy Roper was busily washing harness in a tub of soapy water.

"Huh-hell of a juj-job," stuttered Tommy. "Mum-might as well have a juj-job washing dud-dishes."

"It gives you a good opportunity to get your hands clean."

"Uh-huh, that's right."

"Livingstone went to Scorpion Bend again last night?"

"Uh-huh. He gug-goes quite a lul-lot. Makes gug-good bub-business for us."

"What time did he leave last night, Tommy?"

"Must have bub-been about tut-ten o'clock."

Henry walked back to the office and sat down at his desk. Judge came in from the jail, hung up his coat and sat down.

"Judge, what time did you leave the Tonto Saloon last night?" asked Henry.

Judge looked at him curiously. "Are you checking up on my morals, Henry?" he countered.

"Not at all, sir. That would require the undivided attention of a recording angel."

"Thank you," replied Judge dryly. "I would say that it was about half-past eleven—and sober."

"Was Jimmy Sloan still at the roulette wheel?"

"He was, sir—and well ahead of the game, I believe. Now, what have I said to cause you to smile so foolishly?"

"It was not mirth, I assure you, Judge. It may have been a foolish idea, which leaked out on my countenance."

While they were talking, Howard Beloit came to the office. He seemed in good spirits, and sat down with them.

"I think I have finally convinced my daughter that the ghost of Don Black was merely an hallucination," he told them. "She was so nervous and upset over what happened that day, you know. Why, she would not even leave the room."

"I can understand," nodded Henry. "A terrible experience."

"I believe you witnessed the scene yesterday between Livingstone and young Sloan."

"Yes, I saw it," replied Henry.

"A very unfortunate thing, indeed. Jimmy Sloan is of good family, but not what I would select as a husband for my daughter. He insists on forcing himself on her, and I—well, I merely put my foot down. But not until," he hastened to add, "my daughter agreed."

"I see," murmured Henry. "By the way, Mr. Beloit, has your

office informed you as to the reasons why Arthur Miller came here?"

"My office does not seem to know."

"Then you have no way of knowing what might have been in that brief-case?"

"Not the slightest, Mr. Conroy. It is all very mysterious."

"There are more mysteries, Mr. Beloit," declared Henry. "For instance, can you give me any reason why the copies of telegrams to you have been stolen from the record book at the Scorpion Bend depot?"

Howard Beloit leaned forward, looking keenly at Henry.

"I did not know that," he said. "How do you know it?"

"I went there to see those copies," replied Henry.

"Why were you interested in telegrams to me, Mr. Conroy?"

"I wished to see the copy of the telegram sent you by Arthur Miller. Naturally, we are interested in his murder, Mr. Beloit."

"Yes—certainly. I haven't the telegram. Perhaps Mr. Livingstone has it, although I doubt if he has. But I am sure that nothing could be gained from a telegram."

"The party, or parties, who destroyed those records must have had a different idea, Mr. Beloit."

"It is a strange thing to do," agreed Beloit. "I shall speak to Mr. Livingstone about it, although I doubt that he would have any theory on the matter. He seems very fond of both of you."

"Does he?" smiled Henry. "I like him better drunk than sober. He is almost human when under the influence of liquor. When sober, he becomes pretty much of a plain damn fool."

Howard Beloit squirmed in his chair.

"I believe that is something that should be discussed in the presence of Mr. Livingstone," he said coldly.

"I took the matter up with Mr. Livingstone," said Henry. "He said it was purely a matter of opinion."

"Well," said Howard Beloit, getting to his feet, "I have enjoyed my short chat with you two gentlemen. I shall see you again."

"By the way," said Henry. "Tell your daughter that she can feel perfectly safe in riding out to my ranch. The ghost has never been seen since."

"Thank you—I shall tell her," smiled the millionaire.

AFTER HE had gone, Judge sighed and leaned back in his chair.

"Well, Henry, you managed to make him feel uncomfortable."

"You mean about Livingstone?"

"Not at all—about those stolen telegram records."

"Well, I felt that he should know."

"Do you think there is some plot against him, Henry?"

"Judge, I have quit thinking. My poor brain is bulging, like an overfilled filing case."

IT WAS early morning at the J Bar C. Since Gale Beloit had seen Don Black at the ranch, he had been careful about being in evidence, but early morning seemed a good time for him to take a bit of exercise in the open.

Frijole Bill was busy at the stove, cooking breakfast. Oscar was at the corral, roping a couple of horses for himself and Danny Regan, while Don Black swung an ax at the woodpile. Danny Regan was at the wash-bench, performing his morning ablutions, spluttering and splashing.

"She was a horseman's daughter, and the horsemen knew her well," sang Frijole, as he shook up the bacon on the stove.

"How are yuh feelin' this mornin', Don?" asked Danny, rubbing his face briskly with a rough towel.

"Great," laughed Don. "Soreness almost all gone. My ribs bother me a little, but they'll be all right."

He knelt down and filled his arms with wood, with which to load up the wood-box in the kitchen.

"Grub-pile, Oscar!" yelled Danny. Oscar waved from the corral.

As Don came up to the little kitchen steps, Frijole stepped outside, the pan of bacon in his hand.

"Damn stuff got too hot," he announced, and as Don stepped past him, something struck the pan with terrific force, knocking it out of Frijole's hand.

For a moment all three men were motionless. From back on the hill came the clattering report of a rifle. Don Black sprawled through the kitchen doorway, wood flying in every direction. Frijole promptly leaped over Don Black, and crashed against a table across the little kitchen, while Danny flattened against the ground, shielding himself with a corner of the steps. Out in the yard, Oscar Johnson went flat on the earth.

"Anybody hort?" he called calmly.

"Not yet," replied Danny. "Frijole!" he called. "Frijole!"

"What the hell do you want?" asked Frijole.

"Toss me my thirty-thirty."

"Goin' to shoot somebody?"

"What the hell do yuh think I want it for—to brush my teeth?"

Frijole, shielding himself with a corner of the doorway, deftly tossed the rifle to Danny. To the north of the ranch buildings, and beyond the stable, was the long slope of a hill, covered with mesquite, cactus, yucca and nearly every sort of desert-hill growth, with cattle trails winding through it.

From somewhere along that slope that shot had been fired. While Frijole and Don peered through the kitchen window, Danny Regan crouched against the steps, his eyes searching the slope.

"Va'al, go head and shoot," called Oscar, prone on his back in the yard.

"Throw some gravel on the Swede," grunted Frijole. "I'd like to see him diggin' in out there in that hard dirt."

Danny suddenly jerked the rifle to his shoulder. He had seen a flash of color against the gray of the brush. It was far out to the left. Two horsemen were traveling in single file, moving objects, but indistinct at that distance. They were heading for the skyline of the ridge.

Frijole and Don had seen them from the window, and ran to the doorway. Oscar was sitting up, pointing frantically. Danny was on his feet now, raising the sights of his rifle.

"Yuh can't hit 'em, Danny!" yelled Frijole. "That's five hundred yards to that ridge."

THE TWO riders came out on the ridge-top, silhouetted against the sky. They were following an old cattle-trail, which went up the skyline for a hundred feet or more before breaking over into the next cañon. Danny cuddled the butt of his rifle, lifted the muzzle, following the riders for an instant, and squeezed the trigger.

The whip-like crack of the thirty-thirty clattered back in echoes from the buildings and hills. For a moment the two riders were still moving ahead. Then the leading rider jerked up his horse, and whirled the animal around.

For a moment Danny thought his bullet had struck in front of the horse, causing the animal to whirl. But the rider was acting queerly. So far away that they looked like toy horses and riders, still their movements were plainly etched against the sky.

"My Gawd, I b'lieve you hit one of 'em!" yelped Frijole. "Look! He's off his horse!"

Danny lifted his rifle, hesitated a moment, and squeezed the trigger again. The horseman jerked his horse around as the bullet struck near him. But he quickly swung back. As the four men stood there, watching his next move, they heard the report of another shot… and another, closely spaced.

A few moments later the lone rider, leading the other horse, went swiftly up the slope, and over into the adjoining cañon.

"Figure that one," said Danny grimly. "Who else was shootin'?"

"I'll tell yuh!" blurted Frijole excitedly. "Danny, you hit that feller—hit him hard, too. He went off his horse. That other jigger, plenty leary of that kinda shootin', wouldn't take time to pack his pardner away; so he busted him a couple more times— to shut his mouth—tight."

"My God, could that be possible?" gasped Don Black.

"One of them sons-of-biscuit-shooters shore ruined my skillet," complained Frijole, picking up the utensil and looking at it ruefully.

"Never mind the skillet!" snapped Danny. "We've got to get up there and see if Frijole's correct."

" 'Course I'm correct. Didn't yuh see that feller leadin' the empty horse up the hill?"

Oscar was already down at the corral, saddling swiftly. Don stayed at the ranch house, taking Danny's advice to stay undercover, while the three of them mounted and rode straight up the slope.

They found the man, sprawled on his face, arms outspread. He had been shot three times. Danny made a swift examination.

"I got him through the right shoulder," he said huskily. "Mebbe he'd have lived. But look at these, will yuh? One bullet above the heart, and the other through his head. That head shot was fired from behind."

The man was about thirty-five years of age, with black hair, sallow skin, and a harsh, bony face. He wore a faded shirt, overalls and high-heel boots. A few feet away lay his battered old hat, which did not show any identifying marks. Except for an old handkerchief, there was nothing in his pockets.

"Dead men tell no tales," muttered Danny, looking down at the man sprawling in the sun.

"Who do yuh think he was tryin' to bush, Danny?" asked Frijole.

"Don Black," replied Danny. "We've got to leave him like he is until we can get Henry and the coroner. C'mon."

THEY RODE swiftly back to the ranch house, and sent Oscar from there to notify the sheriff's office. Danny told Don Black about the man.

"Do you think they tried to kill me?" asked Don.

"Just as sure as God made little apples," replied Danny. "That Beloit girl thinks she saw yore ghost—but fellers as hard as the one up there on the hill don't believe in ghosts, Don. I figure they moved in there before daylight and was watchin' us all the time. Mebbe they couldn't quite figure out which one of us was you."

"You made a good shot, Danny," said Don grimly.

"All guesswork at that distance."

"And his own partner drilled him—to shut his mouth."

"Wolves kill all their cripples," reminded Danny. "If he'd stopped and picked this man up, he'd need a doctor awful bad. They're desperate, Don."

Don Black nodded thoughtfully. "Not much use of me keepin' under cover."

Danny laughed shortly. "Three times—and out, yuh know. This is the third time, if yuh want to count that night at the saloon."

"He came to murder me, Danny. These two attempts prove that."

When Henry came out to the ranch he brought Judge and John Campbell, the prosecutor, in addition to Dr. Bogart, the coroner. They climbed up the hill, where they viewed the corpse. None of them had ever seen the man before. Don Black's name had not been mentioned in connection with the shooting, and Don kept out of sight.

John Campbell and Dr. Bogart believed that the shot had been intended for either Danny Regan or Frijole Bill Cullison. They took the body down to the ranch, placed it in a wagon and hauled it to Tonto City, where they attempted to have the man identified.

"Why, I've seen that man!" exclaimed a Scorpion Bend merchant, who was visiting in Tonto City. "He was in Scorpion Bend a few days age, with another prospector. They were both strangers to me. They had three burros, which they loaded at my place, and paid cash."

"Can you describe the other man?" asked Henry.

"No, I don't believe I could. They were about the same size, if I remember correctly. I believe the other man had a short beard, and was older than this one. They talked about prospecting down toward the Border."

"Did they buy any mining implements?" asked Henry.

"No, I'm sure they didn't. But they stocked up on food. In fact," the man smiled slowly, "I remarked that they would have enough grub to last all winter. They also bought three boxes of thirty-forty cartridges—all I had in stock."

"Have you outfitted any other strange prospectors lately?" asked Henry.

"No, we haven't, Sheriff; only these two."

Back in their office, Henry looked grimly at Judge.

"The fog," he declared, "gets thicker and thicker, Judge."

"We might search for one prospector, who has three burros," said Judge.

"And enough food for a year," added Henry dryly. "I have a feeling that these men came here to kill Don Black. I have a feeling that the man Greer, who was killed by Don, was one of these men. It may be that only one of the original three remains; and as long as he is alive, Don Black's life is in danger."

"But why?" complained Judge. "Without rhyme or reason? Surely, men do not seek to murder without a reason."

Henry nodded thoughtfully, ignoring the question.

"Howard Beloit saw three men at the stage robbery, when the driver was shot down. By Jove, perhaps we have accounted for two! Judge, perhaps this wearing-down process will eliminate all of them. We are doing very well, I believe."

"I see little cause for optimism," growled Judge.

"As long as *I* am alive and unhurt, I shall be optimistic, my dear Judge. Prospecting down near the Border. Hm-m-m. That would mean—north."

"The Border is south, sir," corrected Judge.

"I was only thinking aloud, Judge. They merely *said* that they were going south."

"Are you going into the hills, searching for a lone prospector, who is purported to have three burros and a year's supply of grub?"

"My dear man," replied Henry, leaning back in his chair and squinting one eye at Judge, "even with all my eccentricities, have I ever done anything to lead you to feel certain that I am an absolutely complete damn fool?"

"Nearly," replied Judge gravely.

"Well," said Henry dryly, "if I haven't, I probably will—before this is over."

CHAPTER XI

OSCAR RUSHES IN

AT THE FIRST whir of the alarm-clock, one of Oscar's hairy paws reached out and plucked it off the box beside the bed. The bed creaked protestingly as Oscar got up, reaching around in the darkness for his clothes. He did not light a lamp, but dressed in total darkness.

Don Black, Frijole and Danny Regan were sleeping in the house, and none of them knew that Oscar had nocturnal designs. Fully clad, at last, with a gun shoved inside the waist-band of his overalls, Oscar slipped quietly from the bunk-house, and headed for the slope of the hill, where the man had been killed yesterday morning.

Oscar knew every trail on that hill, and in spite of his bulk he went along with surprising quiet, avoiding the clutching thorns of mesquite, and the knee-jabbing devils, known as Spanish-dagger.

Even in the darkness, he kept below the skyline. Reaching the desired spot, near where they had found the dead man, Oscar carefully sprawled on the hillside. It was still an hour before dawn, and a cold breeze swept across the desert hills. Cows bawled softly around the corrals, and far out in the hills an old mossy-horn steer lifted his voice in a mournful call. On the hills south of the house a coyote chorus awoke the stillness. Oscar merely grunted, and drew his neck deeper into his jacket-collar.

After about fifteen minutes of listening he heard a slither of gravel in the adjoining cañon, the sharp snap of a broken stick. Oscar, the Vitrified Viking, smiled to himself, but did not move. It was possibly ten minutes later when he heard the next sound; the soft scruff of boots on hard ground.

The sound was so close that the bristles on Oscar's neck lifted a little. Apparently the man was right behind, and a little above him. Oscar froze, hardly daring to breathe. He could hear the soft sound of cloth brushing against cloth, as the man moved his arms.

Then the grit of gravel underfoot, a shadow just over his head. Oscar tried to jerk aside, but the foot came down on his shoulder. The man had stepped down on him in the darkness, mistaking him for a deeper shadow, no doubt.

Oscar twisted sideways, jerking the man off balance. With a yelp of fright the man came down in the brush, while right into him, like a charging grizzly came Oscar Johnson. Oscar's right hand came in contact with a rifle, which he tore loose from the man's grip, and threw it aside.

There were no rules in this fight, no conversation. They were like two wild animals, suddenly coming to death grips in the darkness, neither knowing who or what the other might be— nor caring.

Oscar was clutching with left hand, while his right fist, like the Hammer of Thor, never ceased swinging. It came in contact with rock, mesquite, elbows and knees, but finally found its target. The man was fighting with tooth and nail, trying to draw a gun, only to have his elbow paralyzed by a smashing blow. Another hammer-like smash knocked all the breath out of his body, and then a pile-driver began bouncing blows off his unprotected face and jaw.

It was then that the man relaxed, unconscious. Oscar, his nose bleeding, one cheek cut deeply, sat up on the limp body of his victim, and said:

"Das ha'ar vars fun."

He felt for the man's holster, found that the gun was missing, and got to his feet. Then he picked the man up in his arms, flung him over his shoulder, the man's head and shoulders hanging down his massive back, and went triumphantly down the hill again.

Oscar shoved the bunk-house door open, felt around in the dark, and dumped his victim on a bunk. Panting heavily, he scratched a match and lighted the lamp. The man was sprawled inertly on the bunk. Oscar picked up the lamp, held it high and looked down at the unconscious one.

WITH A choking grunt, Oscar dropped the lamp, shattering it on the floor. Luckily it did not catch fire. Oscar almost knocked the door off its hinges as he lurched out of the place. He raced to the house and began kicking and pounding on the front door.

After a few moments Frijole's querulous voice said:

"Who the hell's hammerin' on that door, anyway?"

"Coom ha'ar quick!" yelled Oscar.

"What's eatin' yuh, yuh bat-eared Swede?"

"Coom ha'ar quick, Ay said. Hanry is hort!"

"Henry?" queried Danny's voice. "You say he's been hurt?"

"Yah, su-ure, he's hort. Ay am going for a doctor."

"Where is he?" yelled Danny.

"In de bonk-house," replied Oscar, and went running down to the stable.

Danny and Frijole, half-dressed, ran to the bunk-house. Frijole found the lantern and lighted it. Henry was sitting up on the bunk, holding his jaw, his nose fiery red, one eye a deep mauve, his fat face bruised and cut in many places.

"How are you, Danny?" he asked huskily. "Lovely morning."

"My God, what happened to you, Henry?" gasped Danny.

"I do not know."

"Don't know? How didja get here? What happened to your face?"

"I am afraid that someone else will have to fill the blank places, Danny. Last night I had a feeling that someone might come back and make another attempt to murder Don Black.

"About two hours before daylight, I left Tonto City. I rode around the ranch house, into the little cañon over there, just beyond where the body was found. My idea was to get there early, hide on the side of the hill, and make an attempt to intercept the killer.

"I left my horse in the cañon, and came over on the slope. It was very dark, and I—I stepped on a man."

"You stepped on a man?"

"Right—down—on—a—man," agreed Henry. "At least, that is my impression. The rest is sort of a blur, Danny. I remember fighting—a little."

"But how did you get here, Henry? How did Oscar—wait a minute. Did you talk with Oscar?"

"Not this morning, Danny. Where is Oscar?"

"He went after a doctor a few minutes ago."

"Oscar," breathed Henry. "Did Oscar—"

Danny sat down on the bunk, his eyes filling with tears. Henry, in spite of his injuries, suddenly began to shake with mirth.

"The—the busted lamp!" choked Danny. "He saw you—and dropped the lamp! He—he—I'll be a horned—toad!"

"He was out there, too," wheezed Henry. "He thought I was the bushwhacker."

Henry wiped the tears off his swollen cheeks, and looked at Danny, only to have a fresh paroxysm of mirth.

"It don't sound funny to me," growled Frijole. "Oscar ort to have a good kick in the pants."

"No," choked Henry. "What we need is a set of signals."

"It's a wonder he didn't kill you, Henry," declared Danny.

"Oh!" gasped Henry. "Do you really think I'll live?"

"Prob'ly laugh yourselves to death, like a couple damn fools," said Frijole. "How 'bout a drink of prune liquor?"

"On an empty stomach?" queried Henry.

"It might take the dents out of yuh."

"Yes, it might—but what is a dent, more or less, among friends?"

"Instead of actin' as bartender, Frijole," said Danny, "yuh might go get a hunk of raw beef for Henry's eye."

"Caused," said Henry dryly, "by walking into the edge of a door in the dark."

"Or a horse swingin' his head against yuh in the dark," added Frijole. "They've knocked me silly thataway."

"I've often wondered how yuh got the way yuh are, Frijole," said Danny.

"I never have really needed a choice," said Henry. "But if you want to be knocked entirely out—step on Oscar in the dark."

IT WAS about an hour from the time Oscar left the ranch until Dr. Bogart got there. Henry, Danny, Frijole and Don were eating breakfast, but Don went into hiding.

"I am afraid Oscar exaggerated a little," smiled Henry when the doctor wanted to make an examination.

"Possibly," smiled the old doctor. "He was really concerned. In fact, he wouldn't come back here with me."

"Why not?" asked Henry.

"Well," laughed the doctor, "I am not very good at Swedish dialect, but Oscar said: 'Ay vould radder remember him as I yust saw him last!'"

Buggy wheels rattled in the yard, and Frijole stepped to the doorway. It was Laura Harper and Leila, bareheaded and without coats. They climbed out of the buggy and hurried to the doorway.

"Henry," panted Mrs. Harper. "How is he, Frijole?"

Henry shoved Frijole aside, and Mrs. Harper stared at him.

"Henry, are you all—all right?" she choked.

"My dear Laura, I am all right," he replied, as he stepped out and put an arm around her. "For goodness' sake, you are all out of breath!"

Leila grabbed Danny by the arm and pointed at Henry's face.

"What happened to him, Danny?"

"Why—why, he walked into a—a—"

"Horse head, swingin' in the dark," prompted Frijole.

"That's right," nodded Danny.

Mrs. Harper's eyes were full of tears, and she choked, as she said:

"Oscar came to us, Henry. He—he was crying. He—oh, Henry!"

"Oh, Henry?" queried Henry.

Leila's lips were quivering, and she seemed on the border of hysteria, as she said:

"He *was* crying. He said you—that you probably wouldn't live, and he—he wanted to know if we had any crape for the office door."

"Great Heavens!" gasped Henry. "I shall have to get back there. If he tells Judge, they will probably arrange for a funeral."

"But what is it all about, Henry?" asked Mrs. Harper.

"My dear," he said fondly, "there are things that are done, which are much better left untold. I am not hurt—much. Oscar was wrong in his diagnosis—I hope. Shall we let it go at that?"

"Anything you say, Henry."

"Laura, you are a grand woman. Danny, if you will recover my poor steed, I shall squeeze into the buggy with Laura and Leila, and ride back home in comfort and safety."

"After breakfast," said Frijole. "I feel just like cookin'—and it ain't often that I can cook for two pretty women and a doctor."

"That's fine," laughed Danny. "I've tried plenty of times to get 'em out here to breakfast."

"We were frightened out here," declared Laura. "I never rode so fast in my life. I do believe we cut across every curve on the road."

"Oscar straightened out all those curves long ago," smiled Henry.

Leila glanced at the breakfast table, and Henry saw her mentally count the four places at the table, where Danny, Frijole, Henry and Don Black had eaten breakfast.

"Oscar had *his* breakfast early," said Henry.

Leila looked quickly at Henry. He had interpreted her unasked question, and she knew that he was not telling the truth.

"Oh, I see," she murmured. "Those sausages smell good, Frijole."

"Them sausages happen to be bacon, Ma'am," grinned Frijole. "Sit right down, folks; I'm about to deal the pan-cakes."

After the reports spread by Oscar Johnson, Tonto City was surprised to see Henry ride into town with Mrs. Harper and Leila, apparently alive and well, except for the bandage over one eye.

"Ay guess Ay yust overestimated," commented Oscar blandly.

Judge had just been notified, and was saddling his horse. He came and looked keenly at Henry.

"I suppose," he remarked, "you walked into the edge of a door in the darkness, Henry."

"You surprise me, Judge," smiled Henry. "You do select such prosaic things. A horse swung his head and struck me."

"A hurse!" snorted Oscar. "Yeeminee!"

In the privacy of the office, with Oscar present, Henry told Judge what had happened.

"Now don't blame Oscar, Judge. He was sincere, too."

"Das vars a ha'al of a good fight," declared Oscar. "Ay sure enyoyed it."

"It seems to me that you would have noted the weight of your victim, Oscar," said Judge.

"Ay didn't vait for anyt'ing, Yudge; Ay yust packed him down to de bonk-house."

"Two souls, with but a single thought," sighed Henry.

"And," added Judge, "two fools, who beat each other."

"And a ha'al of a good yob ve done," sighed Oscar.

AT ABOUT noontime, in the desert hills around Wild Horse Valley, the sun gets very hot. In fact, it was about a hundred and fifteen in the shade—and the shade was negligible. Henry and Judge, astride two weary-looking horses, went poking along in single file. Judge was not at all interested. Like Sancho Panza, he was willing to let Don Quixote discover his own windmills.

Henry squinted his sun-scorched eyes at the landscape, flicked some drops of perspiration off his nose, and tentatively caressed his one purple optic.

"Judge," he remarked, "you look as fresh as a daisy."

"I am, sir," declared Judge, "almost at the point of collapse. Of all the damnable things I have ever experienced! Two old fools, riding willy-nilly over this devil's gridiron, for no known purpose. God only knows what you are seeking—you don't."

"Granted, Judge. But isn't it a wonderful nature study? For instance, consider the horned-toad."

"Why consider the horned-toad? It is too damned hot."

"All about us," declared Henry, "are the evidences that a wonderful nature takes care of its own. No rain for months, and all this growth is doing splendidly."

"I am one mass of saddle-sores," complained Judge. "Miles from home, traveling through an inferno. A fit contemplation for a Dante."

"Merely a state of mind, my dear Judge," assured Henry. "Think coolness."

"With my poor old tongue sticking out a foot?"

"So that is what it is," chuckled Henry. "And I have been wondering all the while why you wore a red necktie?"

They circled the head of Mummy Cañon, and Henry led the

way on toward the northwest, while Judge, his feet dangling out of his stirrups, groaned softly.

"Adventuring is wonderful," declared Henry. "I feel like Columbus."

"You may feel like Columbus, but you are acting like a damn fool."

"They told him the same thing, Judge. We explorers are always misunderstood. You see, the commissioners of this county seem to think that we are not earning our salaries."

"Is that why we are out here, suffering like this?"

"Partly—yes."

"But they don't know it."

"Granted. But we do, Judge. Our consciences are clear."

"Of all the stupid damn things I ever heard!"

Henry drew rein, wiped his brow with his sleeve and pointed toward a small cañon.

"Judge, have you ever observed the buzzard? Without any visible motion of his huge wings, he circles, gaining or losing altitude at will. No effort whatever. Marvelous, I would say."

"A repulsive, carrion creature," muttered Judge.

"A necessary scavenger of the wilderness, Judge. By jove, there seems to be a convention of them in yonder cañon."

"Dead cow," said Judge disinterestedly.

"Something dead," agreed Henry. "Shall we investigate?"

Judge shrugged his sunburned shoulders. He was not interested in dead cows. Henry led the way over to the small cañon, where a huge flock of buzzards, croaking their displeasure, went flapping away.

BUT IT was not a dead cow—it was three dead burros. And all three of them had been shot down. Judge refused to be interested.

"I cannot conceive any reason why I should get excited over the demise of three burros," declared Judge grumpily. "True enough, they are faithful, hard-working little creatures; and necessary in some lines of work. But if you expect me to sit here on the edge of a cañon, slowly broiling to death in this damnable sun, and shed any tears over those three burros—you mistake me greatly, sir."

"I think it is a great discovery," declared Henry. "In fact, it is of incalculable value to me."

"With your sun-warped mind, perhaps it is. It is really too bad we did not bring a flag with us; so you might plant it on one of those ill-smelling carcasses and claim them for the Sovereign State of Arizona."

Henry climbed heavily into his saddle and looked across the long distance down into the valley.

"As I understand it," he said thoughtfully, "a burro is a very faithful beast of burden. They crave companionship, I believe. For example, if we owned those three burros, and made our home out here in the hills, those burros would stay close to us. Am I right?"

"I believe that is correct," groaned Judge, "although I hardly understand this eulogy to a jackass."

"Probably not," sighed Henry wearily. "But if you were in hiding in these hills, and you owned three burros—"

Judge looked queerly at Henry for several moments.

"You mean—they killed the burros to prevent anyone from—why, Henry, I'm damned if I don't believe we have discovered something, after all. Those three burros, browsing near home—yes, I believe my theory is correct."

"Since when do you get a theory, Judge?"

"The facts are evident, sir. But in what way will it help us?"

"I am sure I do not know," admitted Henry. "Those two men purchased a great quantity of food in Scorpion Bend, it seems. One of the men has gone to his just reward—I hope. Fearing possible discovery through the medium of jackasses, the remaining man, or men, killed the jackasses."

"But," reminded Judge, "all jackasses are not dead. I believe,

He was falling
backward through one
of the old windows

in order to not make it unanimous, we had better ride back to
Tonto City at once. This is no place for deliberations."

"I believe we are perfectly safe here, Judge. These men would
not kill those burros near their habitation. In fact, I believe they
would leave them at a great distance from where they lived. You
are merely giving in to your natural homing instinct. I believe

our best way back would be past the old town of Erin, and from there to Piñon Grades."

"It might save the remnants of my bony old knees from Spanish dagger and mesquite thorns," agreed Judge.

They rode past the old ghost town, and were about halfway to the grades, their horses shuffling along an old trail, when Henry suddenly drew rein. He was gazing curiously at the sandy soil of the trail, when Judge rode in beside him.

"Another important discovery, Henry?" he asked.

"Queer," murmured Henry. "The imprint of a dainty, well-shod foot. See the marks of a French heel, Judge, and a perfect outline of the rest of the foot?"

"Perfectly," agreed Judge. "It could be of indeterminate age, because there has been no rain for months."

"I realize that, Judge. But doesn't it strike you as being queer for an imprint like that to be found here? What on earth would a woman be doing here, walking on this trail? By Jove, I have it!"

Henry looked triumphantly at Judge Van Treece.

"You have it?" queried Judge.

"A discovery," admitted Henry. "They are wearing French heels this year."

"What is wearing French heels this year, Henry?"

"Blond angels, of course. And I laughed at Tommy Roper."

"I think you are suffering from a touch of sun, Henry."

"Anything can happen in Arizona," smiled Henry.

CHAPTER XII

THREATS FOR HENRY

JOHN CAMPBELL, PROSECUTOR, looked gravely at the three men, seated at the office table. He had known the three men for several years. Edward Mitchell was a merchant in Scorpion Bend and chairman of the Board of Commissioners. Al Cooper was a cattleman; and Sam Schroeder was a butcher in Tonto City.

"All right, Ed," John Campbell said. "What did you want to see me about?"

"About the way our sheriff's office is bein' run," interposed Cooper, a tall, gaunt, gray-haired cowman.

"It ain't right," added Schroeder. "Too much funny stuff."

"Too many unsolved murders," declared Mitchell. "Look at this paper, John."

He spread out a copy of the Scorpion Bend *Clarion,* a semi-weekly, and poked a forefinger at the leading editorial, which read:

> Wild Horse Valley is fast becoming a Mecca for murderers, while our estimable Sheriff sits in an easy chair, polishing his all too prominent proboscis, or exchanging snores with his elderly, and never-was-efficient deputy, and his grossly ignorant jailer, murderers roam the Valley, unhampered and unmolested in any way. It is time that the Commissioners put a halt to such conditions. Wild Horse Valley needs wide-awake, efficient peace officers—not a trio of sideshow freaks, known far and wide as the Shame of Arizona.

"That shows yuh what the world thinks," stated Cooper.

"That," corrected Campbell, "shows us what the *Clarion* thinks. I happen to know that Willard Preston, editor of the *Clarion,* is a little, two-faced sneak, without the guts of a jack-rabbit."

"He opposed yore candidacy, if I remember correctly," reminded Cooper, rather maliciously.

"With his customary success," said Campbell dryly.

"Leaving all that aside, we've got to do something," declared Mitchell. "We can't ignore facts, John. Henry Conroy ain't worth a damn as a sheriff."

"We all have, and are entitled to, our own opinions," replied

Campbell gravely. "I have studied these recent murders, and have had several talks with Henry Conroy about them. I don't believe that there is a single sheriff in Arizona who could have done any more toward solving them than Henry Conroy has done."

"Well, what has he done?" demanded Schroeder. "My idea of a sheriff is a feller who goes out into the hills and tries to run 'em down."

"Run down what, Sam?" queried Campbell.

"Murderers, of course."

"I see. Then you think that a sheriff should be able to distinguish a murderer at a glance. You also believe that a murderer commits his crime, stands still and waits for the sheriff to sight him, and gives the sheriff a chance to run him down. I would like to remind you, Sam, that there has never been a book of rules for the conduct of murderers."

"Aw, hell, I didn't mean that—exactly."

"It seems to me," remarked Cooper, "that we could find a good sheriff in this country. I'm shore sick and tired of the way he's runnin' that office—and I don't mind tellin' yuh, John."

"As a matter of fact," smiled Campbell, "you three men came here today, all cocked and primed to ask Henry Conroy to resign. This talk with me is merely to see if I will help to justify your action. You read that snake-toothed editorial in that newspaper—and believed every word of it. Well?"

"John," said Mitchell coldly, "you say that Conroy has done as much as any sheriff could do toward clearing up this situation?"

"Yes, I believe he has, Ed."

"I can't see where he's done a damn thing."

"You haven't discussed things with him, have you?"

"No."

"It seems to me that, in fairness to Conroy, we ask him to come up here and join this conference. Perhaps he can tell you something of the true conditions."

"I dunno what the hell we want to argue with him for," growled Cooper.

"We better have him up here," said Mitchell. "I don't want to be unreasonable."

JOHN CAMPBELL sent a boy to notify Henry. In fact, Henry expected to be notified. With conditions as they were, the commissioners in session, and John Campbell asked to meet with them, Henry felt sure that his office would be under discussion.

John Campbell smiled a greeting, but the commissioners merely nodded coldly. Henry advanced to the table, shoved his hands deep in his pockets, reared back and looked gravely around the table.

"Gentlemen," he said, "I was about to demand an audience, when your messenger arrived. It seems—"

"We sent for you—" began Mitchell.

"Evident, but of no consequence," interrupted Henry. "No doubt, you gentlemen are aware of certain conditions, which I have been investigating with possible hope of success. I am not here to outline each angle of the trouble. Suffice to say that apparently I am becoming, as you might say, the fly in the ointment in the lives of certain murdering gentlemen in this Valley. Read this."

Henry drew out a small piece of brown paper, soiled and crumpled, which he spread on the table. On it, written in penciled capitals, badly formed, was the warning:

> YU HAVE GON FAR ENUF. MIND YUR OWN BISNESS OR WE WIL GIVE YU THE SAIM AS THE OTHERS GOT.
>
> THE ONE WHO GOT EM.

"Well, what do yuh know about that?" snorted Cooper. "Tough, eh?"

"They seem to be worried, Henry," observed John Campbell. Henry nodded grimly.

"By golly, you've got 'em scared, Henry," grunted Schroeder.

"How do you think I feel about it?"

"Well!" exclaimed Mitchell. "Apparently they are afraid of you, Conroy. It must be that you are doing things to annoy them. That is fine."

"For you—yes," agreed Henry.

"But you are not thinking of—well, being influenced by this warning, are you?"

"Mr. Mitchell," replied Henry, "I swore to uphold the law in Wild Horse Valley. That is your answer, sir."

"Good! Go right ahead, Sheriff; we are all behind you. John, I guess this meeting is over, and we all feel better about things."

"I am sure you do," agreed John.

"Gentlemen," said Henry, "you will please not mention that warning note. The less the public knows about such things, the better it will be for all concerned."

"We won't mention a damn thing about it," assured Cooper warmly.

Henry walked to John Campbell's office and sat down with him.

"Henry," said John soberly, "they were all set to ask for your resignation. I opposed their idea as strong as I could, but I could see the handwriting on the wall. That warning note was a godsend."

"I thought it would be—when I wrote it, John."

The lawyer jerked forward, staring.

"*You* wrote that note?"

"Yes." Henry smiled. "You see, I felt sure I should be on the grill. There was nothing concrete to offer them; so I warned myself to behave."

"Then your life is not in danger?"

"John, you forget that Oscar is still with me. Shall we cross the street and have a little drink?"

"I believe we need one. By the way, Henry, did you see the last issue of the *Clarion?*"

Henry nodded gravely. "When I left the office, Judge was reading that editorial to Oscar Johnson. The editor is rather wormish, don't you think, John?"

"I believe that the word 'wormish' covers him like a blanket. What did Judge think of the editorial?"

"Well," chuckled Henry, "he said it rather bore out his own impressions."

WHEN HENRY left the Tonto Saloon he went back to the office, where he found Judge and Oscar. The big Swede was hunched on the iron cot, a picture of utter dejection.

"He has been sitting there an hour, apparently running a temperature," informed Judge. "And if incoherent mutterings are any indication, he is semi-delirious."

Henry looked critically at Oscar, who was rubbing his two horny palms together, his jaw set in determined lines.

"Where do you feel bad, Oscar?" asked Henry. Oscar looked up.

"Ay feel bad in my hort."

"Leaky valve, perhaps," said Henry seriously.

"That Swede," declared Judge, "is too tight to even have a leaky valve in his heart."

"Ay am sore as ha'al," declared Oscar.

"Sore about what?" queried Henry.

"Yosephine."

"Oh! Is she acting up again, Oscar?"

"Yust like a fool. Ay vant to take her to de dance at Scorpion Bend, and she says she is going with Olaf Yorgensen. Dat damn viggler! He is yust as bad as a Hi-vay-yan hoodlum dancer. He should vare a grass skort."

Henry's choking spell left him red-faced and tearful.

"Her decision probably saves a team and buckboard for the J Bar C," remarked Judge.

"Well, I really and truly am sorry, Oscar," said Henry huskily. "I am afraid you are losing your control of Josephine."

"Dass oll right," replied Oscar. "Ay am going anyvay. Yosephine says dat Olaf is a porfect yentleman. He is no yentleman. He vares roober collars and vite ties, yust like a bortender. De trouble vit Yosephine is, she don't know a yentleman ven she sees von."

"Uses perfume, I suppose," remarked Henry.

"By de quart," agreed Oscar. "He smells like ha'al."

"I suppose Josephine likes his smell."

"Yah, su-ure. Olaf is yust a knot-headed dude. He even varshes his teeth."

"Oh, that is the last straw!" exclaimed Henry. "Are you going alone?"

"Ay am going vit Tommy Roper. Tommy asked de Beloit girl to go vit him, and she refused. Tommy got new suit, too—yust as green as ha'al—and yellow shoes."

"Marvelous," whispered Henry. "And he asked the Beloit girl."

"Yah, su-ure. He told her it vouldn't cost her a cent."

Oscar put on his hat, jerked it down over his eyes, and strode out of the place. Henry placed his arms on his desk and buried his head.

"There are times, when I feel that I can't stand anything more," he declared hoarsely. "And to even imagine that *my* vaudeville act was funny."

"What did the commissioners want?" asked Judge.

"Oh, they merely wanted to compliment me."

"On apprehending the criminals?"

"No, Judge; on recovering three out of four bodies of the slain. That is not a bad record. And with Don Black still alive—we have a perfect score."

"I believe you are evading the real reason, and prevaricating, to boot, Henry. But no matter. We, of this office, are getting so damn degraded that we lie to each other. Every time a person asks me a commonplace question, into my mind dashes possible lies to cover the situation. I, Judge Van Treece, a sworn officer of the law, am getting to be such a damn liar that I cannot sleep at night."

"I would not worry about that part of it, Judge," said Henry. "You sleep nearly all day, anyway. Have we any of Frijole's Elixir of Life left?"

"Enough to drown our shame, Henry."

"Great Heavens! What a supply we must have!"

SAM SCHROEDER, the Tonto City butcher, was an honest, well-meaning man. He had sworn, along with the other two commissioners, to not mention that warning note. But Sam had thirst periods, in which he drank entirely too much.

After the meeting was over, Sam grew thirsty; so he went where such thirsts are slaked, and an hour later Samuel was in a very expansive mood.

He met Charles H. Livingstone, insisted on buying the lawyer a drink, and told Livingstone to tell Howard Beloit that in a very few days Henry Harrison Conroy would recover Beloit's stolen jewels, and have the robbers in jail, chained hand and foot.

"Interesting, if true," murmured Livingstone.

"Henry never lied in his life," assured Samuel. "That's why we keep him in office."

"Wasn't he elected to that office?" asked Livingstone.

"Sure," agreed Samuel. "But us commissioners hold him right in the holler of our hands. We can hire and fire him any time we feel like it. He's sure running 'em down. They're scared, don't yuh know it?"

"Not knowing much about local things, I did not know it."

"It's a fact. Why, they even sent Henry a warnin', tellin' him to let 'em alone, or they'll kill him, like they did the others."

"Indeed?"

"Absolutely. Got the note today. I read it."

"Threatening him, eh?"

"With death. It sure shows that they are scared of him."

"Apparently. Was he frightened?"

"Henry? You couldn't scare him with a basket of snakes."

Livingstone smiled and motioned the bartender to fill up the glasses. "Did he say he would recover the jewels lost by Mr. Beloit and his daughter?"

"He didn't say exactly that. But it looks like a cinch, don't it?"

"Well, it seems a possibility," admitted the lawyer. "I imagine it would be quite a feather in his cap, if he merely caught the robbers."

"Feather in his cap? Say," Samuel poked Livingstone with a huge forefinger, "if Henry got a feather in his cap for every smart thing he's pulled off since he took office, he'd look like he was wearin' a war-bonnet. Well, here's to Henry."

"To Henry," murmured Charles H. Livingstone.

FRIJOLE BILL came in from the ranch that afternoon. He stabled his horse in Henry's barn, and came in through the jail. Henry, half-asleep in his chair, took one look at his ranch cook and gasped asthmatically.

Sartorially Frijole Bill was wonderful. He wore a rusty, old Prince Albert coat, which did not fit him by many inches, striped trousers, many sizes too large around the waist, but pleated and tucked under his belt, and a pair of button shoes, with once-white tops.

He wore a red and white striped shirt, celluloid collar, blue tie and riding jauntily on his head, tilted over one eye, was a gray derby hat, presented by Henry. Judging from the nicks on his face, Frijole's razor, was far from keen.

Judge opened his eyes, closed them tightly and shook his head, as though trying to clear his vision.

"Well, how do I look?" asked Frijole, making one complete turn.

"For what?" asked Judge weakly.

"Dancin'," grinned Frijole. "I'm goin' to Scorpion Bend t'night with Oscar and Tommy. Yuh see," explained Frijole, "I've allus been sort of a wall-flower at them dances. I kinda hated to dude up. But I've made up my mind that a feller is jist as old as he looks. As the feller said, I'm goin' for to dip into them flesh-pots."

"Frijole," said Henry in a strained voice, "I believe you are right. You are dressed for dipping. As I calm down a little, I can see that you are the Spirit of the Dance."

"Thank yuh, Henry. This here derby kinda puzzles me. If I pull it down tight on m' head, and shut m' jaws tight, the damn thing pops up like the cork out of a bottle. I can make her jump six inches."

"When some of those Scorpion Bend cowpunchers see you— it will jump more than six inches," whispered Judge.

"I'll kill the first man who shoots at my hat," declared Frijole fiercely. "I ain't never had one of these hard-crusted ones before, and I shore admire it plentiful."

"Oh, Lord!" groaned Judge.

Tommy Roper stepped into the doorway and looked loftily around the office. Oscar had told them that Tommy's new suit was "yust as green as ha'al," but that description hardly did the color justice.

It was the hue of new billiard-cloth, made to order from measurements taken by Tommy himself. It was so tight, especially the pants, that Tommy looked as though he was wearing tights, below a short jacket. On his feet were a pair of glaringly new, bright yellow shoes, while on his head was a stiff-straw sailor, with a scarlet band. He wore a stiff-bosom dress shirt, high, bat-wing collar and a yellow and black polka-dot tie.

"Come in, Tommy," whispered Henry. "You are looking well."

"Uh-huh. I fuf-feel fu-fu-funny. How are yuh, Fuf-Fuf-Frijole?"

"Well," replied Frijole, "you shore duded hell out of yourself, now, didn't yuh?" There was a jealous note in Frijole's voice.

"Everyth-th-thing nun-new," nodded Tommy grandly. He tested a shoe on the floor, and it squeaked beautifully.

"Make it yourself?" queried Frijole.

"Lul-like huh-hell! It was mum-made by the bub-best tailor in Ch-Ch-Ch-Ch—"

"Chicago," prompted Henry.

"Uh—huh. I pup-paid tut-tut-twelve, eighty-five, plus the fuf-fuf-freight."

"Freight!" snorted Frijole. "Why the hell didn't they jist point it this way, and let loose of the damn thing?"

Before Tommy could frame an answer, Oscar came striding in. He took one look at Tommy and Frijole, and grasped at the wall for support.

"Yumpin' Yudas!" he snorted. "Dey look yust like de pictures de medicine show man had to prove what alco-hol does to de human systeem."

"Yea-a-ah, hell!" exploded Frijole. "You ain't never seen nobody dressed up—that's yore trouble."

"Yah, su-ure," nodded Oscar. "Va'al, oll Ay can say is, Ay hope de hurses don't turn around and see what is behind. Is de team oll hitched oop, Tommy?"

"All sus-set," nodded Tommy.

Henry and Judge walked to the doorway, where they watched the trio cross the street to the livery stable, before going back to their chairs.

Henry sighed and folded his hands.

"After all, Judge, who are we to criticize?" he asked.

"True," nodded Judge. "But that is such a damnable green! And Frijole's color combination would shock an aborigine."

"Speaking of Frijole—" suggested Henry meaningly. Judge got up and went back into the jail to find the jug.

CHAPTER XIII

SHOTGUN SURPRISE

HENRY GOT UP early next morning. He intended to ride out to the ranch and see how things were out there. Sitting on the edge of the sidewalk in front of the office was a husky individual, bare-headed, clad in a black suit. He was whittling on a wagon-spoke. As Henry came close to him, he looked up, squinting his round, blue eyes, one of which was slightly discolored. There were numerous rips in his coat, his collar was missing, and around his neck dangled a white, bow tie.

"Good morning," said Henry pleasantly. "Waiting for someone?"

"Ay am looking for Oscar Yohnson."

Henry glanced at the wagon-spoke. The whittling was a subterfuge.

"Are you Olaf Jorgensen?" queried Henry.

"Das is yust who I am, sir. Ay have never met you socially."

"No, that is true," agreed Henry quietly. "Where is Oscar?"

"Ay don't give damn. Sooner or later he vill coom ha'ar."

"Yes, I suppose it is inevitable. Did you have a good time at the dance last night?"

"Ay do not vish to discuss it, sir."

"Excuse me," said Henry, and went back to the stable.

"Socrates," he confided to the horse, "I hope we are back here, when Oscar arrives. I want to see Oscar make Olaf eat that wagon-spoke."

On the way out to the ranch Henry found Frijole's derby, and one of Tommy's yellow shoes. They were both in the middle of the road, about a half-mile apart. Danny and Don were cooking breakfast. They did not know where Oscar was. Tommy and

Frijole were fast asleep in the bunk-house. They came in about daylight, gave three cheers, and went to bed, without unhitching the buckboard team.

"I would like to know what happened in Scorpion Bend," said Don Black. "Frijole lost his hat and coat, and Tommy lost both shoes. It must have been a wild night."

"And," added Henry, "Olaf Jorgensen is sitting in front of my office, whittling on a wagon-spoke, while he awaits the return of Oscar Johnson."

"And me playing the rôle of a ghost," sighed Don. "I'd like to see that meeting."

Olaf was still there, when Henry returned. Judge was just a bit apprehensive.

"He might kill Oscar," he said. "That wagon-spoke, you know."

"Not if he hits Oscar on the head," assured Henry. "I cannot imagine what happened to Oscar."

"Josephine isn't back yet," informed Judge. "I checked on her at the hotel, after observing our friend out there with the wagon-spoke."

"Well," remarked Henry dryly, "it may be a case of winner-take-all. I suspect that Oscar fernangled Jorgensen at Scorpion Bend."

HENRY AND Judge were at the stage-depot, when the stage arrived. Oscar stepped out and grandly assisted Josephine. They both seemed very grim, red-eyed from lack of sleep, and did not speak to each other.

Josephine turned toward the hotel, and nearly bumped into Olaf. For a moment she glared at him, her mouth set in a hard line, and then he stepped past her toward Oscar, who was paying the driver.

Josephine stopped. Olaf, the wagon-spoke gripped in his huge, right hand, stepped in close to Oscar. To Olaf's credit, it may be stated that he was going to wait until Oscar turned around.

Without undue haste, but no loss of motion, Josephine stepped in closer to Olaf, drew back her right fist, swung with every ounce of her raw-boned body, and her fist caught Olaf square on his right ear.

Olaf's knees buckled, and he did a queer, little crow-hop off the edge of the sidewalk, where he made two more little hops and then sat down heavily. On his first hop he lost his wagon-spoke. Before he had completed the next hop, Josephine had the wagon-spoke.

Oscar looked quizzically at Olaf.

"Ha'lo dere, Olaf," he said pleasantly. Then he took Josephine's arm, and they went toward the hotel.

Olaf rubbed his sore ear, got slowly to his feet and went straight toward the Tonto Saloon.

"Imagine that!" exclaimed the stage driver. "That female can *hit*."

Oscar came from the hotel, as Henry reached the doorway. Oscar looked both ways, grinned at Henry and said: "What became of de viggler?"

"If you mean Mr. Jorgensen—he went to get a drink, I believe."

Oscar grinned broadly. "Yeeminy Yudas, Yosephine can hit, eh?"

They walked down to the office, where Judge joined them. Oscar yawned and sat down on the edge of the cot.

"Just why was Mr. Jorgenson trying to club you, Oscar?" asked Henry. "He has been waiting for you since daylight."

"Yah? Oh, that Norvegian dude, he couldn't hort anybody."

"Apparently he and Josephine had a falling out at the dance."

Oscar chuckled foolishly and rubbed his button-like nose.

"Va'al, it vars like dis, Hanry; Olaf took Yosephine to de

dance, and dan he vent away and left her. Ay looked oll over town, but Ay can't find him; so Ay have to bring her home."

"There is a faint scent of skulduggery in the air," observed Henry. "Isn't it possible that Olaf came here with Tommy and Frijole?"

"Yudas Priest! You suppose he did, Hanry? Do you suppose he forgot Yosephine?"

"Our angel child," murmured Judge.

"It vars a funny t'ing," said Oscar. "Olaf hired a hurse and boggy to take Yosephine. Va'al, Ay told her ve might as vell use de hurse and boggy, so long as Olaf sneaked out; so ve did."

"That is all very clear," nodded Judge. "You and Josephine got in the buggy, whipped up the horse, and came home on the stage."

"Yah, su-ure. You see, when Ay vipped de hurse, Ay discover that somebody unfastended de tugs. So de hurse come back here, and de boggy stayed in Scorpion Bend."

"Somebody played a joke on you, eh?" queried Judge.

"No," said Oscar. "Ay yust forgot."

"Forgot what?" asked Henry.

"Forgot dat Ay unfastended 'em myself early in de evening."

"I'll bet you felt like kicking yourself," said Judge.

"Ay didn't need to vorry about dat," replied Oscar blandly. "De hurse kicked me, ven he yanked me over de dash-board."

"As a matter of fact," remarked Henry, "you had everything prepared to humiliate Olaf and Josephine—and then forgot what you had done."

"Yah, su-re," admitted Oscar. "But it vars a good dance, and ve had a ha'al of a good time."

He went away chuckling, and a while later Charles H. Livingstone came down to the office. He was in excellent spirits. The stage had brought him a telegram from the syndicate, saying that their agent would be in Tonto City on Tuesday, prepared to close the deal with Howard Beloit.

"I have enjoyed my little visit in your city," he told Henry and Judge, "but shall be glad to get back. Mr. Beloit and his daughter have stood it well. In fact, for a while, I was doubtful that they would agree to stay here. The accommodations are not—well, just what they are accustomed to having."

"I wonder," mused Judge, "what the bedbugs will think, when they are again obliged to seek nourishment in plebeian blood."

"There *are* bedbugs in that hotel," declared Livingstone.

"After having slept there for about a year, I am afraid that you haven't exactly made a new discovery."

"By the way, Mr. Livingstone," said Henry, "I understand that you and the young Mr. Sloan buried the hatchet."

"I am of a forgiving nature, Mr. Conroy," replied the lawyer. "Mr. Sloan was convinced that Miss Beloit wanted nothing to do with him; so he went away willingly. I forgave him that punch in the jaw. Hot headed youth, you know."

Charles Livingstone chuckled, but without mirth.

"We were all young once, you know."

"Except Judge," remarked Henry. "He was mature at birth."

"And you," replied Judge, "never matured at all."

IT WAS late Sunday afternoon, but no church bells were ringing. High on a rocky point about a mile from the old ghost town of Erin sat Henry and Judge. Thunder-heads piled high above the Wild Horse ranges. It was cooler today, but Judge sat there, grumpily surveying the scene below them.

The old town was on a small flat, surrounded on three sides with brushy hills. West of the town were the abandoned workings of the old Silver Spread and the Grubstake mines, with their crazily-leaning old shaft-houses. The once broad trails to the workings were brush patches now, and the desert had reclaimed most of the cleared spaces about the old town.

Since morning Henry and Judge had been riding slowly, making a great circle from the head of Mummy Cañon. For several hours the storm clouds had piled up behind the hills, and Judge watched them anxiously.

"You seem nervous, Judge," remarked Henry. "Have patience. Remember—Job had patience."

"I know," sighed Judge. "But Job never got caught in a storm in these desert hills. I know what they are."

"I suppose," murmured Henry. "Judge, there is something queer about this old town of Erin. It fascinates me. I can sit here and imagine I can see the miners toiling up to the shafts, wagons clattering on the streets; the sound of tin-panny music from the dance-halls, the laughter of women. Queer, isn't it?"

"You should see a doctor," growled Judge. "It isn't normal."

"You practical old devil," said Henry quietly. "No imagination. I suppose that even your dreams are practical—if any."

"I can't see what good it is doing for us to sit here on this point of a hill and discuss dreams. Do you notice how dark it is getting? I may be a practical old fool; but I know storm warnings out here."

"We need a good rain, Judge."

"The country does—I don't. Listen!"

From far off across the range came the low muttering of thunder.

"We should be in Tonto City, instead of fifteen miles away, Henry."

"I was thinking about that footprint of a lady," said Henry.

Judge jerked nervously, as a flash of lightning blazed down, and seemed to dance on the hilltop. Henry turned and looked anxiously at the skyline.

"By Jove, I believe you are right, Judge!" he exclaimed.

"Of course, I'm right!" Judge cried. "Come on!"

They trotted around to their horses, mounted as swiftly as possible, and spurred off the hill. Spattering raindrops thudded on their sombreros, as gusts of wind swept down from the hills.

Judge led the way to the largest building in the town; a two-story, sagging, frame building, which had once been a hotel. The front door sagged from one hinge, the windows long since broken out.

They left their horses under the remnants of an old shed, where they would be partly protected, and ran for the large house. A sheet of water struck them, drenching them to the skin, before they could get under cover. The old building creaked and groaned under the onslaught of the storm. It was so dark in there that objects were barely visible. Dust was everywhere, inches deep in dust and dry sand.

There was an old stairway, with a sagging railing. Apparently the stairway was carpeted in the center, but the dust was fully two inches deep. No footprints marred the smooth coating of dust, but there was one peculiar mark, which attracted Henry. He lighted a match, and looked at it closely.

Then he moved slowly around peering at the floor. Suddenly he stooped and picked up an object. Lighting another match, he and Judge examined it.

"An empty whisky bottle!" grunted Judge. "You'll find plenty around here."

"An expensive brand of Scotch," said Henry quietly. "I do not believe this brand is sold in Wild Horse Valley. It is new, Judge; *and it was tossed down from upstairs.*"

"Nonsense! Why, there hasn't—"

A blaze of lightning, and a deafening crash of thunder shook the old building. Another flash saw Henry and Judge, standing very close together, looking up the stairway.

"No footprints on the stairway," whispered Henry. "Only the mark where that bottle struck in the dust."

Rain roared on the old roof, and spouted down the gutters. It was impossible to see across the street.

"Do you think there is someone upstairs?" whispered Judge.

"Someone *has* been up there, Judge; and they drink good whisky."

"This damned old place gives me the creeps," Judge said. "It's spooky!"

"It is. The requiem of every lost soul in Erin is being sung in this place. Listen to that one! She must have been a soprano."

"Pup-please don't jest, Henry," stammered Judge. "By the gods, I would rather be wet!"

"Wait," said Henry quietly. "Let us go upstairs, Judge."

"Upstairs? Not by a damned sight! Those stairs are dangerous. The whole place might cave in!"

"I am going to take that chance, Judge. You wait here. If I don't come down—"

"I—I think we better stay together," faltered Judge. "Safety in numbers, or something like that."

Their feet made no sound in the deep coating of dust. At the first landing they stopped and listened. Every inch of the old building shook and twisted. Squeaks, as high-pitched as the E-string of a fiddle, ran a crescendo, ending in a stuttering rasp of tortured, rusty nails.

"A fine pair of damned old fools," whispered Judge.

"Too frightened to run away," added Henry, with a husky chuckle.

There was a steady *drip, drip, drip* along the upper hallway, as the rain beat through the ancient roof. Quietly they went up to the hallway. A flash of lightning illuminated the hall from the broken windows at each end. A crash of thunder caused them both to duck instinctively.

"Whew!" muttered Judge. Another flash saw Henry hunched over, looking at the floor. It illuminated the hallway long enough for Henry to see that the dust had been scuffed away from an end window to the nearest door. He grasped Judge by the arm and whispered:

"That first room to the right, Judge. They came through the window. Wait for another flash."

It came, along with a swirl of rain through the open window.

These old windows were long, and only a foot above the floor level.

"We—we better go for help, Henry!" whispered Judge.

"I am going to see what is in there, Judge. Come on."

Henry was against the door, listening. Except for the wailing of the wind, creaking of a tortured framework, and the sloshing of the rain, no other sound could be heard. Carefully Henry tested the old knob. The door was not locked.

Slowly he opened it. There was an odor of cooked food, stale tobacco smoke. Gripping his gun in his right hand Henry went slowly forward into the room, with Judge close behind him. Henry was feeling with his foot, fearful of falling over something.

"A match, Judge!" he said hoarsely.

A flash of lightning illuminated the hallway, lighting up part of the room.

"Don't move!" rasped a voice. "We've got yuh covered with shotguns, and we'll blast yuh both through the wall!"

CHAPTER XIV

GHOST TOWN THUNDER

HENRY WAS SO startled that he stepped back, caught his heel on something, and a moment later he was falling backwards through one of the old windows. It seemed that he made one complete turn in the darkness and downpour of rain, and landed, sitting down, in a thick bush.

Unable to see him, of course, someone at the broken window was stabbing the darkness with pencils of orange flame, while the reports sounded like a carpenter's hammer against the old boards. Apparently the shooter was wasting lead, taking a chance that one of his bullets might find a billet.

Still dazed and winded, Henry crawled out of the bush, stumbled over a rock and fell down again.

"Something in the nature of an encore, I suppose," he muttered.

Henry had lost his gun, and was unable to find it in the darkness. Going slowly he came to the main street, which he crossed. A flash of lightning showed the two horses under the shed. Stumbling through the wet foliage, Henry led his own horse away to the further side of an old tumble-down shack, where he tied the animal.

As he came back past Judge's horse, he almost ran into two men. They passed within twenty feet of where he crouched, and stopped at the old shed. One of the men swore viciously.

"Jist like I told yuh—he's pulled out! We had them two damned old fools in the trap and one of'em fell out. Hell! We'll leave the other old coot right there, until we git back."

"Do yuh think it's safe to leave him?" asked the other.

"Shore. Hell, it'll take that feller three hours to ride back to Tonto City—if he don't git lost and break his fool neck. We got plenty time."

There was no hesitancy on Henry's part as the two men faded out in the darkness and rain. He went straight up the stairs and into that same room. The window had been covered with an old blanket. Judge was on the floor, tied hand and foot, blinking at the lighted candle. Henry quickly removed the ropes.

There was a small kerosene burner, some cooking utensils, and a big supply of canned goods. Two bed-rolls were stacked in a corner, and a rope ladder was piled up against a wall.

"How did you get out of here?" asked Judge wearily.

"Fell out," grinned Henry. "How are you, Judge?"

"Fell out? You mean—all the way to the ground?"

"I believe it is impossible to do it any other way."

"Well, let's not argue about it," quavered Judge. "I want to get out of here. You and your discoveries! Are you satisfied now?"

"Not yet, Judge."

"Not yet? Oh, well, I suppose not. Don't stand there arguing with me! Fall two stories—and still arguing! Not another word, sir; I'm going home."

It was still raining, but the bulk of the storm had passed. They found their horses, climbed into soggy saddles and headed away in the darkness. Judge was too nervous and excited to ask Henry how he came back to make a rescue, or what became of the two men.

In spots the road had been washed away, but they got through. With their horses stabled, they faced each other in their room; two bedraggled, dirty-looking creatures, who drank gustily from a bottle. Drinking was no formality this time. Water dripped off their boots and made muddy puddles on the old carpet.

"What a damnable way to spend the Sabbath," mourned Judge, shivering in his sogg garments. "And for no use, sir. Spiked by cactus, saddle-galled, soaked to the very marrow of our bones, assaulted in a haunted house, shot at! By gad, sir, all that and more! And for what, if I may ask? Not a damn thing, sir! Do not interrupt me. You cannot point out one single thing which we have accomplished. You are not one whit more enlightened than we were when we rode away from here. You have not proved one single thing, Sheriff."

Henry rubbed a grimy hand around the bottle, his fat face grim with deep concentration.

"Judge, you are wrong," he said quietly. "For a long time I have wondered about a certain thing. Tonight I proved it to my own satisfaction."

"Just what did you prove, sir?"

"That a man of my age and size, after falling two stories, *will not bounce.*"

"I have come to the conclusion," said Judge soberly, "that you are the biggest fool I have ever met."

"Good!" exclaimed Henry. "We have both accomplished something."

IT WAS past noon next day, when Danny Regan rode into Tonto City. Henry and Judge had just finished breakfast and were coming to the office, where they met the young foreman of the J Bar C.

"Greetings, Daniel," smiled Henry. "How is everything at the ranch?"

"All right, Henry. How are yuh, Judge?"

"Better than I expected to be," growled Judge.

"Better than he hoped to be," corrected Henry. "You see, Danny, we were out in that rain last night. It soured all of Judge's milk of human kindness, and this morning he is very grumpy, because he isn't suffering from pneumonia."

"No thanks to you that I'm not," growled Judge.

They went into the office and sat down.

"I've been out, lookin' for horses," said Danny, tossing his hat aside, and reaching for the makings of a cigarette. "I wanted to get that gray team, so Frijole could haul some corral poles."

"Did you find them?" queried Henry.

"No, I didn't. I guess that whole herd is ranging on the north side of Mummy Cañon. I searched the south side, and swung 'way in above Erin; but didn't find anythin'."

Danny lighted his cigarette and leaned back in his chair.

"Somethin' happened up there, and it strikes me kinda funny. I was comin' in toward the main road, west of Erin, down through them rocky breaks. I was up there kinda high, lookin' down along the road toward Piñon Cañon, when I seen a man on foot.

"I wasn't close enough to see what he looked like, but I could see him pretty plain. The way he was actin', I thought he was huntin'. He was kinda keepin' under cover, movin' slow-like toward the road. There was the old road from Erin, but he wasn't on the road. I was strainin' my eyes, lookin' to see a buck break out of the brush.

"But there wasn't no buck. I seen him stop at the forks of the road for mebbe a half a minute. Then he walked over to the stump of an old saguero, and it looked to me as though he put somethin' in the stump. Then he turned around and walked into the brush.

"Well," smiled Danny, "I couldn't go straight down there, 'cause there wasn't no trail. I had to make a wide swing down to the road about a quarter of a mile above the forks, and the man was gone. I watched for him quite a while, but there wasn't no sign of him; so I took a look at the old suguero stump. Here's what was in it."

Danny drew a piece of wrapping paper from his pocket and handed it to Henry, who spread it on the desk-top. Judge leaned over his shoulder, peering down at the penciled capitals.

SGOA GXZ YGK LITKOYF. ITKE SQLZ FOUITZ. DXLZ DXCT EQDH. QFLVTK.
P.

"It looks like Russian," grinned Danny.

"Not enough ski's and vitches," replied Henry. "Danny, it looks as though somebody was using the saguero stump for a post office."

"That's right. But what language is that, Henry?"

"Apparently a code message, or what is known as a crypto-gram."

"Well, how in the devil could *we* read it?"

"Danny, it was not written for us to read."

Henry rubbed his red nose, and considered the message again.

"If those are words," he declared, "the writer was full of bicar-bonate of soda. But I am glad you brought it, Danny. At least, it gives us a diversion."

"As though we had none!" snorted Judge.

"Well, I thought it was kinda funny—postin' notes in that stump," said Danny. "I reckon I'll drift back, and have Frijole go with me across Mummy Cañon. I'll see yuh later, Henry—when Judge is feeling better natured."

"Humph!" snorted Judge sourly.

HENRY PUT the paper in his pocket, managed to elevate his feet to the desk-top, after which he folded his pudgy hands across his bosom, and relaxed audibly. Judge looked sourly at him, tilted against the wall, and clasped his bony hands around his knees.

"The sheriff's office," observed Henry dryly, "is functioning at normal speed again."

"The Shame of Arizona, having its usual siesta, you mean."

"We worked on Sunday," reminded Henry. "Judge, every time I remember your frightened stammerings on that old stairway last night, I want to guffaw aloud. You were actually in a cold sweat. Never tell me that you do not believe in ghosts."

"I do not, sir!" Judge insisted. "There was a terrible draught on those stairs… and my damned rheumatism… all right, laugh like a fool! What did you do, but jump out of a window. No, I suppose you were not at all frightened. Not a bit."

"No matter how I got out—I saved your life. I was smart enough to move my horse so they'd think I'd gone away. I suppose you told them where we left the horses."

"I—I felt obliged to inform them, sir."

Oscar came clattering through the jail corridor and banged into the office.

"Ha'alo, yents!" he beamed. "Ay hope Ay see you va'al."

"Well enough, Oscar," replied Henry. "How are you?"

"Yust as good as anybody in de vorld."

"What became of Olaf?"

"Olaf? Oh, he vent back to Scorpion Bend, a sadder and viser Norvegian."

"Just another flame blown out, I suppose."

"Yah, su-re. Olaf is yust a gold deeger."

"Gold digger, eh? Has Josephine any money?"

"Va'al, su-ure. She has vorked t'ree year at de hotel. She saves tan dollar a month."

John Campbell came into the office, bringing a Scorpion Bend *Clarion*.

"One of the boys from the Yellow Warrior got a first copy off the press this morning," he told Henry. "Look at this."

He spread the paper on the desk and pointed at the leading editorial. Henry read it aloud.

BRUTAL ASSAULT ON THE EDITOR

Last Friday night, as we were closing the *Clarion* office, we were seized in the dark by a huge brute, forced back into our office, knocked half-unconscious and tied to a chair.

Then this fiend in human form proceeded to pour and smear every available can of ink in the place over our head. We were there, until our plight was discovered Saturday morning.

No doubt our scathing editorials against the criminals of Wild Horse Valley are having their effect. This fiend, no doubt trying to disguise his voice, spoke in a badly enunciated Swedish dialect. If the Commissioners of this county refuse to fire the present incompetents from the sheriff's office, it is high time that the public took the responsibility out of their negligent hands.

"John," said Henry huskily, after a long silence, "someone must have turned against the worm."

"I shouldn't say it, Henry; but I can't be sorry about this."

"My tears are all dry, too, John. But he is still vitriolic."

"That is true. Is there anything new developed, Henry?"

"Not yet," replied Henry. "But I believe we are showing progress."

"Good. Well, I must be going. I thought you'd like to see that."

"Thank you, John."

Henry leaned back in his chair and looked keenly at Oscar, who looked straight back at him, a queer smile on his face. Suddenly he broke into a gale of laughter, slapping his knees with his huge hands.

"Wait a minute," said Henry. "Before you have a complete breakdown, I would like to question you, Oscar."

"Shoot," choked Oscar, tears running down his cheeks.

"This man writes," said Henry, "that the Swedish dialect was badly spoken. How do you account for that?"

"Ho, ho, ho!" choked Oscar. "Ay vars trying to speak goot English!"

"Aren't you ashamed of yourself?" growled Judge. "The idea!"

"Das idea vars good," declared Oscar. "Maybe he vars right, ven he said you vars no good; but he vars all wrong ven he said Ay vars ignorant, Yudge."

Henry was leaning on his desk, wiping tears from his eyes.

JUDGE'S NOSE twitched violently, his lips quivered and the ghost of a smile flickered in his eyes. He cleared his throat raspingly.

"Was any of it *red* ink, Oscar?" he asked.

"Red, blue unt green, Yudge."

"Good, good! Now, Oscar, if you will go back to cell number one, and bring in Frijole's latest vengeance against the human race, along with three tin cups, I believe we shall drink to the *Clarion*."

"Yah, su-ure," grinned Oscar. "It vars a ha'al of a lot of fun."

They were drinking, when Charles H. Livingstone came in. He declined to partake of the prune whisky.

"These cursed delays are making me weary," he declared. "Today I got another telegram, saying that the syndicate representative will be here Thursday, instead of tomorrow. Another delay, and Howard Beloit swears that he will call off the deal."

"You could hardly blame him for that," agreed Henry.

"With all his wealth, he should not worry about a million-dollar deal," remarked Judge.

"I suppose not. Beloit is rather queer in what he does. Now he wants to pay tribute to Tonto City, with a big banquet Thursday night. He has told me to invite the whole town. We will hold it at the hotel, with plenty of good food, lots of liquor, and a big time for everyone. In fact, the sky will be the limit."

"Why, that will be wonderful!" exclaimed Henry.

"I believe it will," agreed Livingstone heartily. "You two are the first to be invited. Mr. Beloit thought it would be fine to have the papers signed and witnessed at the banquet. I—Mr. Beloit wondered if you would act as toastmaster. With your stage experience, you know—"

"Why—I—well, I might," faltered Henry.

"Then that part is settled. Judge, will you get up and say a few words? Being one of the leading citizens—and all that, you know."

"I might," agreed Judge. "Yes, I might do that."

"Especially after a few drinks," added Henry.

"Oh, there will be plenty of drinks. Everything from cider to champagne—and very little cider. Miss Beloit is enthusiastic over the idea. Things have been rather dull for her in Tonto."

"One murder and one ghost," murmured Henry.

"That is true. I suppose that is the reason why she quit riding. Her nerves haven't been so good since the ghost episode. However, she is looking forward to this banquet. Well, I must run along. It is very fine of you to act as toastmaster, Mr. Conroy; and I am sure we will all enjoy Judge's talk."

"Well," observed Henry dryly, "he selected two capable men."

"I believe," said Judge, "that I shall talk on the evils of intemperance."

"You?" gasped Henry.

"Well, who should know the subject better than I? You would not hire a blacksmith to repair your watch, would you?"

"After three drinks of Frijole's whisky—I might. But go ahead. By the time I call upon you for your speech, every male creature in the place will be so drunk they'll think you are delivering Lincoln's Gettysburg Address. By that time you may be so drunk yourself that you will really recite that immortal speech. It doesn't really matter."

"I suppose not," sighed Judge. "Pearls before swine."

"Platitudes before pollution," smiled Henry.

"I think," said Judge, "that we should go and tell Laura and Leila about the banquet. I am sure they would want to know about it as early as possible. Clothes, and all that, you know."

"Judge," smiled Henry, "I always suspect you of seeking an invitation to supper."

"Do you think they might invite us?"

"It is always worth a trial, Judge. It might be macaroni and that delectable cheese, or it might be baked beans and brown bread. However, we shall not be finicky about the menu. Let us go."

LEILA AND her mother were in the kitchen, which was filled with delicious odors. Henry sniffed and smiled widely.

"I just told Mother that I would be willing to bet you two would smell that meat-loaf," laughed Leila. "Anyway, we were going to invite you to supper."

"Wonderful!" exclaimed Henry. "Have you heard about the banquet Thursday night?"

Naturally they had not heard about it; so Henry gave them all the information.

"But, Henry, I haven't anything to wear," protested both women in chorus.

"Wear what you have on now," he suggested. "I think you look wonderful."

"Thank you," laughed Leila, "but a house-dress and an apron is hardly appropriate for a banquet."

"I would not worry about clothes," remarked Judge. "You will look better than any other woman there, I can assure you."

"And Miss Millionaire, in all her glory," sighed Leila.

"They are paying the bills," said Henry quietly. "We should not care what they wear, Leila."

"Danny doesn't know about it, does he?" asked Leila.

"Naturally not. But he will."

"I am to make a speech," informed Judge.

"If I ask for it," reminded Henry. "Do not forget that I am the engineer on this train."

They all laughed and started a general conversation about food and clothes, while the meat-loaf sizzled merrily. Suddenly Leila said:

"Henry, have you ever searched any more for the body of Don Black?"

"Yes, my dear, we have," nodded Henry. "I know where it is."

"Where?" asked Mrs. Harper quickly.

"It is probably walking around the ranch house, or slumped in an easy chair, reading a magazine."

"My Heavens!" exclaimed Mrs. Harper. "Henry, what do you mean?"

"Ask Leila," smiled Henry. "She counted the breakfast plates the other morning."

"I—I thought it was queer," said Leila. "But I wasn't sure."

Henry explained what had happened to Don Black, and why they kept him under cover.

"No wonder Miss Beloit fainted, when she saw him!" exclaimed Mrs. Harper.

"It must have been a shock, my dear Laura," agreed Henry. "It was also a shock to Frijole, Oscar and Tommy. In fact, we had to put one new window in the main room of the ranch house, where Oscar and Frijole went through. Tommy would have gone with them, but his legs refused to function. Oscar ran all the way here."

"And wanted to put crape on the office door," choked Leila, her eyes filled with tears. "I don't see how you stand him."

"My dear girl, he keeps me from growing old."

"And he has added years on my already advanced age," declared Judge. "That Swede is positively a menace to humanity."

"Henry, did you see the last *Clarion?*" asked Mrs. Harper.

Henry nodded solemnly.

"Oh, I think it is a shame!" exclaimed Mrs. Harper.

"The Shame of Arizona," murmured Judge.

"I didn't mean that, Judge. But someone with a grudge against that editor tried to imitate Oscar; so he would think it was your office behind the attack."

"A very clever deduction," said Judge soberly. "But I am very glad to state that the imitation failed. Oscar, I believe, has the best line of broken English in Arizona."

"And broken buckboards," added Henry. "My dear Laura, if that meat-loaf doesn't hurry—"

"Everything is ready," laughed Leila.

CHAPTER XV

SHOTGUNNED SHERIFF

DANNY AND FRIJOLE succeeded in finding and roping the pair of gray horses, which they brought back to the J Bar C. They were a big, strapping team, which Danny had intended breaking to drive, but he turned the job over to Frijole and Oscar.

"We'll tame them there babies, y' betcha," declared Frijole. "We'll hook 'em up to the old breakin'-cart this evenin'."

The breaking-cart consisted of the front running-gears of an old lumber-wagon, on which a platform had been constructed in such a way that the seat could be set far back, in order to insure the driver against flying heels. In appearance it was not unlike a chariot. There were no brakes.

In extreme cases the extra man on the seat held a rope, which ran through a bit-ring on one of the horses, and extended down to a single-hopple. Frijole suggested using it, after looking at the size of the two grays.

"Ay don't believe in 'em," declared Oscar. "Ay never seen de hurse yet dat Ay couldn't hold vit lines."

"Yeah, I know," replied Frijole. "Our rollin'-stock shows it. All we've got left is a wagon and this here breakin'-cart."

"Ay have my little accidents," admitted Oscar.

"I hope to tell yuh. Where'll we go ridin'?"

"Ay don't care, Free-holey."

"All right; we'll go to town. I've got a gallon of liquor for Henry. He must be almost out by this time."

Frijole wrapped the jug carefully, placed it on the seat, and wired the handle to the back of the seat. Danny would have worked one of the bronchos at a time, coupled with a steady, well-broken horse; but not these two wild men.

Rearing, lunging and kicking, they went out to the main road, where Oscar managed to swing them toward Tonto City.

"Yentlemen, have a ride!" howled Oscar.

Luckily they did not meet anybody on that narrow road. Not being at all bridle-wise, the team went where it willed, but as long as it was in the general direction of Tonto City—who cared?

They uprooted cactus patches, knocked down yuccas, and went into Tonto City, dragging a lot of brush. They tied the team to the livery stable fence, and untied the jug of prune whisky. Tommy Roper came out, and they waited for him.

"Sus-sus-say, didja huh-hear 'bout the bub-bub-banquet?" he stuttered.

"What the hell's that?" queried Frijole, digging at a cactus thorn in his finger.

"Big dud-dud-dinner and lotsa dud-drinks—all pup-paid for."

"Lead me to her!" exclaimed Frijole.

"Thursday nun-night," explained Tommy. After much stammering he managed to explain to them about the banquet.

"Ay like de idea," decided Oscar, "especially de part about de free liquor. Ay am good drinker."

"Yeah, you shore are," agreed Frijole. "I wonder if Henry and Judge are over in the office."

"Nope," replied Tommy. "I sus-seen 'em gug-going up to Huh-Huh-Harper's a while ago."

"Well, we might as well have a couple snorts out of the jug," said Frijole. "No use deliverin' it to an empty house."

THEY WENT into the tack-room of the stable, where Tommy dug up some old cups.

"Dud-don't give me mum-much," said Tommy. "I'll nun-never forget that dud-dance at Scor-Scor-Scor—"

"Scorpion Bend," finished Frijole. "Yeah, you shore got stiff."

"Uh-huh." Tommy gulped his drink, gasped a couple of times and unfastened his collar.

"That green suit shore knocked 'em cold, too," said Frijole.

"It's fuf-finished," declared Tommy sadly.

"What do yuh mean?" queried Frijole.

"Rur-rur-rain ruined it."

"Faded, yuh mean?"

"Huh-hell no! That suit was fuf-fuf-fast color. It shr-shr-shr—"

"Shrunk?" queried Frijole.

"Uh-huh. I'll tut-tell the world. Them pup-pant-pockets come plumb dud-down to the knees now. Next suit I git is gug-goin' to be su-six inches too dud-damn long to bub-bub-begin with."

"Dat suit vars owful green, Tommy," declared Oscar. "Ay never saw such a ha'al of a green suit in my life before. Have anodder drink."

"Rur-rur-royal green," said Tommy.

"The kind that all the kings are wearin' this year," added Frijole. "Well, here's hopin' yore tonsils are petrified."

"I—I wuw-wuw-wish the kings was wuw-wuw-wearin' short pup-pants; I'd be in sus-sus-style."

"Ay never seen von vit any pants on at all," declared Oscar.

"Yuh never did? Hell, you never seen any kings, Oscar."

"Ay have seen lots of 'em, Free-holey."

"Where the hell did you ever see any kings?"

"Dere is four of 'em in every deck. Ho, ho, ho! Dars is goot yoke!"

They had another drink. Tommy dug into an old trunk and drew out a battered cornet.

"Bub-bought it the other dud-day," he told them. "Ain't it a dud-dinger? Nun-no, yuh can't bub-blow it around huh-here. I dud-did, and I scared huh-hell out of the huh-huh-horses. The bub-boss said he'd fuf-fire me, if I bub-blew it again."

"We ort to start a band here in Tonto City," declared Frijole.

"By Yinks, das is good idea!" exclaimed Oscar. "Ay have got a skveese-organ, yust as good as new, except for few holes."

"That's right, yuh have," agreed Frijole. "And I've still got one string on my gitter. Can you play any tunes, Tommy?"

"I th-th-think so. The feller sus-said all yuh have to-to do is bub-blow like hell and sh-sh-shove down on them th-th-things on tut-top. Then the tut-tune comes out the bub-big end—there."

"'Course," said Frijole, "you've got to have some idea what yo're tryin' to play. The damn thing ain't no mind-reader."

"I wuw-wuw-wondered 'bout that," admitted Tommy.

"Them horns are all right," admitted Frijole, "but I'd rather play somethin' that I can sing with."

"Ay t'ink ve better have anodder drink," remarked Oscar.

"Uh-huh," agreed Tommy. "Then mum-mebby somebody can th-th-think of a sus-song."

IT WAS about nine o'clock, when Henry and Judge left the Harper home. Judge went over to the Tonto Saloon, and Henry walked back toward the hotel. The general store was still open.

Henry stopped and looked at the motley display in the window. In the center was a typewriter, used but still serviceable.

As Henry looked at the machine, his eyes narrowed thoughtfully. With a pencil and the back of an old envelope, he wrote down the letters, as they appeared on the keys of the typewriter. Then he went back to the office, lighted the lamp and sat down at his desk.

He spread out the note that Danny Regan had found in the saguero stump. Counting the alphabet on the layout of the keyboard, he discovered that S was L, G was O, O was I, and A was K. That gave him LOIK, which did not mean a thing.

Henry rubbed his nose thoughtfully. "Let's see what the next three letters show."

Following the same procedure for GXZ, he got OUT.

"By Jove, I've got it!" exclaimed Henry aloud. "Where there is a double letter, they use one of the regular letters. That first word is LOOK. LOOK OUT!"

As swiftly as possible he decoded the rest of the letters. It was not difficult, now. The note read:

LOOK OUT FOR THE SHERIFF. HERE LAST NIGHT. MUST MOVE CAMP. ANSWER.
J.

It was plain enough now. One of the men, who had been in that room at Erin Sunday night, had written a warning to someone, and left it in the old stump. The cryptogram was simple. And yet, in a country where typewriters were not common, the solution was accidental.

"Look out for the sheriff," muttered Henry. "Well, that's—"

The front door opened and closed softly. Slowly Henry turned his head, and looked directly into the muzzle of a six-shooter. Behind the gun stood a masked man, and just behind him was another masked man, a shotgun in his two hands. While the two men looked steadily at Henry, they seemed to be listening.

A huge body crashed into him

"Open yore mouth, and we'll blow yuh through that wall," threatened the man with the six-shooter.

Henry blinked painfully and swallowed with difficulty, but kept his lips tightly shut.

"All right," growled the man with the shotgun. "Have it yore own way. But, damn it all, I'd give it to him right here, and have it over with quick. No use delayin' the deal."

"Keep that shotgun out of this," hissed the other man. "We've got to make this a quiet job. They won't miss this damn fool for a couple days, anyway."

The man chuckled softly at his own joke.

The joke did not appeal to Henry. These two men looked too business-like, and those shotgun muzzles looked like the mouths of twin cannons.

"I tell yuh," insisted the shotgun bearer, "that we can't waste time on this job. Lemme uncock these two barrels into his guts, and then high-tail it out of here."

"And ruin everything, eh?" snarled the other. "Listen! We'll gag the old fool, tie his hands and walk him out of here. Then we'll take him out to Mummy Cañon and throw him off the top—without the gag and rope."

"All right—take a chance. Me—I'd do it here."

"Gentlemen," said Henry huskily, "I don't know—"

"Shut up! You don't have to know anythin'. Put that gag on him."

CHAPTER XVI

NIGHT RIDER

THE JUG WAS empty. Oscar, Frijole and Tommy sat in the little tack-room, by the light of a smoky lantern.

"Yuice oll gone," complained Oscar. "Ay feel like mockin'-birt."

"That's, all ri'," mumbled Frijole. "Wha' time 'zit?"

Oscar managed to get a huge silver watch out of his vest pocket, but it slipped from his hand to the floor, where the crystal shattered.

"Window bruk," observed Oscar, and kicked the watch under a bunk.

"I jus' got good idea," declared Frijole owlishly. "Le's go out to ranch. I got fi' gallons out there. How 'boutcha, Tommy?"

"Mum-me?" queried Tommy. "Sh-sh-sure. Wha-wha-what'll I shing?"

"We're gonna ride out to the ransh, Tommy. Wanna go 'long?"

"Uh-huh. Wait!" Tommy made several ineffectual grabs, before he could pick up the cornet. "Gug-goin' have bub-bub-band mu-mu-mu-musich."

"Tha's fine. We'll sherenade Danny Regan. C'mon, Oshcar."

Frijole took the smoky old lantern along. The huge doorway of the stable was hardly large enough for them, but they got out of the place, and approached their equipage. The two bronchos' eyes flashed balefully in the lantern light, and they moved nervously.

"You get the lines, Oshcar," ordered Frijole. "Tommy, you get on with Oshcar, and I'll untie these jug-heads."

Tommy had a lot of difficulty in getting aboard, but with the dubious assistance of Oscar, he finally got to the seat, still clutching his cornet. Frijole hung the lantern on the fence, while he fumbled with the two tie-ropes.

"I've gotta hunsh, Oshcar, that these horshes wanna go home," he announced. "Hol''em tight, cowboy!"

Frijole slipped off the tie-ropes, jumped aside and ran for the cart. But his aim was poor. He missed the cart entirely and bumped into the fence ten feet behind. Luckily he did. When Oscar drew back hard on the lines, the team whirled, reared and backed into the fence, smashing down a whole section.

"Yowee-e-e-e-e!" screamed Oscar, and at the same instant, Tommy managed to blow a terrific blast on his cornet.

That was too much for that unbroken team. They lunged ahead, a line snapped—and they were free to do as they pleased.

It was just at that time that Henry, his hands bound, and a thick gag between his teeth, was standing beside his desk, menaced by that shotgun, while the other man, hearing the noise at the livery stable, had opened the door an inch, and was peering out.

"What the hell is it?" asked the shotgun man nervously.

And just at that moment Oscar's cowboy yell split the night, followed by Tommy's cornet blast. The man hesitated for a moment, flinging the door wider. Then he whirled.

"Look out!" he yelled, and dived for the corridor door. The shotgun man waited for no explanation, but dived with him.

The next moment there was a terrific crash, the splintering

of wood and glass, a whirl of dust. Henry, his arms tied against his sides, went sprawling across the room. The lamp remained upright, and in its flickering beams Henry saw a gray horse, halfway through the window, snorting, pawing, whistling with fright, while another gray horse was upside down, half in, half outside the doorway, flailing with all four hoofs.

About three feet above the flooring, sticking through the splintered wall, was the tongue of a wagon, protruding at least three feet into the room. Men were running in the street, some-one was yelling:

"Whoa! Whoa!" as though the team was still running.

Judge and several other men came through the rear and into the office, where they surveyed the disaster. Judge saw Henry, and stood there, wide-eyed, jaw sagging. He seemed to be trying to connect Henry with the runaway. Then he stooped and picked up a battered cornet from the floor.

"What the hell's this?" gasped one of the men, and proceeded to take the gag out of Henry's mouth. Then he cut the ropes, and helped Henry to his feet.

More men came in, ropes were thrown, and in a few minutes the gray team, apparently unhurt, except for a few small cuts, were led away. Only one porch-post out of four was left standing. The wheels and axle of the cart were down in the alley.

Frijole was there, partly sobered, but carrying the unlighted lantern.

"Diogenes," said Henry huskily, "art looking for someone?"

"Have yuh seen Oscar and Tommy?" queried Frijole.

"I haven't seen—but I have suspected," replied Henry.

"Me and Oscar are breakin' a gray team," confided Frijole. "Yuh see, we need a work team at the ranch."

A man staggered out of the alley and limped into the lamp-light. It was Oscar Johnson, one eye swelled shut, his left ear bleeding and one sleeve of his shirt missing.

"What in de ha'al is going on ha'ar?" he demanded to know.

"Here's Tommy!" exclaimed Frijole. "He was under the pavement."

"Whu-whu-whu-where is it?" asked Tommy, getting to his feet.

"Where's what?" asked Frijole.

"Th-that cuk-cuk-cuk-cuk-cuk—"

"Well, git it out—or lay the aig," advised Frijole.

"Cornet!" exploded Tommy.

HENRY TOOK Judge by the arm and they moved away. Safe in their room at the hotel Henry told Judge what happened in the office.

"My God!" gasped Judge. "They were going to murder you! I hope you realize that, sir."

"I have a feeling that their intentions were not exactly honorable, Judge," replied Henry dryly.

"Can you describe them?"

"Judge, all I know is that two masked men came into the office, bound and gagged me, and were going to take me out to Mummy Cañon, remove gag and ropes and kick me over the edge. One of them insisted on killing me there in the office, but the other one wanted it done cleanly. Evidently he won the argument. And then those drunks staged a runaway—and saved my life."

"They should be made to pay the damage to the office."

"Pay damage to the office? Judge, don't you realize that they saved my life?"

"Not intentionally, Henry," Judge insisted. "Legally, they are liable for damages."

"I see," sighed Henry. "My life is of no consequence. But will you forget the legal aspect of the case, and begin to realize that, except for those three glorious inebriates, I would be down at the bottom of Mummy Cañon, a mess of tangled wreckage?"

"Perhaps they were merely bluffing, Henry."

Henry groaned and rubbed his sore arms, where the tight ropes had galled the skin.

"Why would they bluff?" he asked. "They were not trying to force me to say anything or do anything. They were the same two men who roped you in Erin the other night. Were they bluffing you?"

"In my case, Henry, I believe they were sincere. But I can't for the life of me understand why they should want to kill you."

"Unless it was for the skin and tallow," murmured Henry. "I don't mind telling you that I am getting worried, Judge. I had no idea that they would make a direct attack on our office. It gives me goose-pimples."

"Well, it might have been in the nature of a joke, you know. I don't see what your murder would accomplish for them."

"I believe," said Henry soberly, "they are striking at the brains of our organization."

Judge snorted and pulled off his boots.

"At least," he remarked, "I am not going to lose sleep, until I find that their intentions are really serious. We may be making a mountain out of a mole-hill."

Judge piled into bed, but Henry did not undress. When Judge was snoring softly, Henry took a sheet of paper and a pencil, hunched across their little table, and proceeded to write a letter. It was a slow job, because of the fact that Henry was obliged to consult another sheet of paper, and do much counting.

When it was finished to his satisfaction, checked and re-checked, Henry put on his hat, went quietly out of the room, down the stairs, and out to their little stable behind the jail.

"I hate to ask it of you, Socrates," he told the horse, "but it seems that we must make a late pilgrimage. The night is still in its infancy; so we need not hurry. I hope you have my interests at heart."

He saddled Socrates, mounted heavily and rode away, avoiding the main street of the town, and came into the road to Scorpion Bend.

"The old lone wolf has left his lair," he told Socrates, "and is abroad in the hills again."

There was no moon. But the stars were bright, and the crooked old road wound like a yellow ribbon through the gray-blue of the valley.

"Socrates," he said, "a year ago my only conception of the West was derived from seeing a stage production of 'The Squaw Man'; and here I am, matched from the jaws of death a few hours ago, riding alone in the starlight—without brains enough to crawl into a hole and play safe."

Socrates merely bobbed his head, as he shuffled along the dusty road.

CHAPTER XVII

DAYTIME COURAGE

IT WAS THREE o'clock in the morning, when Judge awoke, and discovered that Henry was not with him. He lighted the lamp and was amazed to note that Henry had not been to bed at all. Filled with dire forebodings, he dressed hurriedly and went down to the street.

There was not a light showing in the town. Down at the office he found that the door had been broken too badly to function within two inches of the lock. Judge entered the office, noted that the place was empty, went outside and padded around to the stable. He fumbled for the padlock, saw that the door was ajar, and went softly into the place.

He was feeling his way cautiously in the darkness, when a huge body crashed into him, mighty arms encircled his lanky frame, and he was lifted off his feet. The next moment his shoulders hit the door, which banged open, and he and his antagonist crashed to the hard ground outside.

The breath was knocked from Judge's lungs, but he pawed weakly at the face of the attacking force.

"Ay'll learn you to steal hurses!" panted Oscar's voice. "Ay'll make pretzel out of you, you son-of-a-gonn!"

"Oscar!" wheezed Judge. "Oscar!"

"Who in de ha'al!" snorted Oscar, sitting up on Judge.

"Judge," wheezed the suffering old deputy.

"Yudge? Yeeminy Yee! Yudge! Ay t'ought you vars a hurse-t'ief for sure."

Oscar picked Judge up and stood him on uncertain feet.

"What in de ha'al are you doing out ha'ar, Yudge?"

"Looking for Henry," wheezed Judge painfully.

"Yee-zus! Is Hanry lost, Yudge?"

"He's gone," whispered Judge.

"So he vent, eh? Yah, I see now. Ay heard noise at de stable. It voke me up, and I find Soker-tees gone. Ay bet four dollar some hurse-t'ief take him; so I move blanket out ha'ar. Ay say to me, 'By Yee, I save von hurse, anyway.'"

"You almost killed me, Oscar."

"Yah, su-ure. But who de ha'al look for *you*, ha'ar, Yudge?"

"I suppose you are right, Oscar. But that doesn't find Henry."

"Maybe he yust vent for a ride."

"I don't believe it, Oscar. Two men were going to kill him last night. They had him gagged and tied up in the office, and were going to dump him into Mummy Cañon, when that runaway headed for the office and frightened them away."

"Yumpin' Yudas! Ay didn't know it, Yudge. Do you suppose dey got him?"

"I don't know what to think. Let's go into the office."

They went in, and Oscar lighted the lamp.

"I swear, I don't know what to do," declared Judge.

"De first t'ing to do, Yudge," offered Oscar solemnly, "is for you to put on some pants."

"My goodness! So it is. I—I guess I was in a hurry. It isn't often that I forget my trousers. However, I am upset over Henry."

"He never ta'al you he is going out?"

"Not a word," declared Judge. "He seemed preoccupied last night."

"My gu'dness!"

"I would venture to say that he was frightened, too."

"Va'al, maybe he yust storted running, Yudge."

"But be took Socrates. I—by Jove, I wonder! Would he go there all alone? Is he that big a fool?"

"Yah, su-ure," agreed Oscar blandly.

"Saddle our horses, while I get some pants," ordered Judge. "We might save the blamed fool, if we hurry."

Judge trotted back to the hotel, where he secured a pair of pants, and trotted back to the stable, carrying the pants in his hand.

"You better put 'em on, Yudge," suggested Oscar. "Dis vind is pretty cold."

"Yes, I suppose so. I—I must be a little excited about Henry."

They mounted their horses and rode toward Scorpion Bend. This was one time when Judge was willing to ride fast, even if he did have to cling to the saddle-horn.

IT WAS daylight when they came to the old road, which led to Erin. They swung their horses and rode slowly back through the hills to the old ghost town, where they dismounted in front of the old hotel.

Daylight, a gun in his hand, and Oscar beside him, Judge was brave. He led Oscar straight up the old stairway, where they stopped on the landing. The door to that particular room was sagging open. Everything had been removed. In fact, except for lack of dust, there was nothing to indicate that the room had ever been occupied.

They examined the other rooms and went down the stairs, where they sat down on the old, warped porch. Judge, explaining everything in detail, told Oscar what happened to him and Henry in that house. He pointed out the spot where they had left their horses, showed Oscar where Henry fell out through the window, and explained how Henry, in moving his horse, fooled the two outlaws into believing that Henry had gone away.

"Yust like Ay always said," declared Oscar, "das Hanry is a tough yigger and smort as ha'al."

"I am afraid he has met his Waterloo," sighed Judge.

"Is dat his name, Yudge?"

"Whose name?"

"Das Walter Loo."

"I said Waterloo. Oh, never mind; it's a long story. It is the name of a place, where Napoleon was defeated."

"Va'al, das oll right," nodded Oscar. "What de ha'al—anybody might get vipped vonce in a vile, Yudge."

The sun was warm on the old porch, and both men were weary from their cold ride.

"There is no use hurrying," yawned Judge. "My one hope was to find him here—and that hope is gone."

"Hanry vars a yentleman," declared Oscar soberly.

"Was?" exploded Judge. "Was, eh? Damn it, Oscar, you speak as though Henry is dead."

"Ain't he?" asked Oscar meekly.

"Well, now, how do I know? You take too much for granted. As far as I know, Henry may be alive and well."

"Yah, su-ure," agreed Oscar. "And he may be dead as ha'al, too."

"You make me so mad!" Judge got to his feet and yanked at his belt. "Let's go home. You, sir, are impossible! I can well under-stand that you wanted crape for the office door, before you knew Henry was dead. Get on your horse, Oscar."

"Yah, su-ure," said Oscar wearily.

Judge, hunched in his saddle, led the way down to the main

road, where they met Charles H. Livingstone in a buggy, going to Scorpion Bend. He drew up, looking at them curiously.

"Have you seen anything of Henry Conroy?" queried Judge.

"Not today," replied Livingstone. "I left Tonto City rather early, of course. Perhaps he isn't up yet—or wasn't, when I left there."

"Yes, that may be true," nodded Judge.

"Ay t'ink ve might find him in Scorpion Bend," suggested Oscar.

"Yes, we might," agreed Judge quickly. "I never thought of that."

"Is there anything wrong?" asked Livingstone curiously.

"I—I hope not. You are going to Scorpion Bend?"

"Yes, I am."

"I was just wondering if I might ride with you, and let Oscar lead my horse. I crave a cushion."

Livingstone laughed and nodded. Judge handed his reins to Oscar and climbed into the comfortable buggy. Then they went on.

TEN MINUTES later Henry Harrison Conroy rode out from behind a dense patch of mesquite and came down to the road, where he stopped and looked carefully around. Within thirty feet of the forks was the old saguero stump about ten feet off the road.

Henry swung his horse over beside it, felt inside the cavity, but found nothing there. Then he took a folded note from his pocket, dropped it into the old stump, and rode on toward Tonto City.

"Look out for sheriff," he chuckled, as he rode down along Piñon Grades. "I wonder if Judge and Oscar are looking for me, or if they went hunting on their own account."

Howard Beloit and his daughter were having a late breakfast when Henry came in. They nodded pleasantly, and Gale said:

"Thank you very much for offering to be our master of ceremonies, Mr. Conroy."

Henry bowed deeply. "My dear lady, it will be a pleasure. In fact, I am looking forward to the event with the greatest of pleasure."

"I hope that everyone will be there," smiled Beloit. "We do not want to slight anyone, you know."

"They will all be there, Mr. Beloit," assured Henry. "Tonto City has so little entertainment that they grasp every opportunity. It will be an event in their lives—and mine."

"Thank you, Sheriff. Mr. Livingstone is arranging everything, and he has orders to not stint on anything. From four o'clock in the afternoon, until midnight, no one will be allowed to spend a cent for liquor or food in Tonto City. Everything will be free."

"Magnificent!" exclaimed Henry. "I have heard of such prodigality, but have never witnessed it, Mr. Beloit."

Henry finished breakfast, went back to his office, where he hung his hat on the protruding wagon-tongue. No one had cleaned the office; so he took a broom and swept out the broken glass and splintered wood. Then he went back to the hotel and went to bed.

At suppertime Oscar and Judge came home, weary and disconsolate, but Oscar yelped with glee, when he saw Socrates in the stable. They hurried to the office, where they found Henry asleep, his feet on the desk-top, his hands folded over his bosom.

"Look at him!" exploded Judge. "Sitting there asleep, while we have searched Arizona."

Henry opened his eyes, blinked a few times and heaved a sigh.

"Sloth!" snapped Judge. "Damme, I believe he is laughing!"

"No," murmured Henry. "Gas pains. Went to bed too soon after a hearty breakfast."

"And let Oscar and me ride the legs off our horses, trying to find you. Don't you realize what you did, sir?"

"No one asked you to follow me," reminded Henry gently.

"No one asked us, eh? Is that all the thanks—"

"Oh, you are seeking thanks?"

"I give up," sighed Judge. "I suppose it doesn't mean a thing to you. I awoke about three o'clock, saw that you had never been to bed, and—well, after what happened last night I was frightened. I came here, found no one, and went out to the stable, where that Vitrified Viking, mistaking me for a horse-thief, nearly killed me."

"Yah, su-ure," grinned Oscar. "Ay skveesed ha'al out of him."

"Go ahead," choked Henry. "It sounds fine."

"It was damnable," declared Judge. "However, no bones were broken. I decided that you had gone alone to Erin, so we—"

"Yudge forgot his pants," interrupted Oscar.

"Go ahead, Judge—without any pants," prompted Henry.

"I went back and got my pants," said Judge soberly.

"And brought 'em in his hand," added Oscar.

"Never mind how I brought my pants!" roared Judge. "I am trying to explain things to Henry. We went to Erin and searched that old house, but that room was empty."

"I know it was empty," nodded Henry.

"You knew it was empty?"

"I supposed you would find it empty. It was empty when I was there before daylight."

"You were there *before* daylight? Alone? Well," sighed Judge, "how true it is that fools rush in where angels fear to tread."

"Angels?" queried Henry. "Meaning you and Oscar?"

"Oh, that doesn't matter. But what have you accomplished, if I may ask? What good did your night riding do, sir? In going to that place alone and at night, you have, in my estimation, branded yourself as the biggest fool in Arizona."

"I am sorry if I caused you mental anguish, Judge," replied Henry.

"Mental anguish! Nothing of the kind, sir. If you want to poke your nose into danger—go right ahead. I don't want you to think for a moment that it makes any difference to me. You are free, white and at least twenty-one, I believe."

"At least, we can remain friends, Judge—I hope."

"You do the damnest things, Henry!"

"I'll buy a drink."

"I believe I could use one, Henry; I am rather weary."

"Same ha'ar," declared Oscar. "Too damn much yawing."

"Exactly," agreed Henry heartily. "Too much, Oscar."

"I suppose there is no use talking any more about it," said Judge, "but I would like to know why you went to that old house, Henry. I surely would like to."

"Well, to tell you the truth, Judge, I went there to find the gun I lost when I fell out of the window."

"You found it?"

"Oh, yes; rusty, but serviceable. Shall we get that drink?"

"It has always been a point of honor with me, sir, to never take a drink with a liar," declared Judge soberly, "but circumstances alter cases. I accept your kind invitation."

"Have you any scruples, Oscar?" asked Henry.

Oscar started to reach into his pocket, but changed his mind.

"Ay don't t'ink so," he said.

"Well, that is fine. Follow me."

The sheriff's office took no chances that night. Henry and Judge went to their room early in the evening and locked the door, while Oscar moved his bed out to the stable, and slept with a shotgun beside him.

CHAPTER XVIII

HENRY PLAYS FOOL

WEDNESDAY PASSED WITHOUT any unusual incident. Tonto City was busy preparing for the big banquet. Charles

H. Livingstone came in Tuesday night, about midnight, bringing two mining engineers, employed by the syndicate to make
a final investigation and report before the sale could be made.
Both Livingstone and Beloit went to the property with them
on Wednesday.

Leila and her mother were busy on some new dresses for the
banquet, and they were doing a big business in new hats. This
was to be a red-letter night for Tonto City; a real celebration—
and free. Extra bartenders had been hired by the Tonto Saloon,
and several extra gamblers had been brought in to help take care
of the games at the Tonto.

Carpenters were busy constructing saw-horses, which would
be used in putting up the long banquet tables in the hotel, and
in making a platform at one end of the big dining-hall. Henry
looked it all over with an approving eye, and proceeded to
unpack his old dress suit, which had been laid away when he
left the stage.

In the ancient theatrical trunk he found a number of old
publicity photographs of himself. Perhaps he looked a little
older now, and possibly a little thinner. One large head, done in
colors, with the nose a violet red, grinned up at him. He shook
his head slowly, a wistful expression in his eyes.

"Henry the Fool, or Henry the Sheriff," he said quietly. "I
wonder which has been the biggest fool. I believe Wild Horse
Valley would vote for Henry the Sheriff. If all the world's a stage,
I have tried my best to make Tonto City the comedy relief. But
after all, there is only the thickness of a cigarette-paper between
comedy and tragedy."

He turned the pictures face down in the trunk, picked up the
old dress suit, and went hunting for a whiskbroom.

IT WAS about an hour before midnight that night. A huge,
full moon seemed to hang low over the top of Mummy Cañon,
flooding the great gash in the earth with silver. Rays of the
moon, like sunbeams flashed across the cañon, picking out the
details of the old dwellings of a forgotten people.

A huge owl, flapping silently along, swung into full relief against the moon, and dropped quietly into the top of a piñon pine atop the cliffs. A rabbit, crouching against a rock as the shadow came along, suddenly darted for the brush—a silver streak.

From far across the cañon came the yipping cry of a coyote. It was answered by several more of its kind. Somewhere, down among the rocks, a bob-cat snarled angrily, as he missed his prey. He came up past the old trail, crouching on a rock, full in the moonlight.

Suddenly he lifted up, turned around and disappeared as a strangely silent file of five people came along the rim above the old dwellings. They were going slowly, making little noise. At the top of the old trail they halted for a moment or two.

"Here's the trail," said a voice quietly. "Watch yore step—it ain't very wide."

Then they filed slowly down the trail, like shadows, and disappeared entirely in less than a minute. The coyote chorus started again. The bob-cat came in sight again, trotted up the trail, stopped at the top and looked back, before fading away in the shadows.

In about fifteen minutes two of the figures came back along the trail. They were almost to the rim of the cañon, when a voice snapped sharply:

"Stop there and put up your hands!"

The two figures jerked around, ignoring the order, their revolvers blazing toward the source of that voice. Bullets splattered and spinged against the rocks.

Then came two roaring blasts of shotgun fire, the echoes thundering back from the cliffs. The two figures were gone from the trail—and the cañon was more than a hundred feet deep at that point. There was complete silence for several moments. Then:

"Ay always said dat de shot-gun vars a vonderful inwention."

"A perfect anæsthetic, Oscar," replied Henry's voice.

TONTO CITY awoke early next morning. In fact, it seemed that all of Wild Horse Valley awoke early, and came to Tonto City. Evidently the festivities had been well advertised. They came in wagons, buggies and on horseback, while some of those nearer town walked in. They brought their babies and their dogs, and lots of them brought their lunch. By noon the hitch-racks were all filled, and they were using fences as an anchorage for horses.

Charles H. Livingstone was very active. He told Henry that the two engineers were satisfied with the condition of things; so there would be no hitch of any kind in the big deal.

"But I did not expect such a turnout," he declared. "Why, it is like a County Fair."

"There will be more," assured Henry. "I expect there will be a number from Scorpion Bend—and possibly points beyond. How are Mr. Beloit and his fair daughter today?"

"Very well, thank you."

"The syndicate representative will be in on the stage?"

"Yes. He, Mr. Frank M. Stahl, and his syndicate is known as the Pittsfield Mine Owners. They are a wealthy group of Pittsburgh investors."

There was no disappointment for Howard Beloit this time. Frank M. Stahl was on the stage. And with him was Willard Preston, editor of the *Clarion*. Willard was about the size of Frijole, but a very dapper youngish man, with a prominent Adam's-apple and weak eyes.

"The worm," murmured Henry.

"Without an ink spot," added Judge. "I wonder if he wants an interview?"

Apparently Willard did not. He saw Henry and Judge advancing, and immediately crossed the street, where he stood on the sidewalk, self-conscious, but rather defiant.

"Teetering there like a road-runner watching a grasshopper," said Henry. "I wonder if Willard drinks."

"His editorials reek of prohibition," replied Judge.

"Which doesn't mean a thing, Judge. You preach the same doctrine every time you get well plastered."

"I do not get plastered, sir."

"Well—yagged, as Oscar says."

They saw Willard saunter into the Tonto Saloon; so they went over there and found him talking with Edward Mitchell and Al Cooper, two of the commissioners. Willard was making notes, as he talked.

"Would you mind stating, Mr. Mitchell," asked Willard, "just how long you three commissioners are going to tolerate Henry Conroy?"

Henry stopped just behind Willard and looked quizzically at Mitchell, who replied gravely:

"How long would you tolerate him, Mr. Preston?"

"Just long enough to throw him through that doorway."

"Well, go ahead; there he is behind you."

Willard squeaked, ducked and came up behind Mitchell.

"The power of the press!" chuckled Henry. "Like most editors, when cornered, you dodge the issue, Willard."

"We do not care to discuss anything with you, Mr. Conroy," declared Willard defiantly. "We detest your dilatory methods, and we can assure you that we will never—"

"We," chuckled Judge. "You talk like twins. Or is it you and your wormish disposition?"

"I warn you," said Willard, "that you cannot browbeat me, Judge Van Treece. The *Clarion* does not back up an inch in its policy."

"I can assure you that no one is trying to browbeat you," said Henry. "No one is asking the *Clarion* to back up an inch. This is a perfectly free country, Willard. You are just as welcome here as you would be in Scorpion Bend. If there were any keys to this city, I am sure you could have them."

"I see," said Willard coldly. "You are trying to take an unfair advantage of me in public. You are not sincere, I can see that at a glance, Mr. Conroy. No, thank you, I have no need of your keys."

"I think you are a damned little swell-headed fool, if yuh ask me," growled Cooper. "You'd bite the hand that fed yuh. Now go right ahead and put that in yore paper, and ask for a vote on it. I'll betcha it'd be a landslide vote—in favor of what I called yuh."

"I believe," said Willard frigidly, "that I can see how Conroy holds his job. Perhaps I have been scathing the wrong persons."

Then Willard pocketed his notes and walked out.

Over in John Campbell's office, Willard Preston sat stiffly on the edge of a chair and began to question the prosecutor.

"Mr. Campbell, is it a fact that two masked men were going to murder the sheriff the other night?" he asked.

The lawyer smiled slowly. "You might get all that information direct," he suggested.

"Or," continued Willard, "was it merely his way of making a bid for sympathy, after all his failures?"

"Such a thing is possible," admitted Campbell, a twinkle in his eye. "There has been much comment about your editorial, in which you say you were tied to a chair and smeared with ink. Many folks think you did it yourself, in order to get sympathy."

Willard's weak eyes blazed with righteous anger.

"Fools!" he snorted. "Would I tie myself so tightly—"

"Would Henry Conroy?" countered Campbell.

"And that is the thanks I get for my crusade against crime."

"Go home and forget it," advised Campbell. "There will always be crime. You are too serious, Willard."

"I was trying to help," sighed Willard.

"You were trying to dictate," corrected Campbell.

Willard winced, thought it over for a while, and finally got to his feet.

"Thank you, Mr. Campbell," he said. At the doorway he turned. "I really was tied up—and inked," he said.

"Personally, I believe it was justified," replied Campbell dryly.

CHAPTER XIX

THE BIG BANQUET

MORE PEOPLE WERE drifting into Tonto City every hour. The games were running full-blast at the Tonto Saloon. Free liquor would not flow until four o'clock, but few were waiting for that event.

Henry wandered around the town. Livingstone came to him with final suggestions, which Henry discussed gravely. Campbell came to Henry on the street.

"Livingstone has asked me to make a little talk, Henry. Just between us, I shall be obliged, if you do not call on me."

"As you like, John. Was Willard Preston over to see you?"

"Yes, he was over to my office. Quite a character—Willard, eh?"

"Quite. Just now he is as drunk as a fiddler."

"Drunk? Why, from the way he flays liquor—"

"Correct. But Tommy Roper persuaded Willard that sloe-gin is a soft-drink. You should see that pair, John. Tommy is trying to recite 'The Face on the Barroom Floor,' while Willard makes appropriate gestures. When I left there, Willard was sixteen gestures ahead."

Four o'clock was the signal for a county convention at the bar. But Henry and Judge remained cold-sober.

"You and I are to witness the signing of those papers, Judge," said Henry. "John Campbell is to notarize the paper, I believe. Mr. Livingstone has ordered that, immediately following the supper, they will go through the formality of completing the deal. After that, it will be up to me to conduct services."

Judge nodded grimly. "I hope you know your lines, Henry."

"A Conroy never forgot his lines, sir."

"Nor a Van Treece his law."

"Unfortunately," murmured Henry, "with all due respects to your law, Judge, I have more faith in a six-shooter or shotgun. By the way, have you seen our editor friend lately?"

"You mean 'Sloe-Gin' Preston?"

"Exactly."

"Tommy should be thrown in jail, Henry. He took that tired-looking, trusting little soul—and made of him a rampaging rake."

THAT STATEMENT seemed more or less true. Willard Preston stood with his back to the bar, elbows on top of the bar behind him, one foot on the rail, his hat sitting far to the back of his head.

"Thish is r'ally a wonderful day, Misser Roper," he said expansively. "Cer'nly glorioush."

"Uh-huh," admitted Tommy, grinning foolishly at his own reflection in the back-bar mirror.

"I wonner 'f I could secure an interview with Miss Beloit."

"Huh?"

"I wonner if I could shee Miss Beloit and get interview."

"Sh-sh-sh-sh-sure," nodded Tommy. "I'll in-in-in-inter—I'll tut-tell her who you are. Mum-mum-me and her are juj-jist like th-th-tha-that."

Tommy held up two fingers, tight together, and looked cross-eyed at them.

"Good 'nough, Misser Roper. Shall we prosheed?"

"Huh?"

"Shall we go over there?"

"Oh, sh-sh-sure."

They made their erratic way across the street to the hotel. The lobby was crowded with people, waiting for supper time.

"Sh-sh-she's in rur-room tut-two hundred and tut-tut-ten," informed Tommy.

Because of the crowded lobby they became separated, but

Willard went straight up the stairs, intent on room two hundred and ten. He adjusted his rumpled tie, cuffed his hat over one eye and went the few feet to a doorway, where he leaned heavily and scanned the number.

Funny thing about those numbers—they kept moving around. He leaned heavier, putting both hands on either side of the number, when the door was suddenly jerked inward.

With a drunken gurgle of surprise Willard fell forward and was checked sharply. Then he was straightened up, shoved back into the hallway, where a terrific blow on his left ear knocked him to the top of the stairs. There he toppled over and went bumping down the treads to the bottom.

"Vat in de ha'al are you doing in my room, you dronken bom?" exclaimed Josephine's voice. But the sound was drowned in the roar of conversation below.

Slowly Willard got to his feet and felt himself over carefully. Old Matt Corrigan, the hotel clerk, craned across the counter, looking at Willard, who shook himself a few times and staggered to the counter.

"Are you the man who runs thish hotel?" he asked.

"Well, yeah, I reckon I am," replied Matt.

"Lemme tell you shomethin'," confided Willard. "Maybe you don't know it, but shomebody is keeping a horsh in that firs' room up there, at the right."

Then Willard Preston carefully adjusted the hat he did not have on, took deliberate aim, and went swiftly through the front doorway.

"Wha-wha-what happened tut-to him, Mum-Matt?" asked Tommy.

"I reckon he got into Josephine's room by mistake, Tommy."

"Huh-huh-he's lucky."

"How do yuh figure that?"

"Huh-he's alive, ain't he?"

More people crowded the lobby, until they overflowed on the

sidewalk. Henry had arranged for his crowd to enter the dining-room through a rear doorway. There were no reserved seats. It was a case of first come, first served.

At the rear of the room, where the platform had been constructed, there were two big windows, wide open for ventilation. Every bit of available space had been used for long, narrow tables, the full width of the big room, and with barely room for waiters to pass between.

At seven o'clock sharp, the doors were flung open, and there was a general stampede. Men, women and children. Several dogs got in, but were quickly removed. Howard Beloit, Gale, Livingstone, Frank Stahl and the two engineers were at a separate table. At another table sat Henry and Mrs. Harper, Leila, Danny, Judge and John Campbell.

Henry, resplendent in a dress suit, the only one in the place, beamed upon everyone. And it seemed that everyone beamed back at Henry. Willard Preston, at a front table, seemed rather puzzled to find that his mouth had been moved from its customary place. He missed several times, and left fork-marks each time.

A small table had been placed on the platform, on which were papers, pen and ink, and a notary's seal. Gale Beloit seemed to be enjoying things, but her father looked upon things with a cynical eye. Frank Stahl seemed amused; the engineers bored. Livingstone smiled thinly, as he looked often at Henry Conroy.

Corks popped, as Tonto tasted its first champagne. Men made wry faces at each other, and reached for whisky. The room was one big roar of conversation, laughter, the shrill voices of children. Outside the hotel, an exuberant cowboy emptied his six-shooter at the sky, causing some nervous people to duck quickly. Henry and Judge both ducked.

"Force of habit," laughed Henry. "I suppose I shall always be gun-shy."

"I was too hungry to dodge," grinned Danny.

"Isn't Miss Beloit beautiful?" whispered Leila.

"Too much paint," replied Danny. "Her lips look like she was bleedin'."

"I think she is beautiful. Her skin is so white. And her father is such a distinguished looking man."

"As a matter of fact," smiled Henry, "if Howard Beloit was broke, he would look ordinary."

"I wonder how it would feel to have a million," said Leila.

"Even if it were painful, I believe I could stand it," smiled Henry.

"This entertainment will cost a pretty penny," said Judge.

"A mere drop in the bucket," replied Henry. "When you consider that Howard Beloit acquired those two pieces of property for less than ten thousand dollars, he could well afford to spend a few dollars here to show his appreciation."

"I don't reckon he ever seen either mine until yesterday," said Danny. "He bought 'em on an engineer's word."

"That is true," agreed Henry. "Howard Beloit was never in Wild Horse Valley until he came here this time. Charles Livingstone says he was here shortly after the engineer reported on the mines, and spent a few days in Scorpion Bend."

"Has Mr. Beloit always been rich?" asked Mrs. Harper.

"Not at all," replied Judge. "In fact, ten years ago, he was in very moderate circumstances. He married a very wealthy woman, who died about a year after their marriage, leaving all her wealth to him and to her daughter."

"Then Gale is not Mr. Beloit's daughter?"

"Adopted, possibly. He seems very fond of her."

"I have been wondering what was wrong with this party," said Leila. "Where is Oscar and Frijole?"

"That is right," agreed Henry, scanning the crowd. "I believe you will find them over in the Tonto."

"They are missing a good supper," said Danny.

THE SUPPER was finally over, and the waiters began clearing the tables. Cigars were passed, and the room was soon foggy with smoke. When the tables were cleared and order restored, Henry got to his feet and walked over beside the platform. Except for minor noises the room was fairly silent.

Glancing over the crowd, and with a wide smile Henry said:

"Ladies and gentlemen, I am sure that all of us thoroughly appreciate the hospitality of Mr. Howard Beloit."

The room shook with applause. Willard Preston got to his feet, his left ear badly swollen, and announced:

"As the rep'sentative of the *Clarion,* I would shay—"

"Pardon me, Mr. Preston," interrupted Henry. "If you will kindly keep your seat, we will proceed."

Tommy Roper reached up, grasped Willard's arm and yanked him down.

"Sus-sus-stay pup-pup-put, will yuh?"

"Thank you, Tommy," smiled Henry. "Friends, Mr. Beloit and Mr. Stahl have asked me to announce that the first thing on our little program will be the signing of the papers, which will transfer ownership of the Golden Calf and the Shoshone Chief from Mr. Beloit to a syndicate represented by Mr. Stahl.

"This will, I believe, be the biggest transaction ever made in Wild Horse Valley. One million dollars, folks; easy to say, but hard to get. Mr. Stahl has a certified check for five hundred thousand dollars, which will be handed to Mr. Beloit the moment the papers are legally signed.

"This deal will mean a lot to Tonto City and to Wild Horse Valley. This syndicate will immediately begin exploration work on the two mines, which will give work to many men, and greatly increase the payroll of Tonto City."

Henry turned to Howard Beloit.

"If you gentlemen are ready, we shall proceed."

Howard Beloit, Charles Livingstone, Frank Stahl, John Campbell and Judge Van Treece mounted the platform. The papers were all ready for signature. Quickly the papers were signed. Judge scrawled his signature, as a witness, and turned to Henry, who was not on the platform.

"You are the next witness, Henry."

"Oh, yes! I almost forgot it, Judge."

Henry took the pen, leaned over the paper and scanned it closely.

"Sign right there, Mr. Conroy," prompted Livingstone, pointing at the proper line.

Henry straightened up slowly and laid the pen aside.

"I am sorry," he said firmly, "but I cannot witness that paper."

Except for the fretful whimper of a baby, the room was silent.

"You can't witness it?" queried Livingstone. "Why not?"

"Because," replied Henry coldly, "that is not Howard Beloit's signature."

"What do you mean?" asked Howard Beloit. "I signed it. You all saw me sign it."

"Have you lost your mind, Henry?" asked Campbell huskily.

Henry drew a piece of paper from his pocket and laid it on the table in front of Frank Stahl.

"That is Howard Beloit's signature, Mr. Stahl," he said. "You will note the difference."

"Why, yes—but I don't see—" faltered Stahl, puzzled.

"What does it mean, Henry?" begged Campbell. "What about that signature? I don't understand."

Henry turned and looked toward the doorway. Some of the crowd were on their feet, trying to hear what was being said.

"Come up here, Don," called Henry.

Somewhere in the crowd a woman screamed softly. Several men got up quickly and went staggering toward the exit, as Don Black came straight to the platform. Gale Beloit, white as chalk, covered her face with her hands.

CHAPTER XX

A DEAD MAN RETURNS

THE CROWD WAS all on its feet now. They were looking at a man they thought had been dead for days. Don smiled at Gale.

"Good evening, Miss *Beloit*," he said.

Livingstone was on his feet, his face white. Henry picked up the legal paper and held it out to Don.

"Is that Howard Beloit's signature?" he asked.

"It is not," declared Don firmly.

"How in the devil do you know his signature?" asked Livingstone.

"I should know his writing," replied Don. "He is my father."

"You lie!" panted Livingstone, shaking a finger at Don. "It's a damnable trick to ruin this deal. You are not—"

"I remember you now," said Don. "You had a little law office out in the Mission District. That was—"

"Look!" screamed Gale.

Coming toward them through the crowd were two men and a girl. One of the men was Jimmy Sloan. The other man *did* look a little like the man whose signature Henry had denied, and the girl was blond, very pale, and seemed tired.

Charles Livingstone ripped out an oath, as he backed up toward the open window at the back of the platform. A heavy revolver was gripped in his right hand.

"Keep back!" he snarled. "I'll kill the first man who makes a move."

He was at the window now, his eyes darting here and there, as he watched the crowd. Then he lifted his left foot, shoving it back through the open window. From out in the darkness appeared a pair of brawny hands, which grasped Livingstone's arms just below the elbows, jerking them back and down.

Livingstone screamed, jerked convulsively on the trigger, and the bullet smashed into the flooring of the platform. A moment later he was yanked from sight, and a voice boomed:

"Oll right, Hanry; Ay have dis faller!"

But Henry was watching the man they had all known as Beloit. While the rest of the crowd saw the exit of Charles Livingstone, Henry saw this man reach inside his coat, clawing at a shoulder-holster. With a grunt and lurch, Henry went into him with a football tackle, and they crashed off the platform.

A muffled pistol shot thudded in the room. Henry was on top. Slowly he got to his feet, looking down at the man who did not move. The blond-haired girl in the evening gown, her painted face the color of wood-ashes, except where the cosmetics showed, looked down at the still figure.

"It was a rotten game, Jack," she said quietly. Don Black caught her, as she collapsed, and placed her in a chair.

Oscar and Frijole were bringing Charles Livingstone through the crowd. The lawyer was snarling like a trapped wolf, but he was like a child in the grip of Oscar Johnson, who brought him to the platform.

"You seem to have played out your string, Charley," remarked the real Howard Beloit, his face hard and drawn from suffering. "Yes, I know all about your plans to dynamite the old mine, as soon as this deal was completed.

"Because of the fact that this Jack Bronson and his wife, who impersonated Gale and me, refused to go through with the deal if any of us were murdered, we are still alive. But if you had had your way, right now we would be under tons of rock in that old Grubstake mine. You told the four men who were our captors that you were holding all of us in order that you might force me to sign those papers, under penalty of death to all of us.

"While I am giving credit to the Bronsons for not approving of murder, I must give ninety-nine per cent of the credit to

Henry Conroy, the sheriff, who saved the lives of all of us. And, Livingstone, you are going to hang for this work."

"He won't hang—if someone will lend me a gun," declared Jimmy Sloan.

"Hang!" sneered Livingstone. "You can't prove anything on me."

"I believe," replied Henry quietly, "that you underrate Wild Horse Valley jurors, Livingstone. It was a nice plot. You and your four gunmen almost succeeded. You had Mr. Beloit and his daughter kidnaped off the stage, and you murdered Johnny Deal, the driver, to seal his lips. Then you substituted this other man and girl.

"Shortly before that Tommy Roper and Lester Allen got drunk in Scorpion Bend. In their wanderings they came to Erin, where they saw this Miss, or Mrs. Bronson. Fearing discovery, someone of the gang shot Lester Allen. This girl was the blond angel of Tommy's alleged imagination.

"Arthur Miller, secretary of the real Howard Bronson, must have wired some damning information to Howard Beloit, or something that caused the gang to murder him in Scorpion Bend, and steal his brief-case. Naturally, they could not let him contact this man who was not his employer. Am I right, Mr. Livingstone?"

"You're crazy," snarled Livingstone. "It's a pack of lies!"

Henry chuckled and turned back to the crowd.

"Folks, I couldn't quite figure out this Don Black deal. Why would they want to kill him? Ben Greer, a bad-man from New Mexico, made the first try—and Don Black killed him. That night Livingstone was supposed to be in Scorpion Bend. As a matter of fact, Livingstone brought Ben Greer down here to kill Don Black—and had to go back alone."

"Prove it," snarled Livingstone. "You can't do it, damn you!"

Henry turned to the blond girl, who was slumped in the chair, staring into space. Don Black touched her on the shoulder, and she jerked around.

"Ma'am," said Henry kindly, "who was it gave you orders to decoy Don Black to those caves in Mummy Cañon?"

"Charley Livingstone," she replied coldly.

"Thank you. And you came out to my ranch later, trying to find out if Don Black was still alive?"

She nodded. "Livingstone thought he was, when they didn't find the body," she replied. "Then he sent two men to kill him from ambush. He said that some cowboy killed one of them. There were only two left, after that. Livingstone wanted to dynamite the mine, but Jack and I swore we'd quit the game. You see, Jack was my husband."

"Livingstone," said Henry, "I'm afraid you can hardly expect to get away from such testimony."

"Henry," said Campbell, "I can understand some of this—but how did you manage to save these people?"

"Simple enough, John. Danny Regan saw a man put a note in an old saguero stump at the forks of the main road and the old road to Erin. It was a cryptogram message, which I was able to interpret. It was a warning for Livingstone to look out for me. I did not have an ounce of proof that a kidnaping had been done. I felt that Tommy Roper had seen a blond girl. I knew there was a mighty good reason for Miller's murder, and there was a good reason for getting Jimmy Sloan out of Tonto City.

"Livingstone was supposed to have made his peace with Sloan, and taken him to Scorpion Bend at ten o'clock at night—when I knew that Sloan was gambling in the Tonto Saloon at half-past eleven. Well, folks, I used the smoking-out method. I wrote a cryptogram message and left it in the old stump. It told them that everything was ready for the grand finale, but that the sheriff was getting too smart; so they were to move everybody on Wednesday night to the old cave dwelling in Mummy Cañon, and then come to the rear of the Tonto Hotel to meet the writer at midnight.

"They made the move as ordered. Two men came up the trail, but refused to surrender. Tomorrow morning we will recover their bodies from the bottom of the cañon. I could not quite figure out why they wanted to kill Don Black, until we had sort of a family reunion at the J Bar C Wednesday night. You might explain it, Don."

"I hope you folks can understand all this," said Don. "When I was sixteen, I ran away from home. My father's name was Jim Beloit, but he had an H as a middle initial. We were far from wealthy. Long after I was gone, father married a wealthy woman. He became Howard Beloit. Gale Beloit was my stepmother's daughter, who I had never seen.

"When Charles Livingstone came here on this deal he recognized me. Being afraid that I might connect the name of Beloit in some way with my own, he decided to—well, get rid of me. When I left home my name was Lawrence McDonald Beloit. My mother's name was Black; so I called myself Don Black. I think that will explain everything."

"But, gentlemen," protested Frank Stahl nervously, "I hope you do not connect me with any crooked work. I came here in good faith."

Henry looked intently at Frank Stahl for several moments. Then he turned to Charles Livingstone.

"What percentage was Stahl to receive?" he asked.

"Twenty-five," replied Livingstone. "But how the hell did you know that?"

Frank Stahl collapsed in a chair.

"I merely guessed at it," smiled Henry. "I felt that Mr. Stahl must be crooked, or very trusting, to pay over a half-million dollars to a man he had never seen—just on the identification of you, sir."

Henry picked up the legal papers, folded them up and handed them to John Campbell.

"Merely an exhibit, John," he said. "Mr. Stahl, if you will hand over that certified check, we will pin it to the papers. You will not need it any longer. Mr. Beloit, I am afraid you will have to negotiate this deal all over again."

"I don't believe I shall," replied Beloit. "I have decided to exploit the mines myself. Jimmy Sloan is an engineer—out of a job. He seems to want to marry my daughter; so where would be a better place to work—and start housekeeping? I am taking Don into the firm with me, and—" He turned and looked at Henry for several moments.

"I appreciate brains," he said slowly, "so I am offering Henry Conroy the position of general manager of all the Beloit interests, with a salary of twenty-five thousand dollars a year."

HENRY STAGGERED against the table, a blank expression on his face. Slowly he turned and looked over the upturned faces of the crowd. He looked at Judge, Oscar, Frijole, Danny—and then at Mrs. Harper.

Finally he turned and looked at Howard Beloit.

"That would mean—the city again," he said quietly.

"Yes. San Francisco, New York—"

Henry shook his head slowly.

"Thank you, Mr. Beloit. I am deeply honored. But"—Henry's face broke into a wide smile—"I would rather be a hitching-post in Tonto City—than Mayor of New York. You see, I have the best job on this earth—the job of sheriff of Tonto."

"And," declared Willard Preston shakily, "I would like to add that he is the best sheriff we ever had in this county."

"Yah, su-ure," added Oscar Johnson. "And Ay vould like to say dat you don't know good Swedish dialect ven you hear it, Villard. Hanry, what are ve going to do with de prisoners?"

"Oh, yes," replied Henry. "Judge, you and Oscar lock up Livingstone. About Mrs. Bronson—"

The blond girl looked dumbly at him, her hands slowly clenching.

"John," said Henry quietly, "you could convict Livingstone, without her testimony, couldn't you?"

"Why, yes, I—I suppose I could. But—"

"She told us what she knew, John. She admits that she

decoyed Don Black. It was a terrible thing to do. But even at that, I—" Henry shoved his hands deep in his pockets. "John, I'd hate to put a girl in jail; and I know you would hate to prosecute one. Her husband died here tonight. I feel that she will always suffer for what she has done—do we want to make her suffer more?"

"It may not be the law," replied Campbell gravely, "but I do not believe there is a man in Tonto City who would lift a hand to prevent her from leaving here—free."

"Thank you, John. I wonder—where is Tommy Roper?"

"Huh-huh-huh-here I am," stammered Tommy. "Huh-huh-huh—"

"All right, Tommy. The county will pay the expenses of hiring a horse and buggy to convey Mrs. Bronson to Scorpion Bend. It will also pay a driver. Do you want to take her to Scorpion Bend?"

"Uh-huh. Your sh-sh-sh-sh-sh—"

"Thank you, Tommy. Oscar, will you go with Tommy and help hitch up the horse? Mrs. Bronson will want to collect her baggage."

Oscar grasped Tommy by the arm and hurried him toward the doorway, with Tommy arguing. Henry walked down to Mrs. Harper, bowed and extended his elbow.

"My dear," he said, "I believe the party is over."

"Henry," she said, "you are wonderful."

"It was nothing, my dear Laura. Being a master of ceremonies is very simple for a man of my ability."

Judge was lying to Campbell and Beloit:

"Yes, it was rather puzzling. But Henry and I figured it all out that night in the rain at Erin."

And Frijole was saying to Gale Beloit and Jimmy Sloan:

"You jist ask Henry if I ain't tellin' the truth. He's *seen* Bill Shakespeare lick a wild-cat. Bill can do anythin', but lay eggs; so there ain't no chance of perpetuatin' the strain."

And over in the livery stable Oscar was saying to Tommy:

"Ay know yust how you feel, Tommy. But it could be vorse."

"Huh-huh-how?" asked Tommy drearily.

"Va'al, she could t'row you down for a viggle-dancer."

Wagons and buggies were rattling out of Tonto City, riders galloped away. The big dining-room was empty, and Josephine watched the waiters clean up the place. On the sidewalk in front of the hotel stood a girl, a suitcase on either side of her, waiting for the horse and buggy. The banquet was over.

THE ARGOSY™ LIBRARY

1. GENIUS JONES by Lester Dent
2. WHEN TIGERS ARE HUNTING: THE COMPLETE ADVENTURES OF CORDIE, SOLDIER OF FORTUNE, VOLUME 1 by W. Wirt
3. THE SWORDSMAN OF MARS by Otis Adelbert Kline
4. THE SHERLOCK OF SAGELAND: THE COMPLETE TALES OF SHERIFF HENRY, VOLUME 1 by W.C. Tuttle
5. GONE NORTH by Charles Alden Seltzer
6. THE MASKED MASTER MIND by George F. Worts
7. BALATA by Fred MacIsaac
8. BRETWALDA by Philip Ketchum
9. DRAFT OF ETERNITY by Victor Rousseau
10. FOUR CORNERS, VOLUME 1 by Theodore Roscoe
11. CHAMPION OF LOST CAUSES by Max Brand
12. THE SCARLET BLADE: THE RAKEHELLY ADVENTURES OF CLEVE AND D'ENTREVILLE, VOLUME 1 by Murray R. Montgomery
13. DOAN AND CARSTAIRS: THEIR COMPLETE CASES by Norbert Davis
14. THE KING WHO CAME BACK by Fred MacIsaac
15. BLOOD RITUAL: THE ADVENTURES OF SCARLET AND BRADSHAW, VOLUME 1 by Theodore Roscoe
16. THE CITY OF STOLEN LIVES: THE ADVENTURES OF PETER THE BRAZEN, VOLUME 1 by Loring Brent
17. THE RADIO GUN-RUNNERS by Ralph Milne Farley
18. SABOTAGE by Cleve F. Adams
19. THE COMPLETE CABALISTIC CASES OF SEMI DUAL, THE OCCULT DETECTOR, VOLUME 2: 1912–13 by J.U. Giesy and Junius B. Smith
20. SOUTH OF FIFTY-THREE by Jack Bechdolt
21. TARZAN AND THE JEWELS OF OPAR by Edgar Rice Burroughs
22. CLOVELLY by Max Brand
23. WAR LORD OF MANY SWORDSMEN: THE ADVENTURES OF NORCOSS, VOLUME 1 by W. Wirt
24. ALIAS THE NIGHT WIND by Varick Vanardy

25. THE BLUE FIRE PEARL: THE COMPLETE ADVENTURES OF SINGAPORE SAMMY, VOLUME 1 by George F. Worts

26. THE MOON POOL & THE CONQUEST OF THE MOON POOL by Abraham Merritt

27. THE GUN-BRAND by James B. Hendryx

28. JAN OF THE JUNGLE by Otis Adelbert Kline

29. MINIONS OF THE MOON by William Grey Beyer

30. DRINK WE DEEP by Arthur Leo Zagat

31. THE VENGEANCE OF THE WAH FU TONG: THE COMPLETE CASES OF JIGGER MASTERS, VOLUME 1 by Anthony M. Rud

32. THE RUBY OF SURATAN SINGH: THE ADVENTURES OF SCARLET AND BRADSHAW, VOLUME 2 by Theodore Roscoe

33. THE SHERIFF OF TONTO TOWN: THE COMPLETE TALES OF SHERIFF HENRY, VOLUME 2 by W.C. Tuttle

34. THE DARKNESS AT WINDON MANOR by Max Brand

35. THE FLYING LEGION by George Allan England

36. THE GOLDEN CAT: THE ADVENTURES OF PETER THE BRAZEN, VOLUME 3 by Loring Brent

37. THE RADIO MENACE by Ralph Milne Farley

38. THE APES OF DEVIL'S ISLAND by John Cunningham

39. THE OPPOSING VENUS: THE COMPLETE CABALISTIC CASES OF SEMI DUAL, THE OCCULT DETECTOR by J.U. Giesy and Junius B. Smith

40. THE EXPLOITS OF BEAU QUICKSILVER by Florence M. Pettee

41. ERIC OF THE STRONG HEART by Victor Rousseau

42. MURDER ON THE HIGH SEAS AND THE DIAMOND BULLET: THE COMPLETE CASES OF GILLIAN HAZELTINE by George F. Worts

43. THE WOMAN OF THE PYRAMID AND OTHER TALES: THE PERLEY POORE SHEEHAN OMNIBUS, VOLUME 1 by Perley Poore Sheehan

44. A COLUMBUS OF SPACE AND THE MOON METAL: THE GARRETT P. SERVISS OMNIBUS, VOLUME 1 by Garrett P. Serviss

45. THE BLACK TIDE: THE COMPLETE ADVENTURES OF BELLOW BILL WILLIAMS, VOLUME 1 by Ralph R. Perry

46. THE NINE RED GODS DECIDE: THE COMPLETE ADVENTURES OF CORDIE, SOLDIER OF FORTUNE, VOLUME 2 by W. Wirt

47. A GRAVE MUST BE DEEP! by Theodore Roscoe

48. THE AMERICAN by Max Brand
49. THE COMPLETE ADVENTURES OF KOYALA, VOLUME 1 by John Charles Beecham
50. THE CULT MURDERS by Alan Forsyth
51. THE COMPLETE CASES OF THE MONGOOSE by Johnston McCulley
52. THE GIRL AND THE PEOPLE OF THE GOLDEN ATOM by Ray Cummings
53. THE GRAY DRAGON: THE ADVENTURES OF PETER THE BRAZEN, VOLUME 2
    by Loring Brent
54. THE GOLDEN CITY by Ralph Milne Farley
55. THE HOUSE OF INVISIBLE BONDAGE: THE COMPLETE CABALISTIC CASES OF
    SEMI DUAL, THE OCCULT DETECTOR by J.U. Giesy and Junius B. Smith
56. THE SCRAP OF LACE: THE COMPLETE CASES OF MADAME STOREY, VOLUME 1
    by Hulbert Footner
57. TOWER OF DEATH: THE ADVENTURES OF SCARLET AND BRADSHAW, VOLUME 3
    by Theodore Roscoe
58. THE DEVIL-TREE OF EL DORADO by Frank Aubrey
59. THE FIREBRAND: THE COMPLETE ADVENTURES OF TIZZO, VOLUME 1 by Max
    Brand
60. MARCHING SANDS AND THE CARAVAN OF THE DEAD: THE HAROLD LAMB
    OMNIBUS by Harold Lamb
61. KINGDOM COME by Martin McCall
62. HENRY RIDES THE DANGER TRAIL: THE COMPLETE TALES OF SHERIFF HENRY,
    VOLUME 3 by W.C. Tuttle
63. Z IS FOR ZOMBIE by Theodore Roscoe
64. THE BAIT AND THE TRAP: THE COMPLETE ADVENTURES OF TIZZO, VOLUME 2
    by Max Brand
65. MINIONS OF MARS by William Gray Beyer
66. SWORDS IN EXILE: THE RAKEHELLY ADVENTURES OF CLEVE AND D'ENTREVILLE,
    VOLUME 2 by Murray R. Montgomery
67. MEN WITH NO MASTER: THE COMPLETE ADVENTURES OF ROBIN THE
    BOMBARDIER by Roy de S. Horn
68. THE TORCH by Jack Bechdolt
69. KING OF CHAOS AND OTHER ADVENTURES: THE JOHNSTON MCCULLEY
    OMNIBUS by Johnston McCulley
70. THE BLIND SPOT by Austin Hall & Homer Eon Flint

www.ingramcontent.com/pod-product-compliance
Lightning Source LLC
Chambersburg PA
CBHW030516020726
47494CB00004B/1112